CW00859888

CARVED IN STONE

BOOK ONE OF THE ART OF LOVE SERIES

DONNA MCDONALD

WWW.DONNAMCDONALDAUTHOR.COM

Cover by *LFD Design for Authors*

Edited by *Toby Minton* and *Karen Lawson*

ACKNOWLEDGMENTS

Many thanks to my editors T Minton and K Lawson for their continued support. I appreciate your work and you.

Thanks to all teachers, principals, and other educators for what they give to our children and society in general. My daughter was a teacher before she died. My nephew is a teacher. My son-in-law is a teacher. Both my editors were teachers. I too have been a teacher. I hope this book makes you laugh because I wanted to show how very human teachers are as well, as being extraordinary people. Please consider this book a tiny tribute to your dedication and love.

Thanks to my nephew Derrick for calling me out on my word choices. The anatomically correct words in this novel are for you, honey. They aren't exactly what you meant, but hey—I'm getting closer. I love that you are sharing my writing journey with me.

DEDICATION

This book is for all the artists and dreamers in the world.
Please don't stop. This world would be a much sadder place without you.

CHAPTER 1

Will Larson watched the batter bubbles burst before he flipped the current batch of pancakes. When he heard the motorcycle roar up outside, he knew Shane had finally arrived for breakfast.

"Good morning," Will said, smiling as his youngest son came through the door sniffing the air like a hungry dog.

"Banana walnut pancakes," Shane said on sigh, walking into the kitchen of his brother Michael's house. "Those are still my favorite."

Will tossed a grin in the direction of his son and then smiled when Shane walked over and dropped an affectionate kiss on his unshaven cheek.

Shane looked like his blonde Nordic-looking mother, but had definitely inherited his father's size, exceeding Will's height by several inches and the width of his shoulders even more. It would take the same quantity of pancakes he and Michael ate together just to fill the twenty-seven-year-old up, so Will poured out batter to make another six.

"So how's the graphic novel business? Has the Winged Protector solved any more crimes or saved any more damsels in distress lately?"

"Nah. His alter ego, Eric Benton, is mostly a monogamist. He's still enjoying the last damsel. I did get offered a deal for action figures last week," Shane said, going to the coffee pot and pouring himself a cup.

"Action figures? That's cool. Was it a good deal?" Will asked, impressed that his son's creative work was gaining popularity. He was doubly glad now that he hadn't let Ellen discourage the boy's comic book drawing too much.

Shane shrugged. "It's a toy company working with my publisher. My agent said they're offering enough to buy a small house, plus a percentage of sales over time. I guess that's pretty good."

Will stopped and stared. "Pretty good? I would say it's pretty great, Shane." He went back to flipping pancakes, smiling and proud.

"Well, I like the idea of getting a house," Shane admitted. "Guess I'm tired of condo living."

"When you get your house, maybe I can come live with you for a while. I think your brother is tired of me already," Will said, wanting to laugh at the pained expression on Shane's face. It would be hard for his youngest to bring home his one-nighters with his father in residence. Will was seriously tempted to do it for a while just to disrupt Shane's habitual womanizing.

"Yeah, I am tired of you," Michael confirmed, walking into the kitchen, stretching and scratching the six-pack abdominal muscles he worked to maintain. It had been harder since his father had been in his house and doing most of the cooking.

Will laughed at his oldest son's comment about being tired of him because it was half teasing and half-truth. The month he'd been living with Michael had been an interesting social adjustment for both of them. He had been relieved to have some company for a while, even if it was reluctant. The last year in a house with no family had been a really lonely one for him.

When he looked at Michael now and smiled, Will had the same thought he always had that it was like looking in a mirror showing him a picture of his past. Michael had inherited his muscular build but not his height, which his son complained about still at thirty-four.

At five-ten, Michael was average in stature, but his wide shoulders, broad chest, and muscled arms only emphasized the passionate nature promised by his dark brown eyes and equally dark hair that hung nearly to his waist. Will's Celtic heritage had branded his eldest hard, but it looked good on him.

"Why exactly are you tired of me?" Will asked, grinning at Michael's snort.

"You've been moping around my house, not dating, and barely working on your art. I'm sick and tired of being greeted by a giant marble penis every time I go out to the courtyard to work. Carve a damn leg or something, Dad. No matter how artistically impressive, a giant marble penis by itself is still creepy as hell," Michael complained, making his father blush.

To soften his words, he patted his father on a shoulder, sniffing the pancakes with appreciation. He loved to tease, but would never outright criticize his father's art. God knew his mother had done enough of that when she and his dad were married.

Shane was laughing so hard at his brother's comments that coffee was threatening to come out his nose.

"So how long has the marble penis been leading its solitary existence?" Shane asked, pulling a coffee cup out of a cabinet to pour Michael a cup.

"Practically since Dad sold the house and moved in here," Michael said, answering for his father.

Shane laughed harder as he handed his brother the coffee.

"Thanks," Michael said, savoring that first bracing sip. "I think Dad's depressed."

Despite his father's amazing financial success as a sculptor, his mother had never thought his father's art was as important as his other work. As the oldest child, Michael clearly remembered all the fights his parents had had about the time his father had spent carving. Selling the house, which was also the place his father was used to working, had been as bad as the divorce itself.

"Stop talking about me in the third person. I am in the room, not deaf, and not depressed," Will denied, sighing over their concerns, which were way too close to his for comfort. "I just haven't felt like carving. Throw a cover over it if it bothers you so much, Michael."

"Maybe the state of the statue is trying to tell you something, Dad," Shane suggested, his amused but serious gaze on his father's face. "Maybe the marble penis isn't the only penis leading a solitary existence. The divorce was over a year ago. Mom and Luke married a few months after it was final. You're not even dating yet."

Will turned off the griddle and set the mountain of pancakes in the middle of the table he'd already set for three.

"Listen, Mr. All-But-Dissertation in Psychology, when you actually finish that million-dollar doctorate at Johns Hopkins, then you can analyze me and my man parts. Until then you're just my smart-ass son. Sit and eat—both of you laughing hyenas," Will ordered, only partially minding their amusement at his outburst.

"Dad, you know Michael and I love you. At least let me give you my best dating advice," Shane said, sliding into the nearest chair.

He heaped six pancakes on his plate and covered them with a lake of syrup before he paused and schooled his voice into the businesslike tone he had learned from the man he addressed.

"Shave your head, get an earring, and ride your bike around town. Your body is great for a man over fifty. You could be picking up the kind of women I do. Look, I got a tongue stud. You need to get one of these. Women love this kind of stuff."

Shane stuck out his tongue to show his father, who only rolled his eyes. He heard his brother snickering around a mouthful of pancakes, but merely ignored his jealous sibling.

Will studied the tongue stud with a mixture of horror and shock.

He looked at Michael, who only laughed, shrugged, and went on eating. His eldest son was crazy in love with a woman he couldn't get along with for more than two minutes at a time. But even though the woman wasn't in his life the way he wanted, Michael wasn't always out with nameless, faceless blondes like Shane favored doing. Sure he dated, but he also tended to bury himself in his work.

His oldest son had only done that kind of mindless dating when the woman he loved got married. When she got divorced, which was remarkably often, Michael stopped chasing other women and resumed chasing her, which was the stage he was going through currently. While it seemed fruitless to Will to want a woman so badly who so obviously didn't want you back, he still never worried about Michael as much. At least Michael cared deeply about someone. Will wasn't sure Shane even had the capacity to genuinely love a woman.

"Shane, you're missing the big picture. Do you even remember their names, what they did to you, what you did to them? Do you ever want to go back to any of them so bad you ache?" Will asked.

"No. But I've not been looking for that kind of experience," Shane said, shrugging away his father's disapproval.

Will pointed his fork at Shane. "Yes, you are. I raised you. You know I felt that way about your mother because I made sure you did. So I know you're at least subconsciously looking for that whether you realize it or not. There is nothing like finding that one incredible woman who changes everything. There is nothing like exploring the full range of lovemaking with an equally devoted partner."

"What happens when that one incredible woman changes so much that she leaves you and marries a younger man? Do you just give up?" Shane asked sharply, daring his father to answer his question less than honestly.

He and Michael both knew their father had taken the divorce very hard. They knew he had sincerely and faithfully loved their mother. Neither of them had really understood what had gone so wrong between their parents that it couldn't be fixed. The divorce had not been easy on any of them, but their father was the one who hadn't moved on.

"Look—every relationship is a risk in some way. I had thirty-three good years with your mother. We grew apart, and she fell in love with someone else. I don't know why these things happen. They just do," Will said, getting up and refilling his coffee. "I am sad about the divorce but not really depressed. When the right time comes, I'll find someone and start dating again. I have an open mind about it."

"Good. When?" Shane asked, watching his father walk back to the table and sit down heavily with a resigned sigh. He wanted to laugh at his father's irritation with him, but he held it in. There was too much at stake to risk his father thinking it was just a joke.

"When I'm ready and I meet someone, I will start dating again. There's nothing wrong with waiting for the right woman to show up. I don't need to fill the interim with tall, leggy blondes half my age," Will said firmly.

"Fine," Shane agreed easily, his tone dripping with fake resignation. "I'll take care of chasing all the leggy blondes half your age, Dad. Geez, you're hard to satisfy. No wonder Michael is tired of you."

When his father glared at him, Shane turned to look at his brother, his gaze full of wickedness. "What kind of women does Dad pawn off on you?"

"None—and I'm totally pissed now," Michael said, putting as much anger in his voice as he could over the urge to laugh. "Dad's always liked you better, Shane. When you buy your house, he's definitely moving in with you."

"Oh, shut up and eat—both of you," Will said, stabbing his pancakes viciously, tired of being harassed by his adult children. "I'm getting my own damn place as soon as I can."

"When? Mom said you gave all the money from the house sale to her," Shane said sadly, shaking his head side to side in pity. "I guess that means you're broke. That marble penis better grow a body soon."

At the vicious swearing following Shane's comments, Michael shook his head at his father as well and made sympathetic noises with his tongue. "Did you ever even use the f-word when you were a principal, Dad? I don't remember you swearing in front of me or Shane, until *he* ran over your Harley with his car."

Michael used his fork to point accusingly at Shane, whose glare matched his father's, and made him want to laugh.

"Thanks, Benedict Arnold. Did you have to remind Dad about me killing his bike?" Shane asked, pancakes all but falling out of mouth. Backing over his father's beloved Harley was the only thing Shane had ever done in his life so bad that his father had been truly disappointed in him.

"You're the one making Dad mad this morning, not me," Michael said, laughing at Shane's pained expression.

Since it was his house, Michael reasoned he could say anything he wanted to defend himself under his own roof. This included shifting his father's irritation in his brother's general direction and away from him. His obvious success at having done so made his smile even wider.

"I'm definitely getting my own place soon," Will said to his pancakes, even as both his sons laughed harder. "And I'm not inviting you two over for breakfast."

Shane pointed his fork at his brother. "If I never get banana pancakes again, you are a dead man."

Michael grinned and gave his brother the finger to let him know how afraid he was of him and his threats.

"I am serious," Shane warned, stabbing the air between Michael and him with his fork like it was a weapon.

Will rolled his eyes to the ceiling and shook his head. Sometimes he wished they had both taken more after their less passionate mother.

CHAPTER 2

Though celebrating her birthday in the dreary March weather had been depressing, Jessica Daniels didn't mind being forty-seven because she was mostly happy with her life. She was close to retiring from her teaching position, and her daughter who dreamed of being an eccentric college professor was finally about to graduate with a PhD in Philosophy from Ohio State.

While her daughter was just beginning her career at thirty, Jessica had started teaching high school art right out of college at twenty-two. Now she found herself constantly longing for a different life. She wanted to get back to her own art—whatever form it took now—before she got too old to want to do it.

In fact, she wanted to get back to doing a lot of things she hadn't done in a while, before she forgot what it was to want them too. So when one of her favorite former art students, Melanie Simpson—now Melanie Madison—had suggested she come to the café to scope out the biker guy who was fast becoming a regular, it hadn't taken much to talk Jessica into it.

Seeing him now in the flesh, Jessica totally agreed the balding biker was all tall-and-firm-body hunky, except for the massive arms and shoulders on him. The man looked to be six feet tall or better, which was not so intimidating for Jessica's five-foot-ten height. She preferred tall men anyway. But the man looked big as well, which was a welcome deviation from the lanky, lean intellectual men she usually dated. You didn't come across tall, big, and well-toned bodies very often, especially in men over forty.

As Jessica listened to him chat with Melanie, she decided that the biker was very articulate, polite, and well-spoken. She also concluded there was a sort of raw power in his assertive tone. The man had the kind of authoritative voice that was just instinctual to obey, unless you had trained yourself otherwise. Being a teacher of wild and unruly high school students, Jessica had a lot of respect for anyone who could speak with authority and command.

Yes, the biker was definitely intriguing to her, so Jessica stood and walked to perch on the bar stool beside him. She was very glad they were the only two patrons in the café at the moment. Jessica found it easier to flirt boldly when there was a smaller audience.

"Hey, big guy, I'll pay for your coffee if you take me for a ride," Jessica offered, instantly drawing his full attention to her.

His gaze traveled the length of her body before returning to her face and hair. "Very nice offer, but no can do. You need a helmet to ride and I don't carry a spare."

Jessica blinked and grinned at his refusal, but only laughed low in her belly.

Will noticed his body absorbed the sound of her laughter and vibrated pleasantly. Her reddish hair streaked with silver blonde strands revealed her age as somewhere over forty, but no more than his shiny dome revealed he was way over forty himself.

"Well, I wasn't necessarily talking about your bike," Jessica said on a laugh, liking the way his face actually flushed at her innuendo. The man was certainly not accustomed to flirting or playing games, she thought. It was a fact she found enormously appealing, and she appreciated the edge it gave her.

"Well, I don't have any safety of any sort, but could fix that if you can wait a bit while I go shopping," he said on laugh, bringing his mildly embarrassed gaze back to her face, the amusement in his hazel eyes evident. "Does your offer have an expiration date?"

Well, well, Jessica thought, her smile broadening at his teasing tone. There was a fun guy in that great body somewhere, and she was immediately interested in finding him. There was also a little something buzzing between them causing arousal to flare. She really loved that first flaring of genuine attraction. Even though she dated a lot of men, it had been a long time since she'd felt the real thing.

"Well, I'd say my answer depends on what you intend to go shopping for," Jessica said sweetly, leaning an elbow on the ancient counter, intentionally letting her shirt front gape to show both her breasts and the blue lace bra she wore.

Ignoring the cleavage, which Will figured she knew damn well he noticed, he instead studied her intriguing face and the fullness of her hair. Then he let his gaze drop to her jean-covered legs. She had very long legs encased in well-worn jeans that fit snugly and intimately to all of her.

"I would buy a spare bike helmet, of course," Will said sternly, keeping his laughing gaze focused in her lap as he spoke.

Jessica laughed loudly and squirmed in her seat. Suddenly all of her was really interested in what that look of his was promising. Okay, the biker was good, very good, she reluctantly admitted. He just seemed out of practice, and Jessica couldn't help wanting to know why.

"Ms. Daniels, don't be teasing Mr.—" Melanie began.

"—Williams," Will interjected firmly, interrupting Melanie's introduction to introduce himself. "I'm Everett Williams, but you can just call me Will."

Melanie raised her eyebrows, but did not correct the proffered introduction. She did give William Larson—still Mr. Larson, her former middle school principal, to her—a questioning look and grin. He had just recently confided in her about his artistic *nom de plume,* and that he had used it to separate his art from the rest of his life.

Today he evidently wanted to play the bad biker artist for Ms. Daniels. How interesting was *that,* Melanie mused? Brent was going to love this story, and she couldn't wait for his return tomorrow so she could share it with him.

Jessica put out a hand for Will to shake. "I'm Jessica Daniels. Sorry for teasing you. Melanie was my art student a couple years ago. I like to shock her with my flirting. It's the cheapest entertainment I can find."

"Ms. Daniels, I was your student almost ten years ago," Melanie corrected with a laugh.

"Shush," Jessica said, laughing. "I'm sure it was just two. What do you do, Will?"

She ignored Melanie's laugh as the girl wiped the counter.

"I'm an artist—a sculptor. I carve people out of stone," Will said easily. "What medium do you work in, Jessica?" He decided he liked her name and the way it sounded when he said it.

"Life," Jessica answered quickly, well practiced in giving a smoothly polished version of her story. "I teach high school kids to express themselves artistically. I haven't wholeheartedly pursued my own art in years. Maybe you can show me your work sometime."

"How about today?" Will asked, the offer coming from some rusty place inside him. But after issuing the invitation, he smiled at how good it felt, how natural. He really would like to show her his art. "The art center in Berea has two pieces of my work on display, if you're interested."

"Sounds like fun," Jessica said, thinking that seeing his art did sound like fun for a first date. Spending time with a man who genuinely aroused her with just a look was equally appealing.

Melanie walked back to them and slid a small tablet and pen over the counter. "I'm assuming you'll need to exchange phone numbers and addresses," she said to them both, laughing at her blatant interest in their conversation.

Jessica smiled at Melanie, pulled the tablet toward her, and began writing down her information.

Will studied her hands as she wrote, noticing the close trimmed nails and the total lack of a manicure. This was a woman who worked with her hands. He imagined her touch would be explorative but sure of its journey over him. Her grip would undoubtedly be strong.

When his jeans got tighter the longer he watched her write, Will let out the laugh he'd been holding in since she sat down. It was nice to know Ellen hadn't taken *everything* from him in the divorce. Thank you, Jessica Daniels, for being interesting, he mused, smiling at her.

"Something funny about my writing?" Jessica asked him, noticing his warm, intimate smile.

"No—something funny about being picked up by a woman in a café," Will corrected.

"Picked up? If that was the case, we'd be necking in the parking lot by now. Visiting the arts center with you is not exactly the same thing as taking you home with me for wild sex," Jessica said, laughing. "You haven't dated in a while, have you?"

"No. I haven't dated in a while," Will agreed, liking her laughing face and her quick sense of humor, even if it was racier than he was used to. "And I am definitely out of practice when it comes to flirting."

Will slid off the bar stool and put a five on the counter next to his coffee cup. He took the paper Jessica tore off the tablet, smiling at the address on it. She lived in the same neighborhood as Michael, sort of the artists' community in Lexington, Kentucky. She might not be creating art, but Will bet she lived the life.

"You suddenly in a hurry now?" Jessica asked, fighting not to be disappointed that the man was so anxious to leave. "You haven't even said what time we're going."

"How about three?" Will asked, smiling at the mild irritation in her gaze. It was nice to think she wanted to spend more time with him.

Grabbing his jacket, he reached over and turned Jessica's bar stool with one hand, causing her to rise off the counter and bump into him as he stepped between her legs. Score one for the old rusty guy, Will thought, when her surprised gaze met his.

"I need to run to the bike shop to buy a spare helmet. That's going to take a couple hours because going there always does. Then I've got another stop to make before I pick you up," Will said softly, looking directly into her laughing blue-green eyes.

He slid both arms into the butter-soft leather jacket, standing as close as the stool would let him as he zipped it, all the while keeping his eyes focused on her lap, and enjoying the spread of her thighs on each side of the stool. It gave him ideas he hadn't thought about in a hell of a long time.

When Will finally lifted his gaze back to Jessica's face, her color was high and her eyes were full of questions about his intentions. He smiled, his body tightening with the thrilling thought of answering even one or two of them. He might be out of practice, but the laughing Jessica Daniels was certainly inspiring.

"Is three o'clock okay?" Will asked, keeping his tone easy and his smile as innocent as he could.

"My schedule is pretty free this afternoon," Jessica told him, unconcerned with what Will might think of her not having plans. "The most exciting thing I'm doing today is laundry."

"Oh, come on—I'm not *that* much out of practice," Will jokingly told her with a snort, finally stepping away from the stool. "I'm at least a couple notches more fun than washing clothes."

He laughed as he walked to the door and grinned when he heard her sputter.

"Hey—who said I was *doing* you?" Jessica challenged, laughing openly at him now.

She'd bet fifty bucks Everett Williams would run like hell if she made a real move on him, despite the bar stool thing. She hadn't missed the quiver in his hands as he zipped up his jacket.

"You started this, lady. You still want to go for a ride or not?" Will asked back, a wicked glint in his eye.

"Yes. I still want to go for a ride," Jessica said on a laugh. "Pick me up at three. If I don't rush right down, give me a few minutes to put my laundry away. I like to take my time and do things right."

"Good to hear," Will said, grinning as he pushed the door open and headed outside.

Jessica and Melanie said nothing to each other as they watched Will pull the helmet over his head and strap it down. They didn't speak until he started the bike and zoomed out of the parking lot.

Jessica hummed in her throat, contemplating the interest she had seen in Everett Williams's gaze. "I've honestly never wanted to go for a ride more in my entire life," she said sincerely with more than a little bit of surprise.

She laughed when she heard Melanie giggle beside her.

Jessica looked over and grinned at the younger woman, whose face was now beet red. "Now how did that simple statement embarrass you? You're married. I'm not saying anything you don't know by now. If that's not the case, I'm going to have a serious talk with your husband."

"No," Melanie said, laughing. "I know what you mean, but he's at least fifty and you're what—mid-forties? Do you all really feel all that stuff at your age? I admit I had a little moment myself when he turned the stool and stepped between your legs. Brent is not going to believe he did that. We've both known him for years."

"Yes, you sweet innocent child—we still feel everything. Bodies get older, but they remain fully functional in most cases. Now what's his deal?" Jessica asked, even as Melanie shook her head no. "Come on. I want to know the biker's real story."

"Can't tell you, Ms. Daniels," Melanie said.

"For pity's sake, will you *please* call me Jessica?" Jessica insisted, making Melanie laugh. "I can't joke about sex with a twenty-eight-year-old who still calls me Ms. Daniels.

"Okay, fine, but I still can't tell you, *Jessica*," Melanie said on a laugh.

"Tell me why he's out of practice then—just that much at least," Jessica pleaded.

Melanie considered. It was probably a good thing to reveal that much. "Will was married forever. A year ago, his wife divorced him and married a younger man. He took the divorce hard. I don't think he's even been dating."

"Great," Jessica said morosely, "another rebounder. I hate being the first woman for a divorced guy. Their guilt over their ex never lets it work out with anyone new. They have to go through three or four women before they get over it."

Melanie studied Jessica. She could practically feel the woman's disappointment.

"Maybe it will be different with Will. I know the man. If he hasn't dated, there's a good reason. Most divorced men I know date lots of women really fast. Geez, you know I never even thought of him as a hot guy, and now I may never be able to see him again without thinking about the stool thing."

"Yeah, what you witnessed was a prime male putting on a show for new female. And your instincts are dead on—Will is a seriously hot guy," Jessica agreed. "What was his ex thinking? I'd bet my teacher's retirement that man knows where all the buttons are and just how hard to push them. As long as the man was married, he probably learned to make a woman's body sing the hallelujah chorus and hit the high notes. If he does anything interesting at all for an encore, I swear I may actually fall in love this time."

"Oh God, stop," Melanie begged, laughing. "Brent won't be back until tomorrow. It's going to be bad enough sleeping alone tonight as it is. If you get lucky, will you come back and tell me about it?"

"Sorry," Jessica said, laughing. "I'm an outrageous flirt, but very discreet about what I do in the bedroom. You'll have to get your vicarious thrill elsewhere tonight."

"But you are planning to do something interesting with Will?" Melanie asked teasingly. It was still hard not to call him Mr. Larson, but she was not going to blow his cover.

"If that second stop of his turns out to be to buy condoms, I am absolutely planning to ride more than his bike today," Jessica said. "That look in his eye was very promising."

Melanie's body shook with laughter, but she was afraid to ask any more questions, no matter how tempted she was. She knew full well Jessica would tell her the truth and she was missing her husband enough as it was.

"Well, laundry calls," Jessica said, going back to the booth she had left and gathering up her things. "Next time I come by, we're going to talk about some art for the outside of this place. Your food is great, honey. We need to draw in some customers. One lonely biker and a spinster do not a clientele make."

"*Spinster?* That so does not describe you. Come back and tell me about what happens. If it works out, we'll put out the word that we're a hook-up place for mature singles," Melanie joked. Then she pointed a finger at the woman smiling at her. "But this is the last guy I fix you up with. If you don't keep this one, I'm taking down my matchmaking shingle."

"I don't think love works like that," Jessica said, leaning over the counter. "Come here and let me hug you."

Melanie stood on her toes and accepted the hug Jessica offered. "Love is going to find you, Ms. Daniels. You're too much fun not to have a guy in your life."

"You're the sweetest thing—always were. I'm glad Brent Madison III talked you into marrying him. That boy was nuts about you since you were in that freshman art class together. Oh God, that really was more than ten years ago, wasn't it?"

Melanie laughed and nodded. "It was thirteen. I was being kind saying ten."

Jessica sighed. "Well, I'm going home now to soak my old head. How did I get to be forty-seven? Life goes by really fast." She headed to the door. "Bye, sweetie," Jessica said.

"Good luck on your date," Melanie said, sincerely hoping two of the nicest people she knew would find out they actually liked each other.

CHAPTER 3

Jessica walked to the living room window of her second-story rental home and stuck her head out when she heard a bike roar up on the street and stop outside. The man looked just as good from up here, she thought, watching Everett Williams park the black monster, step off, and unzip the jacket to reveal his impressive chest. When the helmet came off, she laughed a little at the top of his shiny head reflecting in the sun. It was only a reminder of how real he was and didn't dim her enthusiasm for him a bit.

"Hang on," she yelled, "I'll be down in a minute."

Will looked up to see a mass of red hair spilling over the laughing face smiling down on him. He hoped like hell they could be friends even if nothing else. Jessica Daniels' sunny disposition turned on a light inside him, illuminating places that had been dark for a very long time. Her cheerful attitude was as appealing as the way she looked.

"Take your time, gorgeous," Will yelled up at her, making her laugh at his attempt at charm. "But don't keep me waiting too long."

Jessica laughed again and disappeared from the opening, leaving Will to wonder what he was going to do while she made him wait. The thought had barely found its way into his consciousness when Jessica bounded out of the house, all but running down the front sidewalk to him.

He didn't know yet how old the woman was chronologically, but he put her mental age at seventeen as she all but ran to him. She wasn't even pretending to be coy, and her excitement to see him was on her face. The closer Jessica got to him, the more Will was reminded of the attraction he'd felt for her in the café. Suddenly, a friends-only option didn't seem quite so appealing. Will ran a hand over his front jeans pocket, patting the just-in-case package it contained, glad now he'd made that second stop.

Then Jessica was standing directly in front of him, and he was surprised as he realized she was almost eye level with his six-foot-two height. Will let his gaze travel down and back up once, not missing the amusement in her gaze on him as he did it.

"You're very tall for woman," Will said, trying to justify his thorough scan of her body by stating the obvious.

"So? Are you one of those big guys who wants a tiny woman to make himself feel even bigger?" Jessica asked, crossing her arms. "I can fake a lot of things for the sake of a first date, but being short isn't one of them. I would fail miserably. I love being tall."

Will ran a nervous hand over his head and laughed softly. "No, I'm not one of those guys," he said, leaving it at that.

There was no reason to bring up his ex or her height or anything about any other woman he had dated ancient ages ago. Unfortunately, those memories were the only things Will could think about rationally with Jessica's long body so close to his.

Not used to dating, Will hadn't had to make conversation with strangers—or strange women—very much since his divorce. He could feel Jessica's energy spiking around him, jostling his nerve endings back to life. It scrambled his brain, along with some other parts of him that had him becoming more cautious around her.

Sighing at his lack of composure, Will flipped open a storage compartment on the back of the bike and pulled out a black helmet with bright blue and green swirls. He'd bought the colors because they just seemed like her, though he was unsure why he could think of only her wearing it. He had meant to purchase a spare just in case he got asked for a ride in the future—by anyone. Which could still happen, he told himself, looking at the helmet with serious contemplation.

The red-haired enigma in front him was vibrating with excitement about wearing it. She charmed him with nothing more than her enthusiasm, and Will sighed at his thoughts.

"Got a sturdy leather or heavy canvass jacket?" Will asked. "Boots would be best, but good sneakers would be okay."

Jessica wrinkled her face and hummed in concentration. "I think so. Be right back."

Will watched her dash off at the same clip she'd run out to him, and it made him laugh. The laughter died when Jessica came back out of the house in less than two minutes wearing well-worn dark brown cowboy boots and a leather jacket that molded to her impressive curves. Her comfort in her clothes and herself had his mouth watering and his hands shaking to get on her. He sighed with longing when she was standing directly in front of him again.

Jessica grinned at Will's sigh and liked him even more for being the kind of man whose passion was visible.

"I ride a lot of things," Jessica teased, the lines at her eyes crinkling under his inspection. "This is my horse gear."

Will stepped up to her with the helmet in his hand. She was even taller in her boots and was meeting his gaze full on. Jessica Daniels was literally the tallest woman he could ever remember going out with, even counting college, which was a hell of a long time ago. He pulled the helmet down on her head, feeling her hands come up to push it back and seat it more comfortably.

"How's it feel?" he asked, his hands on the straps.

She brought her hands up to Will's, brushing hers quickly over them to encourage him, trying to pretend not to be thrilled when he froze at her touch.

"Feels good. Adjust the straps. I'm ready for my ride," she said on a laugh.

Will blinked a couple times, then moved his now slightly shaking hands under her chin to secure the chin strap. She tilted her chin up for greater access and his gaze went directly to her unpainted mouth.

"Just do it," Jessica told him, her smiling gaze taunting him.

"What?" Will asked, still sliding straps to adjust each side of the helmet.

"Kiss me and get it over with," Jessica told him. "I'm as curious as you are about it."

"How do you know I'm curious?" Will demanded, trying to decide if he liked her aggressiveness or not.

She was awfully forward, almost too honest. He hadn't even decided if he was going to kiss her yet, even if he did want to.

"Maybe I'm not as curious as you think," Will chastised, frowning and trying to convince himself her suggestion was too much too soon. He dropped his hands from the straps and took one step back for breathing room.

"Chicken," Jessica taunted, laughing as Will all but scowled at her.

"You flirt this hard with all the guys you date?" Will asked, seriously frowning at her as he slipped on his jacket.

"Only the ones I really, really want to kiss in return," Jessica said, crossing her arms and levelly meeting his gaze.

"Good to know," Will told her, narrowing his gaze at her and wondering just how many guys that had been, not that he cared. He looked at Jessica's mouth longingly one last time and pulled his own helmet over his head.

"We're wasting daylight," he said to her, using a phrase his dad had used often in his youth to hurry him up. He turned and stepped over the bike. "You coming or not?"

Disappointed he hadn't taken her up on her dare, Jessica almost replied with a scathing comment, but in the end she decided to play nice. She wanted the bike ride. It had been twenty years and she was genuinely looking forward to it. So she bit her tongue and dropped the subject.

She walked to the bike and swung herself onto the seat behind him. "Do you want me to hang on to you or the bike?" she asked, sliding her long legs intimately beside his hips and along his thighs, putting her crotch practically against his back. Yoga kept a woman very flexible, and as a fairly large woman, Jessica appreciated being loose in her hips. With a little effort and the right motivation, she could have flattened herself against his back but figured she had already worried him enough.

It was all Will could do not to scoot backward into the heat of her. With Jessica wrapped around him, Will suddenly found himself fighting to breath normally. He started the bike before he answered, hoping the idle would cover the huskiness of his voice.

His level of interest in the woman was way too advanced for a first date, Will thought. Hell, it was way too advanced for him period. He wasn't sure yet what he even felt about dating, much less what he felt about Jessica Daniels, her long legs, or the heat at his back. It was appealing, but damn—he needed time to think about it.

"I haven't had a passenger on a bike with me since my sons were in high school. I guess just put your arms around me and hang on," Will said finally, breathing a sigh when she kept her hands above his belt line. If she let them drop, he would wreck them before they got off her street.

Doing as she was told, and feeling the firmness of his chest under her hands, Jessica thought the women of this town needed to have their libidos checked for letting this man run around alone. It was all she could do to keep her hands off the rest of him.

Not that Will seemed to be having the same problem, which was a damn shame. If she'd been younger that disappointment might have ruined her day, but at her age it was not the end of the world.

And as much as she hated to admit it, she'd been down this road with other men before. There could be only one reason, Jessica concluded, for Will not kissing her when she could clearly see he wanted to. It was the same reason he likely had for not dating up to now. Everett Williams was obviously still in love with his ex-wife.

Sighing heavily at the knowledge, Jessica hugged Will tighter. Her suspicions were depressing and sucked most of the excitement away from the ride. They were halfway to Berea before Jessica could finally quiet her disappointment enough to enjoy the air whizzing past her and the rumble under her rear.

How old had she been when she dated the last guy with a motorcycle? She had probably been twenty-something—twenty-something and still happily naïve about men. They had ridden the bike everywhere and made love on it several times. She had fond, fond memories of those previous bike rides. Riding with Will now, years later, was certainly no hardship either, even if a bike ride was all she was going to get from him today.

Sad, but feeling better about her motives, Jessica decided to just focus on being a good companion to Will. When they cruised into the parking lot of the arts center, she climbed off first without being asked, knowing it was what she needed to do. She could tell she had surprised him. It brought a smile to her face.

Will didn't comment on Jessica's actions as he set the kickstand and climbed off himself. It was obvious he wasn't her first bike ride, and he couldn't help wondering who she'd ridden with before him.

"Great ride," she exclaimed, removing her helmet on her own. "I like how you drive, Will. Bike is smooth as glass, too. It's been twenty years since I've been on a bike. Yours is great."

"Yes, it is," Will replied, basking in her praise, even as he wondered about her change in attitude.

Gone was the seducing siren who had climbed on his bike. It was like they had left her behind in Lexington. Instead of feeling relieved, Will found he was sorely disappointed. He looked at Jessica's softly smiling mouth, wondering what would happen if he kissed her now. She looked away from him, pretending not to notice his study, but Will knew she was aware of everything he did.

Damn it, he thought. The woman was under his skin already. How and when had that happened?

"So where's your work?" Jessica asked, taking a few steps and stretching her legs.

Will unlocked the compartments on each side of the bike. "You can store your gear in here if you want. Hang the helmet off the handle bar."

Jessica did as he asked and bent to check her hair in the bike mirror. "Oh God," she said, running fingers through her wildly curling hair trying to tame the worst of the helmet hair problems. "I forgot about that little side effect." She laughed as she straightened. "Got an ink pen?"

Will pulled his leather jacket back out of the side compartment and retrieved a pen from the pocket before handing it to her. He couldn't imagine what surface the woman intended to write on or what piece of knowledge was so critical she had to write it down.

"Oh, that's the perfect kind," Jessica said sweetly, taking the straight stick ink pen from Will.

Will watched, mesmerized, as Jessica twisted and wound her hair with her fingers, finally using the ink pen to secure it in place at the back of her head. When she was finished, her hair was as tame as her conversation had been since she'd climbed off the bike. It brought yet another frown to Will's face, making him wonder what kind of reaction he was having to her.

The woman was being nothing but pleasant, yet he found her sweetness irritating as hell for some reason. The urge to kiss her was strong. His regret for not doing it earlier was even stronger. Whether he wanted to or not, Will sincerely missed the aggressive woman who had flirted so hard with him before. He wanted that woman back.

"Okay, I'm ready now," she said brightly, smiling at Will without any heat, without revealing anything more than polite interest in his art. "Let's see your work."

"Sure. Fine," Will answered, wondering what else he was expecting.

Whatever it was, he wasn't getting to the bottom of it in the parking lot.

He led her to the side of the center and to a paved garden area filled with budding trees. They stopped at a white alabaster piece consisting of five large interconnected circles, each round ring looking like it grew out of the last one.

"This piece is abstract. I don't do many of these, but now and again the idea for one comes and I usually indulge it," Will said quietly.

"Wow, this is all one piece," Jessica said reverently, amazed at the smooth precision of it, the intricate, graceful design. "Will, this is amazing."

Jessica ran her hand over the piece alternatively looking between him and his art. She couldn't help wondering how Will visualized a piece like this as he was working on it.

"You definitely have a gift," she said, meaning it more than she had imagined she would.

Will watched her running fingertips over the piece, her experience of it as much in her touch as it was in her gaze traveling over it. She used her hands for tactile exploration, a touch meant to learn secrets, but still reverent and full of admiration. She was touching his art exactly how he'd imagined her touching him.

Interested parts of his body started to harden at the enticing idea that it could be next. There was shock followed closely by a deep acceptance of his desire for her, but he didn't have a clue how to tell Jessica what was going on. With erotic thoughts robbing him of the ability to speak, Will said nothing much in reply to her comments about his art, just motioned Jessica deeper into the area when she was done with the first piece.

Set in a paver circle, the seven-foot marble man Will called 'David 13' was a little too realistic to greet modest guests at the center, but he certainly had an impact on those willing to venture deeper.

Naming his work after the statue he considered the greatest of all body sculpting work, Will considered his attempts to create art were only emulation. The numbers were self-explanatory for the attempt. So caught up was he in seeing his earlier work again himself, Will hadn't realized Jessica was still moving forward until she had walked completely past him.

She appeared to be in some sort of trance, Will decided, a small smile tugging at his mouth. His amusement didn't last long. Jessica walked up to 'David 13', reached out, and put her entire right palm flat over the all-too-realistic penis, covering the majority of it with her sizable hand.

Will couldn't stop the shiver that shook him as he watched Jessica's hand travel down and back up skimming and cupping the marble, taking its measure, gauging its proportions. He was suddenly dizzy with a soul-deep longing for her hands on him, and right behind that some unnamed fear rose up that engulfed what remained of his sanity.

He couldn't make himself look away from what Jessica was doing to the statue as she explored it. At the same time, he continued to shake in apprehension of what she was concluding.

"You carve this part first," Jessica said roughly, her throat constricted by her awe of the work. "You start here and that's why the proportions are perfect. This is the most perfectly proportioned statue I have ever seen."

Keeping her right hand covering the marble male organ, she reached her left arm up to its head, out to his shoulder, across to the statue's arm and down to its wrist. She switched hands, and repeated the measurements on the other side.

"I could teach a math class with these measurements. You're incredibly precise and incredibly talented—I can't believe. . ."

Her comments were halted by Will spinning her around hard to face him.

"Stop," he commanded. "Just stop touching. . ." His words drifted off as he gazed into her awestruck face.

Jessica had one moment to register the fear and physical pain on his face, then Will totally robbed her of breath when his mouth met hers in a hard, devastating kiss. His mouth on hers could have been glorious, could have been the stuff of dreams in fact, but his anxiety provoked too fierce a response in her. She fought to free herself from his mouth's invasion of hers, but couldn't get through the anger to coax him to soften his lips.

Jessica felt the evidence of his desire for her pushing against her legs, but what should have been thrilling simply wasn't under the circumstances. In fact, it wasn't even pleasant. It was intimidating, and it hurt her to think that Will likely meant the experience to be as scary as it was. He was purposely silencing her comments, and it was working.

Passion—true passion—seemed totally gone from her as she made herself cease struggling. She let herself grieve the loss and for a few moments just absorbed all the anger Will poured into her through his mouth. And when she acknowledged his anger fully, her heart and soul—the part of her that mattered—retreated as far as possible from him.

Jessica once again exerted some force to pull her mouth from his, but Will only pressed harder, held her tighter. His tongue continuously seeking advantage and taking it, whether she was willing to grant access or not. She pushed the panic away as she'd taught herself to do with aggressive men. It had been a very long time since she had allowed herself to be powerless in the arms of any man.

Then it hit her suddenly, the realization, the understanding of where the art came from inside Will. His embarrassment, his pain, and his punishment of her for seeing it, were all suddenly clear to her.

Jessica struggled against Will with more force as she renewed her efforts to pull away, her rising angst finally giving her enough strength to fight against his hold on her. She was seconds from doing something to physically hurt him when Will finally let her go.

Free of his demanding mouth at last, and more mad and hurt than she'd been in a couple decades, Jessica couldn't have stopped the truth from pouring out if her life had depended on it. She was never, never again going to let her experience of life be silenced or controlled by any man, especially not one she might have liked under better circumstances.

"Self-portrait in stone," Jessica said stiffly, swallowing tightly, upset to have to push remnants of her reluctant arousal down, deep down inside her. "The statue is you, Will. The proportions are yours. The perfect statue of David. The perfect form. It's like I already know your body from touching your work. I'm right, aren't I?"

Will tightened his hold on her upper arms, gripping hard enough to bruise her, but he couldn't seem to help himself. Jessica had stripped away the artistic secrets of several decades from him in under ten minutes. He was suddenly very afraid of the other damage she could cause. It was too late to stop himself from hearing her conclusions, too late to wish she hadn't seen and understood.

"How?" he demanded harshly. "How do you know these things? I've been doing this work for thirty-two years. You're the only person who ever just *saw*."

"What does it matter?" Jessica asked sadly. "Why does it bother you so much?"

She stood in his arms with his hands gripping her painfully, stood there and reeled from understanding. Intuitive knowing poured into her like someone filling a bucket up with water until it overflowed. Looking into the artistic soul of this man was like looking into a mirror and seeing herself. Already she was deeply regretting her insights, and Will's bruising grip was making her sorry for speaking the truth out loud to a man so unready to hear it.

And intentional or not, Will's artistic pride was completely destroying the wonderfully sweet attraction simmering between them. Regardless of how much it grieved her, there had been nothing even remotely affectionate in Will's punishing kiss, even if it had still weakened her legs and cemented her feet to the ground.

Even now the man still looked at her with loathing, and Jessica could feel Will's panic all the way to her bones. Empathy for him assailed her, but she also cursed him to hell and back for making her care. Despite the number of men she had dated and bedded, she was standing by the man's art with her heart breaking for him and for what they could have had if he had been ready for it—for her.

But she wasn't seventeen this time, though the attraction and the capacity to love Everett Williams had come just as hard and just as fast as it had with Nathan Daniels. Older and much wiser, Jessica could and would run, she vowed. This time she would not have to have the pain of loving and losing.

Jessica pulled twenty-two years of teaching around her and summoned her best, most authoritative voice. "Get your fucking hands off me or I'm going to knee you in the balls."

Yanking herself forcefully from Will's grip at last, Jessica stepped away from him in relief. She glared over her shoulder at the artistic perfection he had created, and then glared at Will as well, who seemed to finally have the common sense to look ashamed. Then she turned her back on Everett Williams and his work and strode briskly away from both.

By the time Will got to the parking lot and the bike, Jessica was standing arms crossed, gaze on the pavement, her helmet in her hand.

"You don't have to worry about me telling anyone your artistic secrets," Jessica informed him quietly, but firmly. "I teach art, Will. Go with that explanation about how I knew, and we'll both be better off. I'm ready to go home now."

Even though the apology he owed her was on his tongue, Will didn't say anything in return, just opened the compartments on the bike to retrieve the rest of their gear. Still feeling exposed from her observations, he didn't know how sincere his apology would be anyway—which was just as well because Jessica didn't look capable of hearing anything he might have to say to her.

What in the devil had possessed him to kiss her like that? He had just wanted to stop her from telling him more because he hadn't been able to bear hearing what she saw in his work. But the moment his lips touched hers, the desire that had been building for hours had ruled his actions. Will hadn't even realized how far gone he had been until she wrenched herself from his arms and swore at him. His instant remorse and shock at his actions had frozen his tongue.

Jessica was suited up, zipped, and helmet in place before Will had finished his own. He climbed on the bike and felt her settle in the seat behind him. This time she used her knees to hold his hips, keeping the rest of her as far away from him as possible.

He immediately missed the heat of her, missed the intimacy of her long legs beside his. Her hands around his middle weren't shaking, weren't damp, weren't even moving. It was like Jessica had drawn her entire personality back inside herself to keep it away from him, Will thought regretfully, just as she had now positioned her body as far away from his as she could on the seat.

He started the bike and reached a hand to pat hers as a signal they were going to be moving. She didn't flinch away from his touch, but she didn't acknowledge it back either. All remnants of the vibrating energy of excitement she'd had when he'd picked her up were totally gone. In fact, it was like there was no connection between them at all anymore, Will thought, frowning.

Not only shouldn't he have kissed her when he was so upset, he also shouldn't have all but accused her of—*what,* he asked himself? What had she done? Tell him some truth he wasn't comfortable hearing? So what if all of his male statues were self-portraits? What did he have to be ashamed of?

He still couldn't explain his panic, couldn't explain the magnitude of anxiety he'd felt when Jessica told him the truth about his art. She had reached inside to places he had locked away from everyone, even his children. First he had panicked, and then he had overreacted. Now he was ashamed, but didn't know how to make things right again.

At her house, Jessica climbed off and removed the helmet, handing it to him along with the ink pen that had been in her hair. She leaned down and kissed his cheek lightly, barely a brush. The lack of any emotion in it had his gut churning.

"Thanks for the bike ride," Jessica said, breezily. "See you around, Everett Williams. It was interesting to meet you. Good luck with your work."

With a wave over her shoulder, Jessica walked slowly up her sidewalk until she disappeared behind a firmly closed door.

Maybe he hadn't dated in decades, but Will recognized her actions as a major and very final brush-off. He scrubbed a hand over the still visible part of his face, then turned around and stowed her helmet in the now empty storage compartment.

Jessica's helmet, Will thought miserably, something he'd bought for the sole purpose of taking her for a ride. He wasn't going to be letting anyone else use it anytime soon, no matter how brave he'd been earlier.

Tucking the pen she gave him back into his jacket, Will stared off down the street, letting the reality of what had happened sink in completely. He knew enough about women to know what returning the pen meant. Jessica was done with him. She wanted no reminders of their time together.

Now he wished like hell he'd kissed her earlier in the afternoon when she had taunted him. He wished he'd just stepped into her and hungrily kissed her teasing mouth when her lips had first called to him. She would have tasted like the excitement and energy of wanting the bike ride. She would have kissed him back, laughed against his mouth, and maybe even invited his tongue to play with hers.

Instead, he'd forced his mouth on hers when he was angry, forced an intimacy she obviously hadn't wanted at that moment. As Will thought about it now, he realized Jessica had not for one moment responded with any heat to his kiss in the garden. Not that what he'd done counted as real kissing anyway. He almost wished Jessica had kneed him. Maybe it would have balanced out some of his now growing guilt.

The only thing that helped calm him at all was remembering that Melanie knew her, knew who Jessica really was and all about her life. Will decided he would just give Jessica Daniels some time to stop being so upset at him, and then he would find a way to make this right with her.

Today was not going to be the only interaction he had with Jessica Daniels.

He wasn't a bad guy. He certainly couldn't live with the idea she might think he was one.

Will sighed unhappily, put the bike in gear, and rolled away from her curb.

CHAPTER 4

The statue in Michael's work area now had a leg and the beginning of a hip. Will had found the motivation to carve again when the panic over his botched 'date' had subsided. He had had a full week to think about things, a week where he told himself to forget Jessica Daniels, but found he couldn't. The wound she had opened in him had mostly closed and healed. He had hoped every day the same was true for Jessica because he wanted another chance. He had to find a way to get the warmth of her back into his life.

"No chemistry, huh?" Will said morosely, sighing into his coffee as he took a sip. "I can't believe Jessica said we had no chemistry. She's lying, Melanie. There's enough chemistry between Jessica Daniels and me to blow up a damn science lab."

Melanie wanted to laugh at how upset Will seemed to be over the one and only reason Jessica had given her as explanation of why things hadn't worked out on the date. She had never heard William Larson swear before, never seen him upset for more than a few moments. She'd love to know what really happened between Jessica and him on their 'date.' Jessica had pretty much refused to talk about the details of it.

"That's all she told me," Melanie confirmed with a shrug.

"Do you think she was serious?" Will asked.

Melanie shrugged again. "Jessica's pretty honest. I can't even tell you half the things she said the day she met you here. I blush thinking about them. But I guess if she didn't feel anything when you guys kissed—I mean, she said she didn't feel much, Mr. Larson. Women are usually pretty honest with other women about things like that."

No chemistry, Will thought. Well that was just bullshit. There was chemistry. Granted, he hadn't used any finesse with her, had definitely not shown her his best moves, but there had been chemistry—damn it. Plus he couldn't stop thinking about her.

"She's lying, Melanie," Will said again, absolutely believing it and planning to prove it to Jessica the next time he saw her. "Don't call me Mr. Larson anymore. Call me Will, and tell me Jessica Daniels' story. Why isn't she married?"

Melanie shrugged. "I don't know if she wants to get married. Jessica dates a lot," she said carefully, thinking Will didn't need to know specifics of what that meant. Some men wouldn't understand a woman like Jessica who did what she wanted.

"Jessica told me she got married at seventeen. Her husband was a solider and got killed before she got to go overseas to be with him. There was a guy she dated seriously for a couple of years in her early thirties, but he kept wanting her to cut her hair and dress more—I don't know—not like herself I guess. I saw him a few times. He was very good-looking, but never seemed quite happy with who Jessica really was as a person. They broke up the first year Brent and I were in her class. After that, Jessica hasn't stayed with any one guy very long."

"What kind of art does she do?" Will asked.

"That's too personal for me to share with you," Melanie said quietly, her voice and her tone firm and uncompromising. "If she wants you to know, she'll tell you herself."

What kind of art could the woman be protecting that was more embarrassing than his statues, Will wondered? Jessica had put her hands on his penis for crying out loud. Well not his, he amended, but his statue's—which was practically the same thing—as she had damn well figured out the first time she'd touched his work.

"Her art is too personal? What does that mean? Is she embarrassed by it?" Will demanded.

Melanie looked at him with firmness in her gaze. "It simply means her art is too personal and that I'm not telling you no matter what tone you use on me. I outgrew being afraid of you when I started serving you coffee last year."

Will rubbed a hand over his face. "Sorry. The woman scrambled my brain. I should have kissed her when she told me to the first time. Now I'm haunted by not doing it right."

Melanie burst out laughing. "You did kiss her. Jessica told me about it. She said it wasn't very good—sorry. I don't mean to keep harping on the fact."

"What we did wasn't kissing," Will said morosely. "That was panic, fear, and a bunch of other things. She saw my art, made some comments, and then something erupted between us. I need another chance with her, Melanie."

Melanie sighed deeply, fetched the coffee pot, and refilled his cup. "Why?"

Will thought about that for a moment.

"I don't know for sure," he finally admitted. "I can't stop thinking about her, and I just know I need another chance. I can't let what happened be all Jessica Daniels remembers about me."

Melanie saw genuine concern in his face and mentally crossed her fingers at her decision to help him again.

"Do not make me regret telling you this. Jessica is coming by Sunday to put up some art outside. We'll be closed then, but you might just want to swing by on your bike and see what happens. If you tell her I told you about it, I'm banning you from coming here."

"I won't tell her, and I'm doubling your tip today," Will told her, smiling. "Thanks, Melanie."

Melanie looked at him hard. He didn't seem so intimidating today, didn't seem like anything more than a sad older man who'd messed up with a nice woman.

"You remind me of my father today, and I'm feeling sorry for you. Want me to give you some more advice? It might embarrass you," Melanie warned.

"Sure," Will said. "Can't be any worse than what my sons said about the situation when I told them."

"Do more of that stool thing you did the first time you met her," Melanie said carrying the coffee pot back to the burner, laughing when Will covered his flushing face with his hand. "I know it embarrasses you, but Jessica loved that. She loves to flirt. You don't know her, but she has more life in her than any ten women you will ever meet. I think she needs romance the way flowers need water or human beings need air."

Will nodded affirmatively and sighed again as he sipped his coffee.

"Thanks, Melanie," he said, hoping his screw-up with Jessica Daniels was as redeemable as he hoped.

~

When Will swung the bike into the café parking lot on Sunday, he was greeted by Jessica's jean covered backside bent over a large plywood construction project on the ground. So mesmerized was he by the site of her jeans stretched over her hips, he hit the parking space chock abruptly and stalled the bike. He hadn't done such a dumb thing in years, and it flustered him.

Will saw Jessica's head come up and her gaze swing around to him, but there was no friendly smile or wave, no welcome excited energy rolling off her toward him. He felt the loss in his gut. Then Will finally noticed the other people with her, lots of men of various ages, except for one young woman he would guess to be around Shane's age.

Several of the younger men were openly admiring the bike. Others, like the older two men, moved closer to Jessica. Will watched her shake her head in answer to a question from one of them. Then she turned her back and returned to what she was doing, which seemed to involve a lot of energetic pounding on nails.

Will stowed his jacket in the storage compartment and hung his helmet from the handlebars. Pulling himself up to his full height, he walked slowly over to join the group where Jessica was bent over and working. He scowled at one man across the way, who was sneaking looks at Jessica's bent form when she wasn't looking. It was effective enough to stop the man's leering and to momentarily ease the frown on Will's face.

The young woman, who had blatantly watched the exchange, smiled broadly at Will.

Closer now, he could see the young woman was at least in her late twenties, and he would bet she missed nothing, judging by the knowing smile she kept sending his way. She reminded him of Melanie, only sassier. He also saw her hair was red, like the other sassy woman in his life, who was still bent from her very alluring hips and completely ignoring him.

If Jessica Daniels had been a mind reader and had seen the images in his head that her rear inspired, she would have straightened right up, Will thought darkly. He was not even comfortable himself with where his thoughts had gone, but with the other guy staring at her, Will's need to compete for her ruled his common sense. He imagined his fantasies were affecting the tightness of his jaw as well as his jeans.

"Hello, Jessica. You look busy," Will said, hoping to snag her attention and get her to stand up and look at him.

"Hello, Will. Out for a Sunday drive?" she asked politely, not raising her gaze from her work.

Will debated what to say. He hated lying, but didn't want to admit his intentions and scare her either.

"Not really," he finally said, disappointed when she didn't pry. "I thought I'd stop when I saw you. Melanie said something about you doing some art for the café."

"Okay, it's ready," Jessica said out loud, ignoring Will's last comment and standing up at last. She wondered briefly just what Melanie had told him, then reminded herself she didn't care.

"Kyle? You and Tom stand it up. Let's take one more look before we mount it on the building," she said.

Jessica stepped back to let the boys have plenty of room.

Will watched two tall young boys run to do her bidding and heave the large art piece up to a standing position so she could inspect it. He grinned at the plywood woman's face, her playful nose sniffing daises and fifty other kinds of colorful flowers floating out and up the curved design. It was colorful, eye-catching, and glitzy.

And it suited the café perfectly.

"It will do," Jessica said, perusing it. "We can fix the little things once it's up."

"Hey, gorgeous," a deep voice said nearby, "ready for your manpower yet?"

"Your timing is perfect as always," Jessica purred. "Thank you, Steve."

Will gritted his teeth as the tall, well-built man she called Steve, walked to one end of the sign. The man nodded at Will with his chin. "Can you get the other end?"

Saying nothing, Will just nodded and went to the other side and lifted. While he and the man held the art to the building, ten hammers descended on it. Will felt his teeth rattle as the boys went after the nails with the zest of young men showing off for each other. Their full-out enthusiasm made him smile because he'd always loved kids, and not just his own. It's why he'd gone into teaching in the first place, though he'd ended up a principal for a much longer time than he had taught.

Will was still smiling when he felt Jessica's gaze on him, but when he caught her staring, she only looked away. However, the younger woman by her side had taken her eyes off Will only long enough to look at Jessica and back to him.

It was like she was trying to figure out a puzzle. And that makes two of us, Will decided, smiling genuinely at both the boys and the younger woman.

Steve let go of the sign at last, and Will stepped away as well.

"I'm Steve Lipton," the man said, walking to Will and sticking out a hand.

"Everett Williams. Call me Will," Will said, taking his hand and looking at Jessica again, not willing to tell her about his other life until he had settled the issues of this one, since this was the life he was trying to share with her.

"You a friend of Jessica's?" Steve asked, a knowing look in his eyes.

"Trying to be," Will replied, watching Jessica walk away and out of earshot after hearing his words.

He watched as Jessica walked to a group of kids painting a giant flowerpot and bent from her hips again to inspect their work. Will narrowed his eyes on her very appealing jean-covered rear end and sighed loudly.

Steve laughed. "Good luck with that. Jessica is a tough woman to genuinely get to know. Adam over there is trying the same thing."

Will looked in the direction of a man who had risen from his task of assembling some sort of metal pot hanger. He walked over to Jessica and stood as close to her as humanly possible without actually putting his arms around her.

The man was at least ten years younger than he was, Will observed unhappily. Hell, the man might even be closer to Michael's age. Did Jessica prefer younger men, he wondered?

"What does Adam do?" Will asked.

"He's a math teacher," Steve said, enjoying the big man's obvious jealousy. This was not Jessica's usual sort. Will didn't look like he'd be so easily managed by flirtatious charm. "Adam has been dating her for a while now, but I would say he's gotten about as far with her as you have."

"Really?" Will said, wondering why it hadn't occurred to him Jessica might have already met someone new. "How long have they been dating?"

Steve shrugged. "Let me think. Probably for six months now—something like that. It was after Jessica and I broke up. I think it was before Sam the councilman, and after George the electrician. There were a couple other guys in there, too, but I forget their names. Jessica likes men, and she dates a lot."

Steve laughed openly at the shock on Will's face. "I see you don't know Jessica."

"Why are you here if you broke up with her?" Will asked, not fully believing the man's story. Though he was reconciled to his wife's new relationship, he wasn't rushing over to the cabin on the lake to help Ellen and Luke work on it any time soon. Steve Lipton had to be exaggerating.

Then Steve pointed to the boy Jessica was currently patting on the shoulder.

"My son adores her, and she encourages his art. And she's a great person, like what she's doing today for Melanie and Brent Madison. Jessica and I are friends, Will. Once you know her, you always care about her. She's just that kind of person. I'm engaged but still planning to invite Jessica to the wedding. What we had was great, but is no more."

Will looked at Steve, and then looked at the math teacher hovering over Jessica's arm. If the man had looked at Will, he'd have found him scowling again. If the man put his hand possessively on Jessica Daniels, Will wasn't sure what he would do. Breaking the math teacher's fingers held a certain appeal, but it would only be another show of the same aggressiveness he'd displayed in Berea. Aggression was not going to net him the result he wanted.

"So what kind of work do you do, Will?" Steve said, trying to distract the giant guy and save Adam's butt from violence. Whatever was between Will and Jessica, it was something Adam needed to steer clear of until it had run its course, which knowing Jessica wouldn't be long. This giant man with brooding eyes didn't look like the kind of person to willingly share a woman with anyone.

"I'm an artist—a stone sculptor," Will said.

Steve raised his eyebrows. "An artist? Have you seen any of Jessica's work?"

"No," Will said, fully intending now to find out what it was as soon as he could. "Where can I find some? It may be a while before I get a personal invitation. I messed up with Jessica on our first date."

Steve laughed. "I doubt you go any place where you would ever see Jessica's art. It doesn't really end up in art shows or museums. It's best you just let her show you sometime. Her art is very personal. She doesn't show it to many of her dates."

"So I've heard," Will said, frowning. "She showed it to you?"

Steve smiled, narrowed his gaze. "Jessica and I were very close. I would have married her if I thought she would have ever loved me. I never found a permanent place in her heart."

Will wondered how many other old lovers he was going to have to wade through, and asked himself if Jessica Daniels was really worth it.

Then the young woman, who was nearly as tall as Jessica, whispered something to her after the math teacher stepped away. Jessica's peal of laughter rang out, and every man, regardless of age, looked up grinning to see if he could take credit for her amusement.

When Jessica's laughing gaze reluctantly met Will's, he saw the enthusiastic girl in the woman again. He saw the woman he'd messed up with and the one he wanted. And even though Will could hear both his sons laughing at him now, it looked like he wasn't going to have to worry about dating anymore. He'd found the woman he ached for already.

"You friends with the math teacher?" Will asked roughly.

Steve's laughter was low and conspiratorially male. "Not really, but he's an okay guy. Why? Is it time I go distract him to keep you from pounding on him?"

Will smiled, all wickedness and determination. He shook his head from side to side. "No, I'll take care of discouraging him. I just wondered if you cared. You seem like a nice enough guy."

"I am a nice guy. That's why I'm giving you all this free advice. Jessica doesn't like to be chased," Steve warned him, grinning. "She likes to do the chasing, and you have to pretend to let her."

"That's going to be a problem then because I'm not good at pretending," Will said, reaching out a hand again, "but I appreciate the advice, Steve."

Steve laughed and shook his head. "Good luck, Mr. Williams. You're going to need it if you're interested in Jessica Daniels."

Will grinned and walked off to join the group where Jessica now stood.

"MOM, WHO IS THE HOT BIKER GUY WHO KEEPS GLARING AT YOUR MATH teacher?" Brooke asked.

"He's not hot," Jessica asked. "He's as cold as the stone he carves."

"Cold? I don't think so," Brooke said smartly in a singsong tone. "And just how do you know?"

Jessica looked at her daughter and raised one eyebrow. "I went for a ride with him. Trust me—I know."

"I can tell he makes you nervous," Brooke commented, seeing the slight quiver in her mother's hands as she worked. She tried to remember if there had ever been any relationship that rocked her mother's world, but she couldn't recall one. Her gaze returned to Will, who was looking at her mother like a starving man who hadn't eaten in months.

"He looks older than the math teacher, Mom. How old is he?" Brooke asked, curious as he continued slowly toward them. He certainly had a nice body for an older guy.

"Down, daughter. He's too old for you," Jessica replied, making Brooke laugh.

"So if I made a play for him, what would you do? Glare at me like he's glaring at the other men here? You two sleeping together?" Brooke taunted, already knowing the answer. She just wanted to torture her mother into talking about it so she could figure out what was going on.

"God no," Jessica said. "Everett Williams is still hung up on his ex-wife. I'm not that desperate."

"Doesn't look like he's interested in anyone other than you. And I already know you're not desperate," Brooke teased. "If you were, you'd be sleeping with the math teacher. I mean math—really, Mom? Never go for a man who thinks everything in life is a formula. Their brains don't have room for the more interesting stuff."

The laughter burst out of Jessica. "Says the woman working her way through her fair share of handsome law school candidates who quote cases and objections every five seconds."

Brooke pretended to shiver. "I can't help it. They drive me crazy. I like to see how long it takes for them to stop talking about cases in the middle of sex. Being my mother's daughter, I've broken my own record for distraction several times."

Jessica laughed harder and smiled more broadly. "I'm pretty sure even a thirty-year-old daughter is never supposed to tell her mother that much information."

Brooke shrugged. "I think a thirty-year-old daughter can say pretty much anything to a mother who makes the most beautiful vagina art in the world. You're the world's most honest woman."

Jessica stood, hands on hips, and contemplated Brooke's statement.

"I see you've learned the art of arguing from your lovers. I have no rebuttal to that, counselor," she teased. "You fall in love with any of those legal bozos yet?"

"No," Brooke said, "but I haven't been looking for love. I'm waiting until I decide on a college to teach at next year. Then I'll settle down and marry some tenured professor at thirty-two, have my two beautiful babies eighteen months apart, and write a best-selling novel. Once I've accomplished my life's work, I will then enjoy my old age when I turn forty."

Jessica just looked at her daughter. "Old age at forty, huh? I hope you're teasing. I hope you know forty is not that old."

Brooke laughed. "Yes, I'm teasing. I love you, Mom." She looked again at the man who was still moving slowly and very deliberately toward her mother. "So what does the biker guy do?"

"Absolutely nothing for me," Jessica said archly, turning to see Will step up really close to her. She backed up a step and heard Brooke laugh.

Brooke stuck out her hand to the man. "I'm Brooke Daniels—Jessica's daughter."

Will snorted, grinned, and took the girl's hand. "Explains the red hair. Your mother calls me trouble, but you can call me Will."

Will smiled at her laugh and Jessica's glare.

"This is Everett Williams," Jessica said to her daughter, her haughty tone making Will's eyebrows raise, but she didn't really care what he thought.

"Call me Will," he repeated, dropping Brooke's hand to look at

Jessica full on. "I'm glad to finally have a chance to apologize for the other day, Jessica. I should have followed your advice when you told me to do it the first time."

"What advice?" Jessica asked.

"When I was adjusting your bike helmet before we took our ride," Will reminded her. "When you told me to just kiss you because we were both curious, I should have. I've regretted not kissing you in that moment ever since."

"It was just craziness. I was teasing you," Jessica said, shaking her head.

"I'm still curious," Will said boldly, his gaze never leaving Jessica's. "Aren't you?"

"Not after what happened in Berea," Jessica denied loudly, then flushed when Brooke covered her mouth with her hand. "I didn't mean that so emphatically. I mean it's obvious from what happened that we're not compatible. So no, I don't want you to kiss me anymore."

"You're lying," Will said gently, an easy smile on his face. "I panicked and got upset. Then I got carried away. I shouldn't have been so rough with you. You have every right to be mad about the way I treated you, but for God's sake, Jessica, you're too honest a woman to lie about the chemistry between us."

"You have no idea what kind of woman I am," Jessica said, crossing her arms.

"No, but I'm learning. I know you're dating other men, and I'm about to show the math teacher how much more compatible you are with me than him," Will threatened.

He took a tiny step closer to her, reaching out to cup her elbow in his hand. "Besides, your daughter likes me."

"No, she doesn't," Jessica denied, taken aback by his confident assertion.

"Yes, she does," Brooke agreed, smiling. "Kiss her, Will. She's dying for it. Trust me."

"Brooke Renee Daniels," Jessica said sternly, swinging her startled gaze to her daughter's laughing one.

"Well since I at least have one woman's permission this time," Will said, stepping fully into the now vibrating Jessica. For me, he assured himself, feeling the energy emanating from her. This is not for the math teacher or for Steve. This is mine.

He moved as quickly, but also as gently as possible, pulling a protesting Jessica's arms down, and then put his mouth lightly, but firmly over hers before she had time to step away from him.

Unable to stop himself, Will moaned against the warmth of her lips and ran his tongue lightly over her bottom one. He made no attempt to sneak his tongue inside, even though he badly wanted to taste her. Jessica moaned against his mouth in response, and opened her lips beneath his. His heart started beating again when he finally knew for certain she wanted the soft, exploring kiss as much he did. He allowed himself a moment more then pulled his lips from hers.

Will couldn't wait now until Jessica let him do it right without an audience. He couldn't wait to get his hands on the rest of her.

But he had to wait, had to give the math teacher and her time to adjust to it. Maybe he even still needed the time himself.

Will moved his lips to Jessica's forehead, not caring that his profound relief was obvious to everyone watching the show. He folded her into his arms for a friendly but possessive hug, and then just as quickly let her go.

"Thank you," Will said softly, where mostly only Jessica and her daughter could hear. "I needed you to know how special I thought you were, and to know how much I wanted to kiss you despite the fact you scare the hell out of me. I hope I haven't embarrassed you too much in front of your students. I'll see you soon, Jessica."

He looked at Brooke and winked, liking the way she bit her lip to keep from laughing. His boys would love her sense of humor.

As he walked back to his bike, Will saluted the math teacher, who was openly glaring at him now. He waved to the boys who were giving him thumbs-up signs and laughed at Steve shaking his head as he put on his riding gear.

Will rolled away on his bike with an idiot grin plastered to his face because Jessica had kissed him back and moaned.

That was enough for today.

He was suddenly looking forward to tomorrow.

"YEAH, I CAN SEE THE GUY DOESN'T DO ANYTHING FOR YOU," BROOKE told her mother, who had yet to close her mouth or tear her gaze from the man rolling away on the biggest black bike Brook had ever seen.

Jessica sighed and cursed Everett Williams for kissing her sweetly. "He hurt me, Brooke. I'm not letting him get a chance to do it again."

"Are you being a chicken?" Brooke squeaked the question, honestly shocked at her mother. "That's so not like you, Mom."

Jessica sighed again. "No, it's not. I hurt him, too. I don't want to do it again, Brooke. Will and I are not good for each other. We see too deeply into each other's souls."

Brooke nodded at the longing in her mother's face, a longing she wondered if Everett Williams was going to fill. She didn't like the idea of her mother growing older alone. She absolutely hated the fact that no man ever made her mother smile for more than a few days, even Jack the Jerk who had lasted way too long.

"Who are you—you big coward—and what did you do with my mother? You're never going to get over the biker guy until you get him out of your system. You're going to have to follow up on your attraction," Brooke ordered quietly. "The math teacher doesn't even stand a chance until then."

Jessica nodded. "Will's still in love with his ex-wife. It's only been a year. I'm the first woman he's has gone out with in all that time."

Brooke remembered the profound relief on the man's face when he kissed her mother's forehead, and knew her fear of the ex-wife was just an excuse her mother was using. Everybody in hearing distance had heard them both moan when Will kissed her, though that little lip brush could hardly be called a real kiss to Brooke's mind.

Brooke shook her head as she thought about the obvious chemistry between her mother and Will. What was it that worried her mother about the guy? He seemed like a big teddy bear to her, and she liked the way he glared at Adam whatever-his-name-was.

"Well, okay. You at least have to admit he's hot," Brooke said, laughing and hooking an arm around her mother's waist.

Jessica nodded. "Yes, okay. Will is hot. And evidently he can kiss as good as he looks, when he's not pissed off about something," she admitted, wincing as she looked around to see if any of the kids had heard her swear. "Will makes me crazy, and I forget who I am."

Brooke giggled. "Mom, you *are* getting old if you don't see that as a plus. That's the best kind of guy."

"Maybe when you're thirty," Jessica said, hugging her daughter back. "At my age, you just want consistent talent in the bedroom and to be left alone the rest of the time."

Brooke shook her head and laughed. "Who are you trying to convince? Me or you? You can't flirt with yourself, Mom," Brooke said wisely. "You're not the kind of woman who's meant to be alone. You're too much fun. You need a man in your life."

"Oh, I agree with that," Jessica said, gathering up her paints and brushes to go touch up the sign. "I just don't think Will is the right man."

"Being a sculptor, he would probably understand your art," Brooke said quietly.

Jessica thought about that for a minute and finally answered her daughter as neutrally as she could. "Yes. Will probably would."

But to understand, he would first have to find out. Will finding out about her art was a possibility that worried Jessica much more than the way her body was still humming from his kiss. As long as she was sexually interested in the man, Jessica hoped he never saw anything she had created.

CHAPTER 5

When she walked into the café, Jessica looked at the full tables and smiled. It was Saturday lunch. The booths and tables were filled, the bar stools were busy, and there was no place for Jessica to sit. She couldn't have been happier.

"I guess I need to come back later," Jessica said, laughing, as Melanie rounded the bar with several plates in her hand. "Or are you running a wait list?"

"You could pop back into the kitchen and give Brent a hand. We'll feed you for free," Melanie offered, face flushed but happy.

Jessica sighed, always a sucker for the hard working girl who reminded her of her own daughter. "Sure, but don't tell anyone else I work for food."

Melanie laughed and walked off to deliver what she carried.

In the kitchen, a nicely built young man was lining up chicken salad on beds of lettuce and mixed greens.

"Now there's a task I can probably do," Jessica said.

"Hey, Ms. Daniels," Brent said, smiling. "All that art brought them in, didn't it? I think we're actually going to have to hire real help if this keeps up."

"Are you slamming on my kitchen skills just because I let your wife talk me into helping for a free lunch?" Jessica said, arching an eyebrow at him.

"No, ma'am. They don't get any better than you, but you need to be free to follow your creative pursuits. It would be criminal to tie you to a cash register," Brent said, smiling at her. "Melanie ask you to help?"

Jessica nodded, went to the sink, and scrubbed hands and arms. She grabbed an apron off a hook and tied it over her jeans and T-shirt.

"Let me finish those chicken salads. I know what goes on them. That's one of my favorite things on the menu," she told him.

Jessica lifted a dish of mixed seeds and sprinkled them over the salads. Then she put a few grapes on the sides of the plate. When Melanie came back, she looked at the chicken salads and beamed at Jessica.

"Want a job here when you retire?" Melanie asked.

"No thanks," Jessica laughed, making a mock shudder of fear. "I don't even cook at home. Why would I want to cook here?"

Brent finished off a turkey club and slid two pickle slices onto the plate. He winked at his wife.

Melanie looked at Jessica, her gaze full of nothing but gratitude. "Can you take the club sandwich out to the guy in the last booth? Brent can help me deliver the rest of chicken salads."

"Sure," Jessica said with a shrug. She picked up the plate and headed out of the kitchen.

As she was walking down the café to the end booth, Jessica saw its occupant had his head bent over an art book. He looked very serious in his reading glasses and almost academic in his study.

He also looked very sexy when he raised his gaze and smiled at her in welcome.

Her mind went instantly and immediately back to their sweet kiss, and in her head, she heard him once again moaning against her mouth. She told herself to remember his aggression in the garden, but with him smiling at her in welcome, she couldn't bring Berea to mind for more than a few seconds.

"Wow. All I ordered was a sandwich. I didn't expect a fifties housewife to show up and deliver it. You do nice things for that apron, Jessica," Will told her.

Jessica slid the sandwich across the table in front of him and slid into the booth across from him. "Trust me, a fifties housewife I am not. I'm the least domestic woman you have ever met. I don't even boil water on the stove. I use an electric kettle to make tea."

Will nodded to the other restaurant patrons who had overheard his flirting. Then he picked up half his sandwich.

"Business has certainly picked up in here," he said, biting into the sandwich.

Jessica nodded and smiled again.

"Nice work drawing them in," Will said, taking another bite as he continued to hold her gaze.

Jessica shrugged. "The food is excellent. Now that people know about it, they'll all be back."

Will nodded and took another bite. "Yes, the food is excellent. The service is great. I come back because I also like the kind of people who hang out here."

Jessica grinned and looked at the table nearby with six women all in their seventies and eighties. They were all eating chicken salad.

"You into picking up older women? This place is crawling with those kinds of babes," she told him.

Will laughed, a genuine belly laugh. "Not really, but I got picked up here one day myself. I think the woman was a bit younger. I never got to find out her age. She was incredibly hot. I wouldn't mind running into her again."

Jessica laughed and slid out of the booth. "I think I know who you're talking about. If I see her drop by again, I'll let you know. She picks up men in here all the time."

Will shrugged and narrowed his gaze at her. "Maybe I'm the guy she's been looking for so hard."

"Doubtful," Jessica said, smiling. "If she doesn't show up though, I might come back and join you when my shift ends."

Will grinned and bit into a pickle, watching her face as he chewed.

"Sure," he said finally. "I got nothing better to do today than hang around and wait for you."

Jessica giggled and walked back to the kitchen, smacking Melanie on the arm and making Brent grin.

"That was so not fair of you. He flirted with me, and now I have go back out there and spend time with him. Where's my lunch? I'm taking my break early," Jessica informed the now laughing woman.

Melanie handed her a plate of chicken salad. "Can you at least refill drinks first?"

Jessica rolled her eyes as Brent laughed.

"You're a slave driver. I don't think I could ever work for you full time," Jessica grumbled, but grinned.

Melanie shrugged, returning the grin. "Will drinks unsweetened tea with his lunch."

"Like I care?" Jessica asked.

"He's a customer, Jessica," Melanie said on a laugh. "He needs his drink refilled too."

Jessica frowned, realizing she'd been caught overreacting. "Fine. Unsweetened tea. Got it."

When she left the kitchen, Brent shook his head at this wife. "I still don't believe the stool thing."

"Just wait until you see them together," Melanie said, running a hand over the very nice, very firm muscles in Brent's upper arm. "There's chemistry there—just like Mr. Larson said."

"Chemistry, huh," Brent said, dipping his mouth to his wife's for a quick taste of her sweetness, which went all the way to the bone. "I bet they don't have as much as we do."

Melanie let her hand drop and sweep across his hip, over a very well-rounded rear. Her husband was very well-formed for a man, and his body still delighted her even after seven years. "Maybe not, but they have something going on. You have to see it to believe it."

Brent turned and swept his wife into his arms, pulling her hips to his and showing her just how much chemistry was still there between them.

"I'm so glad we close early on Saturdays," Melanie said, using her hands to pull his hips to hers for a brief moment of bliss. Then she slowly pushed off him and sighed.

Brent grinned wickedly and went back to filling the orders.

~

JESSICA TOOK HER PLATE TO WILL'S BOOTH, PUT IT ON THE TABLE, AND then left again without speaking. She couldn't help noticing that Will did nothing but grin.

She walked around the café refilling drinks, talking to people she knew, and then finally brought a glass of tea to the booth when she returned to Will.

Digging into her chicken salad, she didn't talk much until it was half done.

"Research?" she asked, using her chin to indicate the book open at his elbow.

"Studying a new technique," Will said, swinging the book to where she could see.

"Can't really read without my glasses," Jessica said. "I'll have to take your word for it."

"It's basically just a new way to use the same tools. It keeps it fresh for me to see what new sculptors are doing," Will said, turning the book back toward him.

"Where did you study?" Jessica asked, going back to her food.

"Completely self-taught. I didn't study art in college. I studied social sciences," Will said easily.

That had her dropping her fork to the plate. "Your talent is all natural? You never took a lesson?"

"No, but I had an art teacher inspect the first carving I did," Will said, remembering. "It was my senior year in college. I carved my first statue, which was the size of a twelve-year-old boy, and it took me all semester. I wasn't an art student but had talked the art chair at UK into letting me work on it at the campus art studio. Then I let them critique it. They were harsh but advised me to skip the lessons and just pursue it on my own. Latent talent or something, I think they said."

"How old were you?" Jessica asked. "And I agree with University of Kentucky art department."

"Twenty-one," Will said. "I'm fifty-three now. How old are you?"

"Old enough not to have to admit my age," Jessica answered on a laugh. "Okay. That's not fair, is it? Not quite as old as you but in the same ball park—how's that?"

Will smiled. "Do you ever date men your age or older? Or are they all as young as the math teacher?"

Jessica narrowed her gaze. "Adam is thirty-nine and a little too old to be considered a boy-toy. I dated a man who was sixty-eight not too long ago. He was very nice but still mourning his wife who had just died. I date when I'm interested in someone."

"Are you interested in the math teacher?" Will asked, wanting and needing to hear her say no.

"Adam is an interesting man," Jessica said, hedging.

"Yes, I'm sure he is, but are you still dating him?" Will asked, hoping to get a direct answer to at least one of his questions.

"How did we move from talking about your art to discussing my social life?" Jessica asked, ignoring Will's question.

"It needed to be discussed. I'm a firm believer in monogamy and I don't share well," Will told her, taking the final bite of his sandwich.

Jessica shrugged. "And this concerns me how?"

"Are you interested in me? And don't lie," Will ordered, his voice carrying the same authority that had worked with teachers and students for years. "I'd rather just hear the truth than your flirtatious redirects."

"All right, here's the truth. I think you're also an interesting man, but I'm not interested in dating you," Jessica said, choosing her words carefully. But then she had to look away because saying it as Will held her gaze had been a lot harder than she thought it would be and had felt more wrong than she'd anticipated.

Will studied her downcast eyes and the way she now couldn't look at him. Why in the hell was Jessica lying, he wondered? Maybe she was still mad at him, he thought.

"Okay," Will said finally, letting his tone indicate he was sad but resigned. "No dating. I get it. How about a ride instead?"

Obviously surprised by his answer and the question, Will was happy to see Jessica's head snap up.

"Your bike was very nice, but once was enough. Thanks," Jessica said, raising her gaze to Will's, hoping he took the hint.

Will just grinned at her, wicked male intention in his gaze. "I wasn't talking about my bike, Jessica," he said, his tone quiet, serious, and firm. "The bike helmet wasn't all I bought that first day because of you."

When Jessica tried to escape from the booth, she knocked her still full glass of iced tea over on the table. She made an honest grab to stop it from tipping completely over, but the glass and ice cubes all rolled away from her. Liquid caught the edges of his book, but mostly swept across the surface to the other side dripping onto Will and the seat.

Laughing, Will slid out of the booth before the tea completely drowned his lap. There was some tea on the front of his jeans, but he didn't mind because Jessica's face was completely red as she fearfully stared at his crotch. Which was fine by him, Will thought, since everything going on there was her fault anyway. It just made his wicked smile more genuine.

"If you think that's a substitute for a cold shower, it's going to take a whole lot more than just one glass of iced tea to negate the effect you have on me," Will informed her.

He was thoroughly enjoying the fact that his wicked pronouncement brought on more blushing from Jessica and several giggles from the table of older ladies hanging on his every word.

"I—it was an accident," Jessica said, backing away from the table another step.

Will stepped closer and erased the distance she was obviously trying to put between them. "What are you so afraid of finding out, Jessica? You already know more of my secrets than any other woman."

"Not true," Jessica denied. "I'm not interested in your secrets, anyway."

"That's another lie," Will said quietly, his eyes darkening. "You want to know what I did to my sons when they lied to me? I let them suffer the consequences of their actions."

"I don't know what you're talking about," Jessica said, all but yelling in panic at the determined look on Will's face. She did not know his secrets. She knew nothing except how angry he could get and that he could kiss nicely when he wanted.

"Yes—you do. You looked into my creative soul and put your hand right over the core of it," he said. "Your very large, very nice hand has inspired many fantasies for me ever since."

Will picked up Jessica's hand, brought it to his mouth and kissed her wrist, then he moved up her arm to the crease of her elbow. While there he ran his tongue lightly from elbow to wrist, and when Jessica drew in a surprised breath, Will backed her against the edge of the booth and kissed her the way he'd been dying to do.

He moved his lips smoothly across hers until he felt them open to him, and then he plunged a hard, excited tongue into her mouth. Will felt her acceptance of it and him in every cell.

Gone was her resistance, but to make absolutely sure Jessica understood how it was, Will ground his pelvis against hers for a moment. Then he backed off before he got too physical with her again, which was now a distinct possibility.

If he hadn't embarrassed her the other day, Will concluded, he for sure had just now in a restaurant full of people, and he saw she had the pink face to prove it. He was a little bit embarrassed himself, but desperation for kissing Jessica senseless covered a lot of his discomfort. One of the joys of being a man, Will mused, grinning at her dazed expression.

"Too bad you're not interested in me, Jessica," he said, stepping away. "I'm sure interested in you."

He pulled a twenty and the condom he'd been carrying since he met her from his pocket. He threw the twenty on the table in one of the few dry places left, and then reached out and tucked the condom into Jessica's apron pocket. "Here's your tip. Maybe it will fit the math teacher, though I doubt it."

Will walked down the café with its now silent patrons and past its shocked owners. "Melanie. Brent. Great food as always. See you next week."

When the door was closed behind Will, Brent rubbed his face in shock.

"Well—*damn*," he whispered, laughing. He heard the motorcycle roaring away and laughed harder.

Melanie laughed at her husband's side and looked down the café to see Jessica holding a little packet in her fingers. Recognizing what it was, she had to cover her mouth not to burst out laughing hysterically.

"Mr. Larson was right. There's enough chemistry between them to blow up a science lab," she said happily. "I better go help Ms. Daniels before she starts flipping out over a condom."

"Mr. Larson gave Ms. Daniels a condom? Why?" Brent asked, shocked again when his wife gave him a don't-be-stupid-look. "No way. No freaking way, Melanie."

Melanie just smiled. "I'm telling you—I'm going to put out the word this place is a pick-up spot for mature singles. We'll have a waiting list of senior citizens lined up for every meal."

"If that's true, how can you bear to look at him? Doesn't it creep you out? I mean—geez, Mr. Larson's like fifty at least," Brent said on a laugh.

"Stop being such a guy, Brent. However old the man is—he's still plenty hot," Melanie said caustically. "You should hope you're going to be the same way at his age."

"Right. Hot at fifty. Now there's a goal," Brent said, laughing and heading back to the kitchen.

Melanie carried two towels to the booth where Will and Jessica had been sitting and started cleaning up the mess. She picked up the art book and dried the edges carefully.

"Gee, most people just leave money for a tip," Melanie said, barely glancing at what Jessica had in her hand. "I guess I need to have a talk with Will about inappropriate behavior in our establishment."

"Would it do any good?" Jessica asked meanly, shoving her hand and the condom into the pocket of the apron. The packet was still warm from being in Will's pocket, and God help her, she couldn't stop touching it or thinking that Will was probably right about it not fitting Adam. Not that she could confirm that though, damn the man.

"You're right. Will is pretty sure of himself," Melanie said. "He reminds me of my dad. Sometimes he's the calmest man in the world and you think nothing is going on in his head. Then suddenly, you're having to bail him out of jail."

"You had to bail Will out of jail?" Jessica asked, startled.

"No," Melanie laughed, "I had to bail out my dad for being a public nuisance. I can't even imagine Will doing anything illegal."

Then she glanced at Jessica's doubtful face. "You have a strange effect on Mr.—I mean, Will. He's usually so nice."

"Yes, well that nice man accused me of lying," Jessica said, hurt in her tone.

"Really? Will always had a sixth sense for when someone was lying. Well, were you?" Melanie asked, all but laughing now as she watched Jessica flipping the packet over and over inside her pocket.

"Of course I was," Jessica confessed. "My self-preservation kicked in. I'm scared of him."

"Scared of him or of how he makes you feel?" Melanie asked, knowing her face was the picture of confusion. "Will would never physically hurt anyone. I can understand the second one though. In fact, that's what he said about you too. I can see it could go both ways."

"Will is scared of me?" Jessica asked, surprised at that. He sure hadn't acted scared today.

"Of how you make him feel—well, he was scared plenty after your date," Melanie said, grinning. "Based on what he did to you today though, I think Will must have gotten over it, unless you ticked him off by lying. He hates lying. When he kissed you and walked off, I thought the other women in here were going to chase out after him."

"Hand me his book so I can take it back to him. Do you know

where he lives?" Jessica asked, taking the book from Melanie and staring hard at the girl. "It's time Mr. Williams and I got a few things straight between us."

"Will sold his house recently. I think he lives with his son Michael now. I don't know his address," Melanie said with a shrug.

"I'll find him. How many people named Michael Williams can there be in this town?" Jessica asked smartly.

"Uh—not Williams. His son uses the name Larson. Michael Larson. He's an artist too," Melanie said, wondering if Jessica was going to figure it out or assume it was a pen name.

"Michael Larson? I actually know him already," Jessica said, thoughtful. "He lives three streets over from me. I met him at an art show in Cincinnati last year. I even thought about asking him out because he was interesting, but he had some leggy blond on his arm."

Melanie's eyes grew wide at that one. "Close call on that one. That would have been awkward."

Jessica snorted. "If I was seriously interested in Will, I guess it might have been. From what I remember, Michael Larson had a ponytail, very intense good looks and created giant metal sculptures. His work was very symbolic."

Melanie gathered up the dirty dishes from their lunch, stacking them on her arms. "You don't have to take the book to Will. He usually drops by several times during the week."

Jessica pulled the condom out of her pocket and heard the table of older ladies start giggling again.

"This is what I need to talk to him about. The book just gives me a good excuse to track him down. I refuse to spend my week thinking about the things he insinuated. I want this over and settled as soon as possible. The next time I see Everett Williams, I want to do nothing more than just nod and go on."

CHAPTER 6

Michael pulled a shirt over his head as he went to answer the insistent buzzing at his front door. His scowl faded when he noticed the very tall, very attractive redhead standing on his front step.

"Mr. Larson," Jessica said, saying his name instead of hello.

"Yes, and frankly I've never been happier to be myself," Michael said, smiling and letting his gaze take in her completely.

Jessica snorted at Will's son flirting with her. This one was very practiced at the game, she concluded. There was no mistaking who he was now that she saw him up close. Michael Larson was a smaller replica of Will, only with a head full of hair.

"I'm Jessica Daniels. You're a lot quicker on the uptake than your father. He has to dig deep for charming social banter."

Michael laughed, and gestured her in. "I should have known you were already taken. The good ones always are. Come in and tell me more."

When she walked by him and he got a look at the back of her, Michael just smiled wider. Way to go Dad, he thought enviously. Fine looking woman, and tall—in fact, she was probably almost as tall as his father.

"You look familiar," Michael said, smiling warmly at her. "Do I know you?"

"We met at the art show in Cincinnati last year. You had a lovely blonde on your arm most of the time. I also remember your work was very interesting. A person couldn't stand near one of your art pieces and not feel what's going on. Your art is very powerful."

"Forget my Dad and the blonde," Michael said easily, morally lifted by her praise more than the fifteen thousand dollar check he had just cashed for one of his pieces. "Want to go out with me?"

"Too late. You should have dumped the blonde and asked me a year ago. I'm here to fight with your father, who gave me this," Jessica said, holding up the condom packet in two fingers. "One horny man in your family is all I can handle at a time."

Michael let loose a bark of laughter that shook the hallway of his house.

"No shit?" he said proudly. "My brother Shane is not going to believe this. Dad must *really* like you."

Jessica snorted. "Hardly. If anything, your father and I seem destined to crash and burn together. He's determined to make me his rebound woman after his divorce. I'm really not interested in playing that role in his life. Where is he, so I can get this fight over with?"

Michael raised his eyebrows at her vehement statements but motioned her to follow him down the hall.

At the patio door leading out into the work area, Michael stopped and turned around to face Jessica Daniels again. He could feel the energy emanating off her, feel her looking ahead trying to get a glimpse of his father. Michael mentally crossed his fingers that his father got this right.

"You know, for a year now my father has been passing up leggy blondes half his age looking for you," Michael told her, grinning at her consternation. He pointed to the condom in her hand in case Jessica Daniels tried to pretend she didn't understand what he was explaining. "I just thought you should know that before you pass up the chance to use what Dad gave you. Frankly, Ms. Daniels, my father is the best man you're ever going to come across in your life."

"Children often idealize their parents, Mr. Larson. Maybe there are unpleasant things about your father's personality that have eluded you up to now," Jessica told him, irritated more when Michael Larson only smiled at her as if he knew something she did not.

"I didn't say he was perfect. I said he was a good man. Be careful out there. Dad's probably covered in marble dust," Michael told her, sliding the door open for her, "and he probably has his music cranked up too loud to hear you coming. Just stand where he can see you. He'll eventually leave the zone and notice."

Jessica nodded. She stepped forward, stopped, and then sighed as she turned back. "You're a good son, Mr. Larson."

"Michael—please. If Dad bought condoms to use with you, we're practically family," Michael teased, laughing at her frown.

"I hardly think that's the case," Jessica said sarcastically, walking out into the work area.

What could have been a beautiful arbor was covered with a metal roof shielding a long expanse of courtyard from the weather. There was an eight-foot privacy fence surrounding the whole yard, which was nothing but work area. Near the house were piles of metal, several toolboxes, and a dozen or more weld spools. These were obviously the tools of the metal worker.

As she walked farther down the area, she heard the distinct chink, chink of a hammer and chisel chipping away at some stone. Then she saw him. Behind safety glasses, his amber gaze was focused intently on what he doing. A man's figure was being further revealed with every stroke of the hammer, she saw.

And just as Michael Larson had warned, there was a set of white headphones running from Will's ears to his front jeans pocket, the same pocket he had pulled the condom from earlier. Jessica couldn't stop herself from wondering if everything in Will's pocket was just as warm as the condom packet had been.

Shaking her head to clear the erotic distraction, Jessica strode forward and placed herself in his view. Will stopped hammering immediately. Walking to a nearby table, he laid the tools from his hands next to others on it. He motioned her forward, pulling the headphones from his ears and the player from his pocket.

With little other choice, Jessica had to move forward. Then her gaze went immediately to the new statue. Her breath caught. The part of the torso that was finished was even more perfect than the one he had taken her to see.

"What number is this one?" she asked, forgetting for a moment why she had come.

"Seventeen," Will said, picking up a small, fluffy brush and running it over his body to sweep the worst of the dust away.

"You've improved since the one I saw," she said softly. "You really are exceptional."

Will walked over to her. "You can touch it if you like, but be careful of the edges. It's not smoothed out yet."

"No," Jessica said, clearing her throat. "That's all right." She took a step back from him. "I brought back your book."

"Thanks," Will said. "I completely forgot about it. I could have picked it up later in the week."

He took the book and tossed it on the tools table. It wasn't the real reason she'd come by, and they both knew it. Though he had to give her credit for coming by so soon.

Will studied her nervousness and fought a grin.

"Is the book the only reason you're here?" he asked bluntly, his knowing gaze daring her to lie again.

"No," Jessica said, pulling the condom from her pocket and holding it out to Will, who just smiled at it. "This is yours. I don't want it."

"Actually, it's yours. I'm not planning to use it unless it's with you," Will informed her.

"Stop saying that," Jessica ordered loudly, her voice rising with her anxiety. "We are not dating. We are not doing anything else. I don't want you to be interested in me that way."

"Who are you trying to convince? You picked me up, remember? Besides, the truth was in your kiss," Will said sternly, reaching out a palm. "Give that to me before you rip the package."

Relieved he was acting sensibly regardless of his words, Jessica put the condom packet into Will's hand only to be surprised when he reached out his other hand and pulled her forward by the pocket of her jeans. He slipped the condom into one of her front pockets, and then pulled her hips against his firmly.

"I've been waiting for you, Jessica Daniels. Don't keep me waiting too much longer. But in the meantime, I really, really want you to kiss me with some real passion," Will whispered against her mouth. "I want it as badly as you wanted me to kiss you the first day we met."

"Will," she said his name starkly, shaking her head from side to side. He was so stubborn. Jessica hated his persistence, but she also couldn't remember the last time she'd craved a man's kiss as much as she did Will's.

"Ssssh—kiss me. Let me kiss you. We owe it to ourselves to explore this attraction between us," Will whispered. "I'm sorry I messed it up the first time."

"No, really I don't want this," Jessica protested, but Will's hands stroking her hips and lower back were starting to change her mind.

"You told me the truth about my art, so I'm going to tell you the truth about us," Will said softly, his lips on her cheek. "We are going to be so damn good together that you're going to forget all the other men you've known."

Jessica snorted despite her fear that Will was right. The only man she ever still thought about with any regularity was the one she married, even though she couldn't remember the details anymore. She only remembered the want and the want never left her. She had often thought that all the men after her first had just been a way to fill the lonely years without her husband, but she certainly wasn't confessing that to Will.

"I've known a lot of men, Will," Jessica cautioned. "Most of them were good men. Many of them were good in bed. If you want honesty, then you're going to have to accept I've lived the kind of life most men dream about living."

Will sighed and pulled her tighter. "Stop trying to piss me off. I got that much information from Steve Lipton's warnings. Right now, I just want you to kiss me so we can find out what *we* have. Damn it, Jessica, I want your permission and your cooperation this time."

Frowning, Jessica ran her hands over his shoulders, his very broad, very attractive, very masculine shoulders which ran down to a chest men decades younger would envy. It was honed from what he did, she now realized, honed by the hammer, the chisel, and who knew what other tools he used to coax people out of the stone.

"Will—this is so not a good idea," Jessica insisted, even as Will ran a hand up the middle of her back to her neck, lining her entire body up with his in a very exciting way.

"*Chicken,*" he taunted, laughing with his mouth inches from hers. He could see the longing in her today just as much as she saw his the day of their bike ride.

This level of need, Will decided, this was the only reason to ever kiss someone.

"Damn you," she said, leaning into him and putting her lips urgently on his. His moan of pleasure against her mouth had her hand going to the back of his head. She kissed him, pulled away, and then dove back, slanting her mouth in another direction. He tasted just as good from every angle, Jessica thought, falling against Will in relief.

With Jessica's full weight in his arms, Will had to plant his feet more firmly to hold them both up. Mother Nature was making the urge to get horizontal almost overwhelming. Jessica's mouth on his was all energy and motion, all encompassing desire, and gloriously all for him today. Her desperate kiss was even better than he had imagined.

He locked strong arms around her, lifting and pulling her onto him as he leaned back. Her toes almost left the ground and her thighs went around one of his legs. Deciding to oblige her, he lifted a thigh to rub against her crotch, making her shiver and groan.

"Okay. Stop," Jessica said hoarsely. "Just stop. Please."

"If I start begging you to let me use the condom, would you change your mind? I'm only a few seconds away from it," Will informed her, pulling her hips against his and putting the evidence of his need against her fully.

"Will," Jessica said, trying weakly to push herself off him, "I don't want to get this involved with you."

Will lifted his thigh against her crotch again, gaining another groan from both of them. "Really? You sure have both of us fooled then. I pegged you for a more sexually honest woman."

"Will, that's all this is—it's just sex," Jessica said.

Will lifted a hand trembling with passion to her face. "Who disappointed you so badly, Jessica Daniels? What experience sent you into the arms of men who couldn't touch your heart? *This,*" he insisted, pulling her tight against him, his leg firm and hard against the ache he was purposely creating, "*this* is not just sex. This is me telling you, showing you that you are the most incredible woman I have ever met. Yes, I want inside you. I ache for you, just like you do for me."

Her heart was going to explode, Jessica thought. The panic was so large she almost couldn't breathe around it. All she could do was shake her head in denial.

"No. No, you are weaving a dream around me just because you haven't been with anyone since your wife," Jessica whispered softly. "What we have—this is just sex, just chemistry. I admit we have a lot of it. I admit I—I admit I want you back."

"My marriage was over long before it was officially over, Jessica," Will answered firmly, feeling the words in a way he hadn't since the divorce was final. "And this is a hell of a lot more than just sex. If all I wanted was sex, that's easy to find."

"Yes. It is," Jessica agreed.

"This is more than just sex," Will denied emphatically, lifting her hips to his again, sliding her up his leg until his erection was pressed between them. "This is the best kind of foreplay. This is me letting you know that I want to see you fly apart for me. I want to learn what you like, what turns you on, what you need. Then I plan to exceed all your expectations."

Jessica used her hands to push away from Will's chest and off his leg. She put two steps' distance between their vibrating bodies. Her instinct to push him to the ground and climb on top of him was almost strong enough to make her do it. Getting physical with Will literally robbed her of common sense every time.

"I'm not emotionally equipped for anything more than sex in my relationships," Jessica said quietly. "I haven't felt more for a man since my husband died. And I've dated some good men, really good men, Will."

"Yes, I know you have," Will said harshly. "Steve Lipton seemed like a great guy, and I think he really cared about you, but I'm still glad it didn't work out with him. I want you for myself."

Jessica couldn't have been more shocked. What in the hell had Steve told Will, and why had Steve said anything in the first place?

"I swear it always amazes me to find out how much guys talk to each other. Used to be only women shared the intimate stories of their lives," Jessica said, running a nervous hand through her hair.

Will smiled at her embarrassment. "Don't worry. Steve didn't share any of your preferences in bed. I'm sure he instinctively knew I'd prefer to find out for myself. He just said you never loved him."

Jessica stared at the partial statue without seeing it as she was wondering what had possessed Steve to confess the details of their relationship to Will. "No. I never loved him. There's no sense in denying it."

"So is that the problem? Are you afraid you're going to love me, Jessica?" Will asked.

Jessica laughed mirthlessly. "Will, I already know I'll never love you. I'm afraid of disappointing you and hurting us both if we get involved. I'm not a heartless woman. I don't enjoy the suffering of the men I've ejected from my bed. I bleed and hurt, but then I move on because I know that's the only sensible choice. You're the kind of guy who wants to own a woman, body and soul. I am not that kind of woman," she said tightly, but meaning every bit of it.

"How do you know what I'm like, what I would expect?" Will asked, unable to believe she thought so little of him and what they could be to each other.

"The very first day we spent time together, you shut me up by kissing me roughly. You punished me for speaking what I considered only a truth," Jessica said softly. "I've been with men like you before, Will. I won't be silenced or controlled by my attraction to a man. It's just not who I am."

Will walked to his tools table and started rearranging them, getting them ready to store away. He'd never be able to work calmly now. He was too upset at Jessica and her stubborn ideas about them.

"I told you I panicked. That's not the kind of person I am normally. I've honestly never done anything remotely like that to any woman before you. Damn it, Jessica, you stripped me bare with your insights and I overreacted. I was already attracted to you, even though I was in denial then. Then when I touched you, I got carried away. *I'm sorry,*" Will said emphatically, packing his tools into a wooden box he retrieved from beneath the table.

"Will?" a soft feminine voice called.

Jessica swung a startled gaze to the willowy, sleekly groomed blonde standing near them with tears in her eyes. She would be barely five foot six on a good day in heels.

Will also swung a startled gaze to the woman, then his forehead wrinkled. "What's wrong? Are the kids okay?"

She shook her head, sending her chin length bob swinging and more tears flowing. "It's not the kids. It's Luke. He's asked me to leave."

Jessica watched as the woman ran the rest of the distance across the pavers and flung herself into Will's arms. To be fair, the woman didn't really give Will a choice except to catch her and hold her. Will's irritated gaze went to Jessica's over the woman's head.

"I knew it. You're one of those guys after all," Jessica said snidely. "Now look who was lying."

The tears that threatened moments ago vanished with her wry amusement and what she was going to regard as divine intervention. Maybe it helped that Will did not look pleased with the other woman.

"I was not lying. Keep up the smart-ass comments, and I *will* end up being the kind of guy you accused me of being," Will warned, his arms gripping the blonde's arms and pushing her away from him a little. "Ellen, this is Jessica Daniels. Stop pretending you don't see her and say hello."

Ellen turned and crossed her arms, her tears still flowing as she hugged herself. "I'm sorry to interrupt, Ms. Daniels. I—Will and I have remained good friends since the divorce. My husband and I separated today, and I just needed to talk to someone."

Jessica waved her hand. "No need to explain anything to me. I just came by to return a book."

She turned on her heel and started out of the courtyard.

"Jessica." Will stalked after her, leaving what he guessed was a very surprised Ellen staring after him. He stopped when Jessica halted. "We need to finish our conversation."

"It's over, Will," Jessica said wearily. "So is our conversation."

"The hell it is," Will said automatically, his face darkening with determination.

"Go back and help Ellen. You just got offered a second chance with a woman who is probably better equipped to be what you want all day every day," Jessica told him.

"If we got along, Ellen wouldn't have divorced me in the first place," Will said harshly. "She left me for somebody else."

"Exactly. Now you can fix it." Jessica shook her head, slid the patio door open, and walked through the house.

"Will?" Ellen said softly. "Are you okay?"

"No, I am not okay," Will said harshly. "Couldn't you have waited in the house? Don't tell me you didn't see a six-foot tall redhead standing out here with me because I won't believe you. And I'm sick and tired of hearing about the soap opera your marriage to Luke is, Ellen. You know damn well he'll be home before you get back there tonight."

"Why are you so angry at me, Will? Jessica Daniels was the one arguing with you. I heard her tell you she couldn't be what you wanted," Ellen said, then blushed, ashamed for confessing it.

"That's because she doesn't understand yet," Will said, stomping back to the table and throwing his tools into the box with enough force to rattle the metal. "Jessica already is everything I want."

"You are never going to get to be the aggressive man you naturally are with that woman, Will. Don't you know who she is?" Ellen asked.

"She's a high school art teacher, Ellen," Will said, angry at his ex for eavesdropping on his private conversation with Jessica.

"You honestly don't know who she is, do you?" Ellen said softly, then the light dawned. "I'm not surprised she didn't tell you. She faded out of the limelight almost a decade ago. You should do an Internet search on her before you get too involved."

"I am already involved, and I plan to get more involved," Will said firmly, rounding on the woman who still knew how to push his buttons by insinuating he had a lesser understanding of life than she did. "What the hell are you dying to educate me about, Ellen?"

Ellen was shaking her head. "It's a personal matter for her and connected to her art. You need to find out for yourself or ask her about it."

"I carve *disgusting naked statues* as you so eloquently put it a thousand times. What the hell could be so personal about Jessica's art that no one wants to talk about it?" Will demanded, disgusted with Ellen's hints. He slammed the lid shut on the toolbox.

"Fine, I'll tell you then. Jessica Daniels was violently raped when she was young and pregnant. Her husband had been killed in the military only a couple months before it happened. The three guys who raped her hurt her pretty badly. Doctors had to deliver the baby early because both of them were traumatized. She went through some serious therapy after she got well and came out socially swinging. She brought charges and testified against all three men, got involved in women's issues, and created art that—well, I can't really describe it," Ellen said quietly, alarmed at last because Will's face had lost all its color.

"Will?" Ellen began, wishing now she had refused to tell him.

Will ran both hands over his face, as scene after scene of how aggressive he'd been with Jessica flashed through his mind.

"Hell," Will said in pain, unable to stop remembering how often he had grabbed her and forcibly held Jessica against her will. He'd even done it again today.

"What did you do?" Ellen said, walking to Will and putting a comforting hand on his arm. "I know you would never really hurt the woman, William. You didn't, did you?"

"Not the way you mean, but I certainly scared her. I certainly made sure she knew I could hurt her if I intended to do so," Will said, shocked at how close to tears he was. "Damn it. I didn't mean to be so rough when I kissed her that first time. She just shocked me so bad. She was commenting on my art."

"Well," Ellen said, rubbing his arm in sympathy though she didn't know what he meant. She just knew how much Will's heart would hurt if he even suspected he'd harmed the woman. "Your art is a little shocking, William. If you put a fig leaf over some of the parts, people might not insult it so much."

"Thanks. Thanks a lot for your typical show of support. Jessica didn't insult my art, Ellen. Jessica figured it out, figured me out. Now I know why she instantly saw the truth. It makes all the sense in the world now," Will banged a fist on the table, making the toolbox rattle. "She likes to chase. Of course she does. Why the hell didn't you warn me about this, Steve? You told me damn near everything else."

Will stormed off, leaving a still shocked Ellen staring after him. He was heading to the library and not coming out until he knew everything there was to know about Jessica Daniels.

When he got back from the library several hours later, Will went to his room, curled up on the bed, and thought about what she had endured. After a while, he had to make a trip to the bathroom to throw up, and then he came back and cried.

Eventually, after he was both exhausted and disgusted with himself, Will fell asleep just to escape having to deal with what he'd done to add to Jessica Daniels' pain.

~

AFTER HIS MOTHER CALLED HIM, MICHAEL TRACKED HIS FATHER DOWN and found him sprawled on the bed asleep, his face haggard, tears drying on his cheeks.

Pulling the phone from his pocket, he sent a text to Shane to get his younger brother over there as fast as he could. When Shane came tearing into the house about fifteen minutes later, and barreling down the hall like a raging bull, Michael shushed him at the doorway. He pointed out and they walked to the kitchen together.

"I met Dad's new girlfriend today," Michael said softly.

"She made Dad cry already?" Shane said, running a hand through his hair. "I saw his face. He'd been crying, and crying hard. He didn't cry over the divorce that much."

"It wasn't anything Jessica said or did. Mom came and interrupted their discussion," Michael explained.

"Oh, shit," Shane said, covering his mouth to keep the torrent of swearing he wanted to do from escaping.

"No, that's not the problem either. Hell, I wish it was something that easy," Michael said tiredly, running a worried hand through his own hair and watching Shane do the same. Odd how all three of them did that when they were nervous.

"Mom felt guilty about what she'd told Dad about the woman, so naturally she had to purge her guilt by confessing her sins to me. That's when I finally remembered that I had seen some of Jessica Daniels' art, and frankly I wish I hadn't," Michael said, staring the wall and unable not to remember it. "I think I had blocked it from my mind."

"What?" Shane demanded. "What are you talking about?"

Michael threw up his hands. "Where do I start? Jessica was raped when she was pregnant as a teenager. She turned all the violence, all that hurt, into art. Her early work is not for someone without a strong stomach. She made some pretty realistic clay figurines of what happened to her, to show the world what rape looks like. I looked her early work up because of the new work I saw last year, something she calls *vagina art*. That's what she had at the art show, a beautiful glass vagina incredibly erotic to the touch. The raw sexuality in it was mesmerizing. She's probably almost as old as Mom, but I still wanted to ask her out simply because she was fascinating. I didn't because I had a date with me. Thank God for that now. Dad's nuts about her."

"So you think Dad was shocked?" Shane asked.

Michael shook his head. "Shocked at her art—no. I think Dad's been giving her a full court press and using his best guy moves on her. She showed up here mad as hell with a condom packet in her hand that she said Dad gave her. She was intending to give it back. When I saw them getting a little extra friendly during their discussion, I left thinking they might have come to some agreement about the condom. Then I guess Mom showed up with another story about Luke leaving her, from what I gathered. If I had stayed, I'd have stopped Mom, but it was really only a matter of time before Dad found out about Jessica's art. I was already trying to place her myself."

"Wait. Is this the same woman that Dad said figured out his art? The one he said he was too rough with on their first date?" Shane asked.

"Yes. I think so. I think that roughness is what upset him once he knew about her past. That's why I called you," Michael said. "You going to be able to use that million dollar doctorate to help him?"

Shane closed his eyes. "I don't know. I hope so."

Michael nodded. "You're a pain in the ass, Shane, but also the best man I know next to Dad."

Shane smiled at his brother's praise. "Right. You're just trying to get me to share my leggy blondes with you."

"I've had my share of leggy blondes and got stuck on a brunette instead. That's why I pound the hell out of metal every day," Michael said, rolling his eyes. "Let's have a beer and order some pizza. I don't want to talk about this anymore until Dad wakes up."

Shane nodded. "Give me two beers. If I have to counsel my father about his sex life, I prefer to do it slightly buzzed."

Michael shook his head and walked to the refrigerator.

"Wise choice, Dr. Larson," Michael said, bringing back two opened beers and patting his brother on the shoulder "Unfortunately, this is what you get for being the smart son."

Shane laughed without humor and shrugged.

CHAPTER 7

After several days of watching their dad walk around the house like a zombie, Michael and Shane had had enough. They had not been raised to sit around and wait for things to get better. They had been raised to fix things. Neither thought their father's depression was going to fix itself, and they had jointly decided there was really only one solution worth pursuing.

But Michael still gave his brother a worried look as they pulled into the parking lot of Henry Clay High School.

"What if she tells us to go to hell?" Michael said. "She didn't strike me as a woman who did anything she didn't want to."

"You said you left because they were kissing, right?" Shane asked, scanning the area, looking for a tall redhead.

"Yeah, but that doesn't mean much. I'm pretty sure Mom did a good job of busting that up. I mean, God forbid that after a year Dad actually gets to meet someone nice and maybe fall in love with a woman who actually likes him," Michael said sarcastically.

Shane gave him a look that said *get over it* and shook his head.

"Don't give me that attitude. I love Mom, and she's great about many things, but she's being selfish as hell about Dad. She likes being able to run back to him when Luke disappoints her. She likes that Dad is sitting at home not dating. That's a bunch of shit, Shane," Michael said, his anger getting the better of him for a moment.

"Look, I agree with that—which is why we're going to find this woman Dad likes, and talk her into talking to Dad," Shane said quietly, firmly.

He put as much confidence into his voice as he could because he did not want his emotionally excitable brother to know how unsure he was about this plan. The last two things in the world Shane wanted to deal with were an upset older woman and a meltdown with Michael, but he had to do something because it was breaking his heart to see his father hurting again.

"So sitting in the car is not going to get it done," Shane said, cracking his knuckles, which was the only indication of nervousness he was going to allow himself. "Let's go find her."

As they got out of Michael's car, two boys heading to their own car stopped to stare at them. At six foot four with shaggy blond hair and massively big shoulders, Shane knew he looked like a throwback to some ancient Viking. Added to that, the tattoos and piercings he had been sporting for six months produced an immediate stupefying effect on everyone who didn't know him.

"Hey," Shane called to them, wanting to laugh when they swallowed hard. "Where can we find your art teacher, Jessica Daniels?"

Michael had to fight not to laugh at the boys' reaction to Shane. It was damn tempting to have some fun with them. He wondered how Shane could resist it with all the ammunition he possessed in just scary looks alone. Michael wanted badly to say something, but instead he just chuckled at their obvious fear. The last thing he and Shane needed was for the two boys to report them to a principal before they found Jessica.

The boys looked at each other, had a brief conversation about Shane's question, and then looked back at Shane. "Why do you want to know?"

Shane looked at Michael, his gaze twinkling, his tone deliberately condescending. "Young males. They're protecting her. Speak art to them, Michael. You know the language better than I do."

Michael snorted and gave his younger sibling a look promising retaliation before swinging a friendly gaze to the boys.

"We came to see Ms. Daniels about some art for an exhibition in Cincinnati this weekend. She asked us to drop by the school this afternoon," Michael lied easily, then had a brainstorm about how to smooth things over. "Do we need to check in at the office?"

The boy that had not talked elbowed the one who had. The talking one held up an arm and pointed to a building entrance.

"Ms. Daniels is in the art room. If you walk by the shop area in that building over there, you'll see it. She was still in there a few minutes ago," he said.

"Thanks," Michael said, smiling and throwing up an arm. Shane lifted a hand to wave as well.

Michael looked at him after the boys got into their car. "Okay. I have to ask. Why the piercings and tattoos? You were already intimidating without them. Now you scare the shit out of people, even teenage boys who normally don't have the good sense to be afraid."

Shane laughed at his brother's observation about the lack of fear in teenage boys. "If I told you why I got them, you wouldn't believe me."

They took off walking in the direction the boys had pointed.

"Oh, try me," Michael coaxed his brother, grinning. "With seven years difference in our ages, it's already like we're in different generations. I find the workings of your younger, albeit marginally intelligent mind, endlessly fascinating."

"After the divorce, you could tell Dad wondered how much his art contributed to his problems with Mom. I was glad he didn't give it up, so I got the tat to remind me to respect my art no matter what else happens in life. I like the tat, but I got the piercings specifically because they scare people, and frankly they keep most of the women away," Shane said on a sigh.

Michael looked sideways to see if Shane was joking as usual and was surprised to find his brother's face completely without amusement for once. "Why the hell would you want to keep women away? You serious about someone?"

"No, I'm just tired of one night stands. Dad was right. I don't even remember their names or anything else about them. I'd like to have a normal girlfriend, someone to hang with instead of just—you know what I mean," Shane said, frowning.

Michael nodded, and for once he didn't tease back. "I wondered when you were ever going to get over Angela and be normal again."

"This is not about her," Shane denied. "Why would you think that?"

"Aren't you the one with the psych degree?" Michael asked, incredulous that Shane hadn't figured it out for himself. "You haven't gone near any smart woman since you two broke up. You probably don't even like all those leggy blondes."

Shane laughed. He was disillusioned, not dead from the waist down. "If you seriously thought that, you'd be wrong. I haven't given up sleeping with beautiful women. I just want them to have some real personality to go with the great body. And it would be nice if they could talk about something other than the way they look."

"Yeah," Michael said on a laugh. "You're done with the superficial blondes, which just leaves more for the rest of us. I have a thousand dollars that says you end up with a tiny smart woman who turns you inside out before you even get your doctorate approved. The relationship will be so shocking to you that you'll have to devote a whole chapter to it in that book you claim to be writing."

Shane thought about the dissertation languishing in his desk at home waiting for him to send it out for review. He was close, very close to being done. As soon as the next graphic novel was out to the inker, he could easily go back to working on the dissertation. If he did, he could probably finish his degree in December if he wanted.

"You're on," Shane told his brother at last, telling himself not to worry even when Michael laughed. "You just lost a thousand dollars bro. You better head back to your work when we get this done. Make sure you have the money by December. I'm finishing my doctorate this year."

Michael just laughed at his declaration. "Well, the ink isn't dry yet on anything except that tattoo on your arm." His attention was suddenly caught by several kids carrying paintbrushes and cleaning rags into a room in the hallway. "Shane, I think we found the art room."

When they walked to the door, they saw a tall, wild-haired woman in tight faded jeans and cowboy boots milling around the room. She was a good six inches taller than most of the students.

Shane whistled under his breath. "Wow," he said, making Michael chuckle beside him.

"Yeah. And she looks just that good from every angle," Michael said easily. "She likes my art. I want to keep her."

"*You* want to keep her? Why? You got something going on for Dad's woman?" Shane asked in shock, making his brother laugh again.

"Yeah, I do," Michael said easily, staring at his brother with what he suspected were laughing eyes. "I'm mercenary, but it's not as creepy as it sounds. I want another artist in the family and a stepmother who isn't going to make Dad feel guilty for what he loves to do. We've all ended up with women who criticized or outright hated our art. You'd think making money at something would prove it was worth doing, but no—that's not enough either."

Shane snickered at the tirade he'd heard a hundred times since their parent's divorce and put a hand on his brother's shoulder. "Gee, Michael, why don't you tell me how you really feel?"

"You're lucky we're in a school," Michael warned.

Shane laughed and shook his brother's shoulder. "Relax, bro. We're here. We'll do what we can for Dad. We'll have to work on us some other time."

Michael rolled his eyes to the ceiling, but ended up making eye contact with Jessica Daniels as his gaze came back down. She walked across the room and stood in front of them, hands on her hips.

"Mr. Larson—" Jessica began.

"—Michael," he corrected quickly, holding up a hand to stall her questions and comments. "And this blond giant next to me is my younger brother Shane."

Jessica had to look up slightly to meet the gaze of the tall man flanking Michael Larson. She studied his eyebrow piercing and tattoo. The intimidating body art didn't match his eyes, she concluded. His eyes were thoughtful, caring, and intelligent. To her artistically trained eye, he was obviously a big faker, even if a cute one.

She snorted and narrowed her gaze until her eyes were slits.

"Who are you trying to scare with that disguise," Jessica asked, letting her gaze rake Shane from head to toe. "I had the unfortunate pleasure of meeting your mother. You look just like her with all that jewelry you're wearing."

Michael burst out laughing, but stopped at Shane's glare.

"Maybe redheads have a natural immunity to you," Michael said, shrugging, earning an even more furious look. "You know, like they do to poison ivy."

"That's a myth," Shane retorted, then sighed at taking the bait his brother loved to dish out. Shane looked away from Michael, back to the person they came to see. He reached out a hand to her. "It's a pleasure to meet you, Ms. Daniels. We came by to see if we could talk to you about a situation we have with our father."

Jessica took Shane's hand, shook it briefly, then dropped it. The younger Larson sounded like he belonged in a suit and tie instead of ripped jeans and T-shirt with a rock band on it.

"Well, your brother's manners are nicer than yours at least," Jessica said, swinging her gaze to a still snickering Michael before walking back into the room and away from both of them. "I'm sorry, but your father and I have nothing more to say to each other. I think it's very sweet of the two of you to come by on his behalf, but I'm just not interested."

"That's too bad. Dad's really interested in you," Shane replied softly back, mirroring her speech and tone. "In fact, Dad was so interested in you that he looked you up at the library the other day. He knows about what happened to you, and he spent three hours studying your art."

Jessica heard the mild accusation in Shane's tone, but she wasn't offended. She admired his nerve, but refused to let him, or his charming brother, convince her to get involved with a man her instincts were warning her against. She especially refused to be influenced by the fact that they obviously loved their father enough to come and confront her, though it was dreadfully awkward.

Sure, it was proof Will's sons had more integrity than most young people, but Jessica still didn't have to feel obligated to care about what was going on with a man she wasn't even dating. Besides—whatever Will was feeling right now, he would survive it. Jessica couldn't worry about Will when she had her own emotional survival to worry about.

Turning her back to Michael and Shane, Jessica went back to tidying the room. The students had all vanished, and as usual, most had not put their art tools back in storage.

Typical, Jessica thought, very typical. It would take another half hour of cleaning before she could leave for the day.

"So now Will knows all about me and my terrible past. If I could have, I would have made sure he never found out," Jessica said honestly. "There was no reason for him to ever have to know."

Michael cleared his throat. Revealing a hard truth always choked him, but he had learned in his life that he couldn't hold it inside and stay sane.

"Our mother told him," Michael said quietly. "She recognized you, but I had already started figuring it out myself. Whatever Dad's ideas about who you were when he met you, he didn't see this coming. You have to understand—he's the kind of guy who cries at the sad part of movies. Since he cares a hell of a lot about you, needless to say he took finding out your truth pretty hard."

"Well, I appreciate it might have shocked him, but I don't need his pity or anyone's," Jessica said confidently, carrying items to stack by the sink, and carrying a rag back to wipe the now empty tables. "It all happened thirty years ago. I almost never think about it anymore. I took the actions that made sense to me at the time. I have a good life and I regret nothing."

"How do you feel about Dad's regrets about how he's handled things with you? Would you want deal with that?" Shane asked, pleased that she finally stopped wiping the tables to listen. "He's made himself ill worrying about how he's treated you."

"What in the world would Will have to regret with me? You father never did anything terrible. He got a little angry with me once, but I'm a hell of lot tougher than that. He came to his senses long before I felt the need to—maim him," Jessica said on a laugh, remembering at the last minute to keep her language less expressive within the school walls.

"Would you be willing to come tell him the same thing?" Shane asked. "He's been in his room, brooding and not eating, since he found out about you three days ago. First he cried himself sick, and now he thinks he's the worst man in the world. He's convinced that he's scarred you further. I'm sure he's replayed every interaction you've had and not seen any of them in a good light."

Jessica stopped, swallowed hard, and closed her eyes. She couldn't bear to think of Will suffering for her, so she simply refused to acknowledge it.

"Your father is a smart man. He'll eventually get over this. The reason I'm not interested in him has nothing to do with him getting angry and kissing me while he was upset. He kissed me twice after that and should know that I—well, whatever. Will's a grown man. He can figure this all out on his own."

"Maybe," Shane agreed easily. "He could probably get over it much faster if you would come talk to him."

Michael walked over closer and looked around her until she finally met his gaze.

Jessica had to close her eyes to shut out the sincerity in his pleading look.

"Please, come see Dad," Michael pleaded, not caring about begging. "You're all he can talk about now that he knows. We're really worried he's not going to get over this until he knows he hasn't done you any serious harm. Seeing your rape art made him feel guilty for how he's treated you."

Damn Will and his sensitive sons, Jessica thought. She opened her eyes then, but instead of looking at Michael, she ended up looking directly into Shane's soft, worried gaze. If that giant man got teary-eyed she would be a goner, Jessica thought.

"What's the tattoo on your arm about?" Jessica asked to distract them from their pleading, nodding at the ink peeking from the edge of Shane's sleeve.

Shane took the change of subject with grace. He could see Jessica Daniels was wrestling with herself about getting involved.

"I'm a graphic novelist. This is my hero," Shane said, pulling up his sleeve to his shoulder so she could see the whole piece. "I call him *The Winged Protector*."

"I've read your work. My nephew loves those books," she told Shane, sighing. "You definitely know how to create a hero."

"I used a great role model," Shane said, not afraid to use the opening she unknowingly handed to him. "He's having a dark moment right now and has locked himself in his room to brood. Want to be the heroine in this story and save him?"

"I doubt I'm as good as your heroines, but at least that's an original line to take in your argument," she said quietly.

To keep from bursting into tears, Jessica turned and looked down at Michael from her few extra inches.

"You look just like your father," she told him resentfully. "But you're not as nice as he is, are you?"

"No," Michael said, unsurprised at her observation. "I'm too honest to be considered nice. Shane looks like Mom, but I got the rest of her personality. Shane's more like Dad on the inside."

"Well, I'm not very nice either, certainly not as nice as your father. I really, really do not want to do this. I feel a need to save myself," Jessica told Michael, gaining a relieved smile from him as he figured out what she was admitting. "I'm not sure what good it will do, but I'll be over later tonight. I will expect you two to make yourselves scarce after I get there. I don't want an audience when I talk to Will about my personal stuff."

"You have our word," Shane promised, grinning in relief. "I won't let Michael stay and listen, no matter how much he begs."

"I am disowning you as my brother," Michael told him. "Don't believe him, Jessica. He tries to make me look bad all the time."

Jessica laughed tiredly at their bickering. On impulse, she reached out to hug Michael. "I bet you inherited more of your father's personality than you realize, and I still really like your art."

"I like yours too, especially the new stuff," Michael told her, hugging back. "Thanks for coming to see Dad. We really are worried."

"Coming over tonight still doesn't mean that I'm interested in him," Jessica told Michael, straightening and going back to her work.

Michael just smiled as he walked back to Shane. "Yeah, but Shane and I have faith in Dad being able to change your mind."

"Don't count on it," Jessica warned, putting her hands on her hips again.

Shane and Michael exchanged a knowing look but only smiled at her as they left.

After they had gone, Jessica stood in her classroom shaking her head and sighing. She'd had some very unusual men pass through her life over the years, but this was the first time she'd ever had someone's grown children playing matchmaker. Worse than Brooke pushing Will to kiss her, his sons were actually hoping their father would seduce her. If she hadn't been practically ill herself about knowing Will had seen what had happened to her, Jessica would have laughed more at their involvement.

As it was, she was struggling damn hard not to break down about Will finding out that she had been raped. Though why she had ever held the fantasy that she was going to avoid Will finding out was beyond her. Her violent past had ruined every relationship Jessica had had for so long that she had learned to insulate herself from the pity, the reaction, and the physical withdrawal when the man she was sleeping with found out.

It was at least a little easier with Will because they weren't lovers. It was also a little harder because she knew her past would prevent them from ever being lovers now. But what did she care, anyway? Getting more involved was what her instincts were warning her not to do.

Maybe they could be friends, Jessica mused, sniffing back tears and wiping her nose on the sleeve of her paint-covered shirt. Will would probably be okay with that now. He would probably be one of those men who felt the need to save her from her sexuality. She had known plenty of those.

Tears of regret flowed steady as Jessica locked the door and walked to her car. She'd had to gather a handful of toilet tissue from the bathroom to stem the flow.

Despite her assurances to herself that she wasn't interested, it was still damn hard to accept Everett Williams was never again going to back her against a booth or hold her too tightly in his arms. Playfully restraining her was the kind of thing her husband used to do to her, the kind of action she hadn't let anyone do since him. At least, she hadn't tolerated it from anyone until Will had come along.

"Damn you, Will," Jessica said, cursing him again for what she felt.

CHAPTER 8

"Shane, I'm fine," Will told his youngest son, who sat arms-crossed in a chair beside his bed. "I'm not ill. I'm just not feeling very social. You and Michael go on and eat without me. I'll grab something later."

"You're lying," Shane accused baldly, not flinching from the weak glare his father managed to send his way. "You need to eat a normal meal. It's been three damn days, Dad."

"Look, you bullied me into the shower and I took one. I'm going to rest now, and then I'll get up and eat later. Don't you have a date or something?" Will demanded, knowing Shane could be just as stubborn as he under the right circumstances.

"Michael and I are going out. We don't want to worry about you while we're gone, so we got you a babysitter," Shane told him, hoping his Dad would erupt in anger over it.

"Good—they can watch TV and I'll sleep," Will said resentfully, stretching back out on the bed, careful to keep his wide-opened eyes focused on just the ceiling. If he closed his eyes too long without really sleeping, he would just see her art all over again. He'd see piece after piece of four figures, three men doing unspeakable things to a woman, an obviously pregnant woman.

At the thought of what she had depicted in her work, his stomach clenched. Will was seized by urges so violent he was frightened of what he might do under their influence. It was the closest he'd ever come to wanting to kill someone. Each man had only served a term of ten years, and all three were out now. Will thought a lifetime in prison would never have been enough punishment for what they had done.

He also thought making the rape art was the bravest act of creating he had ever seen done by anyone. Neither the rapists nor the world would ever be able to forget it as long as knowledge of Jessica Daniels and her work survived.

Jessica, Will thought, his heart contracting with pain for her. She probably still carried what had happened inside her like a ticking bomb. She probably had memories and triggers that defied analysis. Her daughter Brooke, the woman he'd met, was the child that had survived the attack. And Jessica had lived through it too, if you could call never loving anyone again living, Will concluded.

He remembered pulling Jessica across him as she rode his thigh, how they had both been turned on and trying to come to terms with it. The thought of never having that innocent level of arousal with her again made Will want to sleep and just forget about ever getting up. Three days ago he had gotten everything in the world he wanted, and learning about her past was like having it brutally yanked away.

"Dad," Shane yelled, clapping his hands together loudly. "Stop that. Stop drifting off and pay attention to me. Michael and I are going to be leaving shortly. I was saying you can send us a text when you want us to come home."

Will did close his eyes then, sighing at the edge of panic in Shane's tone. He wasn't intentionally trying to worry anyone. He just needed some time to figure out how to be reasonable about this information before he went insane.

Will finally heard the doorbell ringing and was relieved. It meant both boys would be leaving soon. He'd pull himself together until they left and then send the well-meaning babysitter away as soon as the boys were gone.

All he wanted was to be alone.

~

Michael pulled open the door and saw a freshly showered, still wet-haired woman standing there. She smelled lovely, but looked way too fragile to be dealing with his father.

And she'd been crying.

Seeing her red and swollen eyes tore at Michael's gut. He had a fleeting moment of wondering if it was right to ask for Jessica's help when she didn't look a whole lot better than his Dad did at the moment. Then he pushed his concern aside. Maybe his father wasn't the only person who needed to talk, Michael decided.

"Everything took longer than I anticipated," Jessica explained. "Finally, I just decided to come over as I was because I couldn't pull myself together more."

Michael shook his head. "Don't apologize. You look great, and we're glad you're here. Shane has finally lost patience. Dad keeps drifting off when we try to talk to him and can't seem to hold a conversation for two minutes."

Jessica nodded and let out the sigh she had been holding in for hours.

"Can I call you something other than Ms. Daniels? Formality seems odd in this situation," Michael said.

"Sure. Call me Jessica," she agreed quietly. "Point me to him so I can get this over with."

Michael reached out his hand and took one of Jessica's in his. "Thank you for doing this Jessica—whatever happens. Shane and I are leaving as soon as you give us the word."

Jessica nodded and sighed. She took a deep breath, and Michael squeezed her hand.

"Okay," she said, "let's get this confrontation over with."

~

"DAD, YOUR BABYSITTER IS HERE," SHANE SAID, WHEN HE SAW MICHAEL and Jessica Daniels standing in the doorway of the bedroom. "Wake up and say hello."

Will opened his eyes and rolled his head to the side. When he saw Jessica, he rolled his head back and closed them again.

"Whatever you think you're doing boys, stop right now," he ordered. "Go away, Jessica. Don't let these two tug on your heartstrings. They're master manipulators, which I am blaming on their mother. I know you would never have shown up here if they hadn't coaxed you into it."

It was the truth, Jessica conceded, when she heard Will saying the words, and any other time she would not have been worried about confessing to it. She had thought the boys had been exaggerating about Will's condition. Now she could see they had not told her how bad it really was.

Jessica walked into the bedroom and smartly smacked the bottom of one of Will's bare feet, making him yelp. He was wearing sweats that had seen better days at least twenty years ago, and he looked like he hadn't shaved in several months.

"You could have at least shaved," she said caustically. "You look like a deranged serial killer."

Will's eyes lit with anger for a moment as he took in her wet hair. "Look who's talking. You look like a wet dog."

Well, they were off to a good start, Jessica thought. She walked to the bed and sat on the edge of it taking off her shoes.

Shane averted his gaze and pretended not to be interested in the woman crawling into bed with his father as he asked the inevitable question. "Uh—are you ready for us to leave now?"

"Not yet," Jessica said smoothly. "You can leave when Will tells you to go."

"Tell them to go? You've got to be kidding. I've been trying to get them to leave me the hell alone for days," he declared. Then he looked at each son individually for a couple of moments. "Go. Leave now."

"Not yet," Jessica said firmly to the boys, grateful they were obeying her and not Will. She swung her legs up beside his on the bed. "Move over."

"No," Will said. "Go away."

He closed his eyes to shut out the sight of her. It was bad enough he had to smell her. She must have just taken a shower and washed her hair. Desire curled inside him, but Will ruthlessly pushed it away. Never again, he vowed. Never again would he push unwanted attention on this woman. She could strip and fondle herself, and he still wouldn't lay a hand on her.

"Fine," Jessica said, turning to her side and stretching out her length on what little bed Will was allowing her. "If I fall onto the floor, it will be your fault if I get hurt."

Will scooted over then, moving his head to another pillow and his body to the other side of the queen bed. "There. Happy now?"

Jessica studied him as she moved her body closer to his. "No. I'm not happy, but I'm not curled up in a ball brooding in my bed either. Stop doing this sulking thing and talk to me. Send your sons away so we can be alone, but tell them you're okay first. They've been worried sick about you. Now I can see why. I didn't know being stubborn could turn into a chronic illness until I saw you today."

"I don't need your false sympathy. Just why the hell are you here anyway?" he demanded. "You're not interested, remember?"

Jessica rolled to her back and looked up at the ceiling. "I lied. I was scared of you, so I lied."

"Well, for the record, I will never do anything to scare you again. I'm sorry I did the first time. Now go away," Will said quietly, the knots returning to his stomach.

"I didn't mean I was afraid of you physically. I'm afraid of how you make me feel. The last time I was this emotionally involved with a man, he left me and died. Are you planning to die on me too?" Jessica asked, her throat tight.

The genuine pain in her words took the angry bluster right out of him. Will rolled to his side, putting an arm around her without thinking about it. "No. I'm not going to die."

Jessica patted his arm. "Good. Now tell Michael and Shane to go have dinner and catch a movie, and that they can come back in a couple of hours."

Will looked at his sons standing in the doorway together, faces drawn tight in concern for both Jessica and him. They had been worried about him for days, and now they were worried about leaving Jessica alone with him. He could see it in the way they were trying not to glare at him.

In his whole life, Will couldn't remember ever feeling less like a good man. His sons didn't trust him right now to treat her well. He closed his eyes, breathed quietly a few moments, and tightened his hold on Jessica. His relief to be with her again was profound, and he decided to stop fighting it.

When he opened his eyes, Will looked at his sons with sincere regret. "I'm sorry I worried you. Make sure you lock the door on your way out," he said softly to them. "Jessica and I are going to be fine. I love you both."

"We love you too, Dad. Call us if you need us," Shane said.

"We'll be fine," Jessica said. "Your father and I are going to be friends if he's still alive when you get home."

Michael laughed nervously. "No killing allowed in my house. You sure you don't want a chaperone?"

"Go away, Michael," Will ordered, feeling Jessica's laughing belly under his arm.

He and Jessica listened to the boys walk down the hallway, gather up keys and jackets, and head out the door. There was a deep silence in the house after they had gone.

Jessica turned her head to Will and let her tears flow at last. She had never wanted anything about her to cause him this much emotional pain. She had never wanted it to bother any man, but her regret for Will's suffering was ten times more than she usually allowed herself. All she could do was try to explain.

"Look, you never hurt me the way you've been imagining. I knew eventually you'd discover my past, and I admit it had occurred to me that I would need to talk with you after you found out. I was just trying to spare myself getting more involved, so it took your sons' interference to make me do what was right."

Jessica pulled a tissue from her jeans pocket and used it on her eyes. "The only hurt you have ever caused me is in reminding me too much of the boy I married long, long ago."

Will tilted his head down. It had not occurred to him that he would remind Jessica of anyone. She was the first woman like her he'd ever met. He'd just assumed he would be unique to her as well. To be fair, he guessed Steve Lipton had tried to tell him he wasn't original when he mentioned all the men Jessica had dated.

Male arrogance, Will admitted, was not something a man could easily discard, no matter how old he was. "Help me understand. Tell me about your husband."

Jessica closed her eyes. The last thing she wanted to talk to Will about was another man when she was lying in his arms. However, she knew Will was not going to rest until he was convinced that what she was telling him was the truth.

Jessica took a breath and just began. "I was still a child when I married Nathan. My husband was my first lover, and a very insistent, highly sexual man. I loved him madly and as his wife gladly gave him whatever he wanted from me. But I've never been able, no matter how much therapy I had, to separate what happened to me from the sexuality I experienced with him. They were too close together in my timeline. The violence I endured took his memories from me. For years after the rape, I had no good memories of sex at all. My therapist called it Post Traumatic Stress Disorder. It doesn't just happen to soldiers. It can happen to anyone."

Jessica turned her head away from Will's intent gaze to stare at the ceiling again. "When you kissed me to stop me from talking, you reminded me of my husband Nathan. Frankly, I'm not sure I'm ready to remember him or what he used to do to me. I was pretty shocked that I tolerated it so long without stopping you."

"I wasn't trying to remind you of the past," Will said softly. "I never meant to hurt you in any way at all."

"I know. Don't care about me this much, Everett Williams. Don't dwell on pain that is thirty years old for me. I have emotional scar tissue on top of emotional scar tissue built up inside me. I refuse to blame myself for your pain, and caring about your mental condition is a responsibility I do not want right now," Jessica told him.

Will put his forehead against Jessica's shoulder for a moment, then brought his gaze back to hers.

"Well, I may remind you of your dead husband, but whether you like it or not, you're my first. You're the first woman to pick me up in years, the first I wanted to kiss so badly I ached, and simply the first I have wanted to make love to in a long time. When Ellen interrupted us in the courtyard, I was upset at her for doing it, and that was the first time I had really felt divorced. It's too late to ask me not to care about you. You're the only woman I want. Now tell me the truth. Do I scare you physically?" Will asked, the question not much more than a whisper between them.

"No. You don't. What is it with you macho men? I'm not scared of you even though I know you can overpower me with your greater strength," Jessica said sarcastically. "That's biologically true with a lot of men, Will. Despite what happened between us, and my reaction to it, it never occurred to me that you would intentionally want to hurt me. I'm not lying about that. I wouldn't have crawled into bed beside you or let your sons talk me into coming here if I was physically afraid of you. If you knew me better, you'd have no trouble believing that."

"You might change your mind if you knew how violent I can be when I'm upset," Will said honestly. "If I saw those men today that hurt you, I would still want to kill them, even thirty years later. They should never have been set free. I've seen your art. I can never pretend otherwise."

He moved his hand on her arm in soothing circles, and then wrapped a leg across both of hers. He hoped it felt comforting and protecting to her instead of restricting.

"If I found a way to be alone with the men that hurt you, I'd probably kill them without remorse," Will said, splaying one large hand across her stomach, covering where her daughter would have been. "You could make an argument that I'm not much better than those men."

Jessica stared hard at the ceiling. Past conversations with other men merged into this one with Will. Most men were good inside, she had learned. Most men felt like Will did. Neither his words nor his attitude were a surprise to Jessica. Other men had tried to love her despite the past, but it just hadn't worked out for long.

"Will, I believe you would only use your strength to protect me," Jessica told him, rolling to her side and into his arms. "So hold me tightly and let's sleep together. Make me feel safe and cared for tonight, and maybe we'll both get some rest."

Will put his arms around her, careful not to hold her too tightly, despite what she requested. He pulled her body against his to comfort both of them, and within a few minutes they both drifted off into an emotionally exhausted sleep.

~

WHEN MICHAEL AND SHANE CAME HOME SEVERAL HOURS LATER, THEY found their father and Jessica sleeping peacefully together on the bed, wrapped in each other's arms.

"Well, at least he kept her here," Michael said wistfully. "I'm not waking them up."

Shane shook his head. "It's a good sign, but it doesn't necessarily mean things will work out. If they want each other but aren't acting on it, then this is just a temporary truce."

"Well, I'm not listening to your analysis tonight, bro," Michael said quietly, walking with Shane to the door. "I'm just letting them sleep and wishing for a happy ending. There's nothing wrong with that."

"No—no there isn't," Shane agreed. "Call if you need me. Seriously. I don't mind."

Michael threw his arms around his brother and hugged him hard before letting him go. "You really are the best man I know next to Dad."

"Geez, Michael. I was tired of the leggy blondes anyway. Take them. Take them all. Just stop with the hugging already," Shane said on an embarrassed groan when Michael laughed and let him go.

CHAPTER 9

Because he'd spent several depressing days sleeping, Will awoke at four in the morning still wrapped around Jessica. He used the bathroom to shave and brush his teeth before he crawled back into the bed to hold the still sleeping woman again.

He lay awake for almost an hour just holding her and studying her face as the room brightened with morning light. He used the time to learn every surface and memorize every line, crevice, and hollow. If he never saw Jessica Daniels again after today, Will thought, he would now always remember enough to carve her face.

At almost exactly six thirty, her eyelids finally fluttered and opened. Probably her normal wake up time, Will thought smiling. She didn't look surprised to see him, but she did bring up an exploring palm to his now smoothly shaven face.

"Thanks for not making me wake up to a serial killer," she said, smiling softly.

Will laughed at her teasing. "I figured I owed you that much for staying the night."

He brushed her hair back and cupped her cheek. "You have an expressive face, Jessica Daniels. I really would like to kiss it good morning."

Before she could formulate an answer through the brain fog, Will's peppermint flavored mouth was on hers, his teeth nibbling her lips, his tongue sweeping the area his teeth grazed. Desire shot through her like a lightning bolt bringing instant and complete arousal with it. She curled her fingers into the material covering his shoulders.

Never taking his mouth from hers, Will rolled onto Jessica like they were already lovers, lining their hips together, suggesting the best of all possible ways to wake up. His heart beat in time to the blood rushing through all of him.

This woman, Will thought moving instinctively against her, *this woman* was definitely the one he wanted.

Jessica could feel Will's erection straining against her through his thin sweats that revealed everything he could offer. And he could certainly offer a lot, she concluded, sighing in happiness to be under him. Will's weight bore down on her as he kissed her more deeply, and Jessica groaned at the increasing pressure of his mouth. Then it was simply the most natural thing in the world to part her legs and let Will and his impressive hardness fall between them, to shift under Will until his erection was cradled intimately against her.

Yes, she thought. God yes, and now.

When Will rocked hard between her thighs, the only thing Jessica wanted more than him inside her was to have their clothes magically gone so she could feel his skin on hers. She ran hands down Will's back, pulled his hips into hers, and almost climaxed when Will pushed hard enough against her to move both her and the bed. She groaned against his mouth and was thrilled when he kissed her harder in response.

The hell with worrying, she thought dizzily, honestly wanting Everett Williams more than she could remember wanting a man in a really long time. Tired of holding back, Jessica realized there was no longer any choice about being less involved.

Her heart expanded with the decision and beat frantically in anticipation.

But when she started to pull off his shirt, Will deliberately moved out of the reach of her hands. Just as quickly as he had rolled onto her, Will rolled off and moved to the other side of the bed, putting all the distance he could between them.

"I'm sorry," he said, his voice ragged from the effort to breathe in his aroused state. "I got—carried away. I didn't mean to crawl on top of you like that."

Stunned, Jessica could only look at Will as if he was insane, and then she realized he meant they were really stopping.

Well, she was wide awake now, Jessica decided, staring at the ceiling in shock when she could no longer bear to look at Will's guilty expression. She was breathing like an exhausted marathon runner and aching in places she knew she would feel all day. Her legs still trembled with arousal and wanting him back between them. She cursed Will and his misgivings for ruining the most sincere moment of desire she could ever remember feeling.

"Will, if you didn't interpret my actions just now as an indication of my willingness, you are definitely not as smart as I thought you were," Jessica said tightly. "Or else you still have a hell of a lot to learn about women even at your age."

"I refuse to force you or coerce you into doing anything else with me you don't want," Will said firmly. "Seducing you when you aren't fully awake was not fair either. That's why I stopped."

"Did I act like you were forcing me? Was I not part of the damn seduction?" Jessica asked, not caring that her emphatic tone revealed how far beyond rational thinking she was. "What the hell did your wife do to let you know she was okay with your sexual advances? I did everything but beg you to be inside me. If you hadn't moved away, I was only a few seconds from doing that. You felt me reaching for your shirt to undress you."

Will sighed, and gritted his teeth. "Okay, yes. I knew you wanted me, but this is not the right time. I'm not going to take advantage of you. And being with you is sure as hell not the same thing as being with Ellen."

"Oh, you made that very clear just now," Jessica said harshly. She sat up and swung her feet to the floor, giving Will her back so he wouldn't see how much his rejection had hurt her. "I get that I'm damaged goods, a fragile woman, someone you can't be passionately honest with now. Don't you think I've been down this road before?"

"That is not what I meant," Will said, surprised and hurt by her interpretation of his self-control. "Look—can we talk about this tonight? I know you have to go to work shortly."

Jessica stood, grabbed her shoes, walked to the chair and started putting them on. "No. We can't talk tonight. I have plans tonight."

"You got something more important to do than talking this out?" Will asked, fighting not to be seriously hurt by her refusal.

"Yes. I have a date with a man who doesn't know anything about me other than I seem like a fun woman. It beats the hell out of looking at the pity in your eyes any day," she said honestly.

"*You have a date?*" Will asked, disbelief in his tone. "After you came over here and crawled into bed with me, and then admitted you were interested in me, you have a damn date tonight? What did you do? Make the date before you even came over here yesterday?"

"Yes. That's exactly what I did," Jessica said, mocking his anger. "I plan to have a date every night for the next two weeks until this whole thing with you blows over. I don't have the time or the inclination to work through your masculine guilt complexes hoping we might eventually get to some sort of normal relationship. Despite my misgivings—which is a long damn list—I offered myself to you two minutes ago, and you refused the offer. That makes things pretty simple for me, Will."

"What if I had accepted your offer? What if I'd made you late for work and did what I wanted with you anyway? Would you still have a date tonight?" Will asked, unable to keep the belligerence from his tone.

"I guess we'll never know," Jessica admitted, her voice suddenly quiet and sad. "I never meant to fall asleep here or to let you kiss me this morning. I never wanted you to know the truth about me, and for damn sure I don't want the pity you now feel for me. I got over the rape, Will. I've been sexually intimate with a lot of good men who have treated me well, and the good sex lasts until they find out what happened. Then they become like you and end up reminding me of the past, which brings the shame all back like it was yesterday. Sex and shame do not mix well."

"You're just not going to cut me a break here, are you?" Will asked, angry at her now, angry enough to say ugly things, angry enough to throw Jessica back onto the bed and make sure she knew how much he wanted what she had offered him.

It wasn't about not wanting her. It was about doing the right damn thing by both of them. And it didn't help his already raw emotions to know he was angry enough to demonstrate his own version of possessive violence. He wasn't sure of his boundaries this morning. He hadn't been sure of them in three days. How was he supposed to just get over everything in a single night of being in her arms?

Hell. He didn't even want to let her out of his sight today. He for damn sure wasn't capable of being rational about his actions yet.

"I want you, and I care about you," Will said, sitting up in bed to glare at her.

"Well, obviously not as much as I want you, Will," Jessica said, marching out of the bedroom and down the hall, yelling as she went. "If I'd been shot instead of raped, you'd have been inside me a few minutes ago without a second thought about it. So don't patronize me. You stopped just now because I was raped. I'm not the one with the problem—you are. You don't know yet how you feel about it."

Will bounded to his feet and stomped after her to the front door.

"I stopped for a lot of reasons, none of which had to do with not wanting you. If you sleep with those men you're dating, you will be cheating on me—on us, Jessica. Those other men will be nothing more than substitutes," Will warned, hoping what he told her was as much the truth as he felt like it was.

"You still don't get it. I don't care if the other men are substitutes," Jessica said, her hand on the doorknob to ensure her escape. "Do you know what the success rate is for relationships to survive when the woman has been raped, Will? It's less than ten percent. That means ninety percent of all relationships a raped woman ever has in her life will likely break up due to PTSD issues from the rape. I have to date a lot of men to find the ten percent of relationships that might actually work out for me. I refuse to feel guilty about looking."

"Jessica," Will said, anxious for her to hear him at little, believe him when he said how he felt. "You can stop looking. I'm the right man for you. I swear it. I'm the one you've been searching for who will understand it all. I just have to get my head straight. You need to give me a little time."

"If you were the right man," Jessica said, her voice tired, her body still yearning for his, "you'd have been grateful for what I wanted to give you this morning, and for damn sure not turned me down when I was finally ready to take a chance on us. You're a good man, Everett Williams, but you just proved you're not the right one for me."

"Yes. I am," Will hissed, when he wanted to swear and yell until she listened to him. *"I damn well am the right man."*

Will slammed a hand on the front door to close it and to prevent her escape. Then he used one shaking hand to turn a surprised Jessica around, and push her back as gently as he could against the door. It killed him to use force to restrain her, but he had to make sure she heard him. He absolutely couldn't let her out the door to run away until he'd gotten through to her.

"Listen to me, you damn stubborn woman," he said harshly. "You said I reminded you of your husband. Do you know why? It's because I'm affected the same way Nathan Daniels would have been if he'd lived to know his wife had been violently raped. Can't you look at it from my side for even one moment?"

"No. I do not want to see how you feel about my thirty-year-old past. Let me go, Will," Jessica ordered.

"I can't let you go. I need you in my life, Jessica. If you can't forgive me immediately, give me two weeks at least," Will ordered harshly, even while she shook her head from side to side, "*Promise me* —promise me not to sleep with anyone else for two weeks. That's not a long time. If I can't convince you of my feelings in two weeks, or we're still fighting about this, I'll leave you alone to do what you like. You can even have the super-sized box of condoms I bought because I sure as hell am not going to use them without you."

"Stop making fun of me," Jessica commanded loudly, punching Will hard in the shoulder. "I don't care how noble you think you are. I refuse to apologize for my life or my dating habits whether you understand them or not."

Will could see her unwillingness to hurt him in her gaze, but it was probably too much to expect her to admit it when she was so upset with him.

"I don't want an apology or a damn justification. All I want is two weeks, Jessica," he said, fighting the urge to sigh in relief as he watched her close her eyes and drop her head to her chest. Jessica was never going to find a man who wanted her the way Will knew he did.

"Promise me," Will said quietly, the words a plea now more than a command.

He wasn't an idiot. The only idiotic thing Will had done was not take what she offered when he'd been waiting so long for her to want him back. All this time they'd spent arguing could have been spent doing something else. If he could wind the clock back just fifteen minutes, Will thought, they'd both be having an orgasm right now. The idea of how close they had been made him crazy.

"No. No promises," Jessica said coldly, but then was shocked when Will fiercely covered her mouth with his demanding one again.

His hands slid down behind her, lifted her hips to align with his again, and just like that they were back to where they had been in the bedroom before he'd rolled off her. Again, her arousal was instant and complete. If her mouth had been free, Jessica would have simply begged Will to take her back to bed, even with her common sense warning her to run now before it got worse.

With his mouth on hers again, Will couldn't believe how quickly the heat grew between them. Oh god, why hadn't he just taken what she offered this morning? When Will finally forced himself to let her go, his body was screaming for hers. He was pretty sure he'd never wanted a woman quite so much in his entire life. Today was going to be a miserable, frustrating day without even a chance of being inside her.

"Honor this. Give me two weeks," Will ordered fiercely, kissing her hard one more time. Then he opened the front door and pushed a very surprised Jessica Daniels outside the house, slamming the door closed behind her sputtering protests, and throwing the deadbolt to keep himself inside.

If he hadn't done all that, he would have chased down the sidewalk after her.

When he heard her walk away swearing, Will leaned his forehead against the locked door, cursing himself again for not just sinking into her when he'd had the chance. He turned around to find his son Michael standing in the kitchen doorway sipping coffee and smiling at him.

"Sorry. I didn't intend to eavesdrop, or watch the show. You two were just oblivious of me," he said, taking in his Dad's wild eyes and flushed face with interest. "Want some coffee now or after your cold shower?"

"Don't start with me. Your teasing is getting to be more like Shane's every damn day I'm here," Will said darkly. It was all he could do not to turn Michael into a target for his frustration with Jessica.

"Well, lately you're giving me a whole new opinion of you too, Dad," Michael told him honestly, not even trying to hide the smirk. "I'm starting to understand where Shane and I got our—well, never mind."

When his father had stopped Jessica Daniels from leaving, when he had ordered her not to sleep with other men, Michael had had to stop himself from hollering out his support. It would definitely not have endeared him to Jessica, who already had a semi-poor opinion of him. So he'd settled for a quiet fist in the air in the kitchen.

"I have a newfound respect for you after how you handled this morning, though I have to tell you, if that had been me with Carrie, I would never have refused her anything. I don't know how you managed it with Jessica," Michael said sincerely, taking a long drink of coffee.

"I managed it because I want more than she's given those other guys. I want it all," Will said fiercely, running a hand through what was left of his hair. "I don't want her pity any more than she wants mine. I want her in my life, willing and accepting of what is between us."

"Great," Michael said, laughing and walking into the kitchen. "I want that for you, too. I might even be able to help you make that happen."

He poured his father a cup of coffee when he noticed he'd followed him into the kitchen. *Ah, the dead really has returned to life,* Michael thought relieved, letting himself smile at his father in approval. He would need to share the news with Shane so his brother could stop worrying as well.

"Help me?" Will asked, almost fearful about what his grinning son had in mind. "How can you help me?"

"I know where Jessica Daniels is going to be on her—what did you call it—oh yeah, her *damn date* tonight," Michael said, grinning at the sudden look of determination in his father's gaze. He would love nothing more than to help his father bust up Jessica's date.

"Where is she going to be?" Will demanded, surprised.

"There's an art show in Cincinnati. Jessica is registered to show several pieces of her vagina art," Michael said.

"Vagina art?" Will repeated the unfamiliar phrase. "What's that?"

"A celebration of the feminine," Michael quoted carefully, using the art show's description of it. "She's only released the new work in the last year or so. You'll have to see it to understand it, but trust me, you're going to like her new art a whole lot more than her other stuff. Most of them are glass, which only makes them better. I bid on the one I wanted already, and I'm the highest bidder so far. I saw it when I met her last year, but I confess I submitted the bid under an alias to keep her from finding out it was me."

Will laughed and shook his head. Because Michael's name was so well known in the art community, he often turned in cloaked bids on art pieces. He didn't want others to know he was such a patron of the arts. "I can see you're dying to tell me, Michael. What name did you use this time?"

Michael smiled, glad to see his father back to normal—or almost normal. "I used the William Larson identity. When Jessica finds out, she'll think it's you."

Will spit coffee all over the table while Michael laughed. He pulled a handful of paper napkins from a nearby holder.

"Doubtful," he said, mopping up the spill. "Since she thinks my name is Everett Williams and that I'm just an artist."

"You never told her your real name?" Michael asked, wondering why his father would want to hide his former day job from a fellow teacher.

"It hasn't exactly had time to come up," Will defended.

"Do you think she'd be less interested in you if she knew?" Michael asked, truly puzzled.

"It's not that," Will said. "I just wanted to make sure the next woman understood I was an artist first. I didn't want to be with anyone who didn't accept it."

"Well, I think you hit the jackpot in Jessica Daniels. I can't imagine a woman who could understand you or your work any better," Michael told him. "I'm damn envious."

"I'll tell her about the other career eventually. I intended to tell her before now. I guess I liked her thinking I was just some rebel biker artist type," Will said, running a hand through his remaining hair.

Watching his father do the Larson-male-hair-sweep-thing again made Michael laugh.

"You are a genuine rebel biker artist type, Dad. You always have been, but now you get to be that all the time. Mom may not have liked that part of you, but it's always been who you were on the inside. Jessica seems to like it fine. I saw you two kissing when you were covered in marble dust. She had white palm prints on her ass when she left," Michael said, enjoying his father's flushed face.

"She did not," Will denied, the heat growing as he remembered kissing her.

"You know I don't lie about those things. Mom even mentioned it," Michael said, heaping the embarrassment on his father's head without remorse. "And frankly, it was a good thing for both of those women to know the truth about your intentions."

"Shane really is going to make a fortune writing a damn book about us one day," Will complained, crossing his arms.

"Good," Michael said. "He needs to make more money. He's going to owe me a thousand dollars when he finishes his dissertation this December."

"Did he say he was finishing?" Will asked, curiosity overriding his temper about dealing with Michael's version of honesty. "That would be great. I hadn't seen any more bills for tuition. I sort of assumed he temporarily dropped out."

"No. We made a bet. I bet him he was going to fall in love with a tiny, smart woman before he finishes," Michael said with glee. "This is going to be the easiest money I've ever made. Last night I hugged him, and he offered me all his blondes. He even confessed that the piercings were to scare the women away. I'm using the power of suggestion on the psych man. I love it."

"And to think I was worried Shane was never going to grow up," Will said, ignoring Michael's joking and smiling at the idea of Shane trying to scare away the girls. That boy had never had to chase any female. They fell at his feet, and he picked one up now and again. Will could see the logic of why Shane would choose to alter himself to discourage them.

"You need to set a good example for Shane and me, Dad. Get your divorced shit together and come with me to the art show," Michael said. "Shane and I can help you look good enough to seduce Jessica away from anybody."

"Boy, I was sleeping with women long before you came into existence. I can do my own seducing. Thanks anyway," Will told his oldest son dryly.

"It will be harder looking like you currently do. Face it, you need a little updating, Dad. You have to look better than her date, who may be close to my age," Michael said on a laugh.

"Great, Michael. Thanks for the pep talk," Will said dryly.

"Look, the woman is worth at least buying some new clothes for, isn't she?" Michael asked, sipping his coffee and fighting not to smile too much.

"I guess I could use some new clothes, but no piercings or tattoos,"

Will said firmly. "I hate older men who do that, and I draw the line at mutilation. I don't need to try to imitate you or Shane."

Michael pulled out his cell and held up a hand as he pushed a button to dial.

"Hey, Shane. Yeah, of course it's seven-thirty in the morning. Look, we need to get Dad a new look so he can go bust up Jessica's date tonight and seduce her. No, not yet. She stayed all night, but he turned her down this morning. I don't know. He just did."

Will watched Michael direct his impatient gaze to the ceiling as he waited for Shane to finish what he was saying.

"I don't know why Dad turned her down. Come over here and analyze him yourself," Michael said into the phone, laughing as his father put his head in his hands.

"Now listen. You're not hearing me. We're just going to get Dad updated so he looks better than the other men in Jessica's life. I think we should do what you suggested and buy him a great jacket to wear with his jeans. Oh, and some new boots too, big enough to make him at least a few inches taller than her. Yeah, we want him to be your height. Great. Come on over. I'll make breakfast."

"I mean it, Michael. No piercings or tattoos," Will said firmly, glaring at his oldest son as he hung up the phone. "Don't even ask."

"Trust me," Michael said, grinning. "I look just like you. I know exactly what needs to be done. It's like planning my future."

CHAPTER 10

The complete lack of hair on his head was hard to get used to, even though Will had to admit being completely bald looked much better than sporting a giant bare spot on top. He thought of all the movie stars and sports figures with shaved heads as he checked out his own in the mirror, and he figured the boys had been right about getting rid of his hair.

Not that Will thought he looked like a movie star now, but his shaved head definitely shifted the focus to the rest of him, which had for the last decade looked better than his head.

The brown tweed jacket was great, and he liked it a lot. And the boots were surprisingly comfortable despite the thick heel.

As Will studied himself in the fitting room mirror, he liked what he saw. Or at least he mostly liked it all. He reached two fingers up to play with earring now gracing his earlobe, still trying to figure out how his sons had talked him into it. He was getting soft as he got older, Will decided. He used to be a lot better at saying no to them and meaning it.

Sighing, Will strode out of the fitting room to the sales floor where his sons waited patiently to check him out.

Shane nodded and grinned when he saw him. "Nice," he said in approval. His father was practically eye-to-eye with him now.

Michael just smiled as his gaze swept over his father. Then he smiled more when he saw several women giving his father the once over before repeating it several times. They had been looking at Michael, and then Shane, until his father walked out of the fitting room almost as tall as Shane and much, much better dressed.

Jessica Daniels was in for a real surprise, Michael decided, and maybe some competition if she kept playing hard to get. His father sure didn't look like some run-of-the-mill retiree now. Michael just had to say something about what he was seeing.

"Dad, if the sales girls had seen you roll in on your bike, you could have gotten laid right here in the fitting room," he teased.

"Michael, that's enough," Will said harshly. "You're being crude." And it didn't help that he could definitely imagine Jessica and him in that tight little room together. He barely fought off the frustrated sigh.

Michael saw one woman point his dad out to another woman and grinned. "No. I'm just being honest about how great you look. Jessica is damn lucky you don't think like Shane or I do."

Will looked at himself standing next to both his very attractive sons. He had to admit that he did look younger and more confident. No matter how he felt on the inside, he wasn't going to be mistaken for an old washed-out guy dressed like he was.

"I do like most of this, but is the earring really necessary?" Will asked, touching his earlobe again.

This got a chuckle out of Shane, who up to now had just been nodding at what Michael said.

"Yes. Jessica is going to love the earring," Shane told him firmly, pulling his dad's hand away from his ear. "There's something about the contradiction of a giant man wearing a tiny piece of jewelry. It says you can break the bed but be completely sensitive while doing it."

Will snorted. "Oh, good—sensitive, but extremely horny. That was exactly the look I was going for," he whispered dryly, making them both laugh.

"Great. Then you're all set," Michael replied, laughing. "Want to ride to Cincinnati with me or drive yourself?"

"I'll get there on my own," Will said, "if I have any money left for gas after all this."

"Dad, it's a few hundred dollars. When was the last time you bought new clothes?" Shane asked. "I bet it was before you and Mom broke up."

"Okay. You're probably right," Will said. "Listen, I'm heading to the café for a bit to try out my new look. I'll see you at the art show."

"HEY, MELANIE. BRENT. HOW'S IT GOING?" WILL SAID, CLIMBING ON A bar stool at the counter. His gaze took in the crowded tables with a smile. "Looks like business is still booming."

Melanie and Brent Madison both walked over to him like zombies and stood looking at him in shock.

"What?" Will asked. "Is everything okay?"

"You—well. . .I mean," Melanie stammered, and then flushed. She might have melted to the floor in shock if her husband hadn't put an arm around her shoulders for support. First the stool thing and now the hot-guy look. It was almost more than her brain could take in about William Larson.

"Nice earring, Mr. Larson," Brent said breezily, unable to stifle a grin at the sight.

Will's hand went automatically to his earlobe. "I've had it for several hours now and almost forgot about it. I told my son Shane it was too much."

Brent moved his arm down to squeeze his wife's hand as he shook his head and smiled at William Larson.

"No. It looks good. Nice haircut too, Mr. Larson. Makes you look younger," Brent said as casually as he could. "In fact, you look so good that I may have to shave my head now to compete."

Will laughed at the idea of Brent shaving his full, thick hair all off. He knew he was teasing. "Yeah, right. A shaved head isn't great, but at least it beats the bald spot."

Melanie walked up and peered into his face. "Is that really still you, Will?"

Will ran hand over his face, trying to minimize the embarrassed flush. "Why? Is this all too much? I let my sons do this to me. They said I needed updating."

Melanie shook her head from side to side. "It's not too much. You look great, just very different. You don't look—well, you don't look as old as my dad anymore."

"I still feel as old as your dad," Will said softly, smiling regretfully. He had never minded being a surrogate father to any child.

"Has Jessica seen you yet?" Melanie asked.

Will shook his head. "No. Apparently, she has a date tonight," he said, frowning. "I couldn't talk her out of it, but I'll probably see her at the art show."

"I wish I could be there when she sees you," Melanie said earnestly, as she poured him a cup of coffee. "I'd love to see the look on the math teacher's face too."

"Math teacher? Is that who's she dating tonight?" Will demanded, glaring at Melanie.

"You can't be mad at the messenger," she told him, arching an eyebrow at his glare. "I shouldn't have said anything. It's just that you're going to shock Adam whatever-his-name-is too. You don't look like anyone's gray-haired dad anymore. You look like a movie hero."

"Movie hero? Oh good, that's exactly the look I was going for," Will said sarcastically, rolling his eyes and laughing at what he was sure was a joke. "I was going to leave a good tip anyway you know. You don't have to flatter me."

Melanie looked at her husband, who bit his lip and stared at the floor to keep from laughing out loud. It was very obvious to both of them that William Larson had no clue how big the transformation was.

CHAPTER 11

Jessica had chained off her area and left her art unattended for a short while to walk around with her embarrassed date who obviously didn't understand the artistic value of a glass vagina. After he'd criticized several other artists' work, including Michael Larson's metal sculptures, Jessica was fed up with trying to be polite and had left Adam to browse alone so she could return to her own work.

As Jessica neared her display table, she saw someone had stepped around the rope barricade. All she could see was the man's back as he reached out a tentative finger to stroke the finely crafted clitoris on the *Blue Blaze* model. Jessica shivered and laughed at herself for doing so, letting her gaze openly admire the man from behind. He was a little taller than she was, broad shouldered, and completely bald with an earring.

And if the front looked as good as the back, he was also going to be totally hot. Her interest had her smiling at her carnal thoughts. Maybe her attraction for Will hadn't ruined her for other men after all, she mused. In fact, she might even be tempted to ask the man out for a drink. It would give her an excuse to send Adam on his merry way, and one guaranteed to make sure he'd never ask her out again.

Will, on the other hand, would not be pleased. Jessica thought of the promise he'd tried to extort from her this morning and sighed.

There was simply no reason to feel guilty. It wasn't like she had agreed.

She ruthlessly pushed away her memories of kissing Will and immediately imagined Brooke calling her "chicken" again. Well, she was a chicken about getting more involved with Will. So what? The sexy bald stranger looked a lot safer to her and a lot less trouble.

"Looks like you're a man who knows his way around one of those," Jessica said, intentionally teasing him so she could judge him by his response.

Will smiled at the flirtatious tone he hadn't heard from Jessica in a while, but he didn't turn for a moment.

"Oh, I've touched a few of these in my time," he said finally with a laugh, turning and meeting her gaze directly. "But I think I prefer the real ones to art."

"Will?" Jessica all but choked, her arms uncrossing as she came a bit closer to study him. She looked down to his boots and back up to the top of his shaved head. "That's a very nice look for you. I really like your earring."

Will made a mental note to thank Shane later. His son's other comment had also been dead on too because he could definitely see himself stretching the limits of a bed with this woman tonight. In fact, he had never seen Jessica look so tempting. Memories of how close he'd come to enjoying all of her this morning came rushing back.

"You look pretty good yourself, Ms. Daniels. I knew you had legs, but not mile long ones that went all the way up to heaven," Will said, teasing.

His gaze dropped to her low-heeled shoes and slowly made its way up to the denim skirt stopping several inches above her knees. He couldn't quite see over her head, but he was looking down at her for the first time since they had met. The rush it gave him put a wicked smile on his face that Will suspected would have only made Jessica mad if she knew the cause.

Over the short skirt, Jessica wore a gauzy white top and a denim vest too small to button over her breasts. Will forced his gaze away from them before he gave in to the urge to reach for her.

Instead, Will looked at her wavy red hair and the long metal hoops almost brushing her shoulders. He used a finger and sent one hoop swinging, appreciating the flirty smile it brought to Jessica's face.

"I like your earrings, too," Will said, drunk with the need to get her alone and try to appease the ache he had for her.

Jessica laughed cautiously at Will's intense perusal. Kissing her so desperately this morning, Will had taxed her nervous system to its limits. Now he was making her awareness much worse with his new look and open flirting.

Though she wondered what had possessed Will to make these changes, Jessica pushed down the answer that came immediately to mind. No, she wasn't going to believe Will had made these changes for her, she decided, no matter how thrilled she might be to think it. Not that she *was* thrilled. It was mostly surprise—just surprise.

Well, okay, she had to admit that Will did look *really* good.

And judging from her reaction even before she recognized him, Jessica concluded she was probably always going to be attracted to Will. A scary thought, but not one she wanted to analyze while smelling his cologne and thinking about kissing him.

"So what do you think of my art," Jessica said, trying to distract herself from her hyperawareness of Will by nodding with her chin to the table.

"I like it better than your earlier work," Will said honestly. "And I'm finally understanding how you figured out my secrets so quickly. We're kindred souls in looking to our own bodies for inspiration."

"I know it's bold to show such an intimate part of yourself to the world, but I wanted to celebrate my sexuality and encourage others to do the same. I think people either get it or they don't. I'm sure you know how challenging it can be to have an artistic vision that embarrasses people," she said to Will.

"Yes," Will said softly. "I know exactly how that is."

Jessica's gaze was locked on his and in her face Will saw both understanding and acceptance. It was the same look she'd given him in Berea. He just hadn't been ready for it then.

"Jessica, what you said this morning—well, you were right about me being caught up in my own reactions. It actually helps me to see what you feel comfortable revealing to the world. Your boldness helps me believe you when you say you're over the past."

"Well, I think I am for the most part, and I work really hard to live only in the present. I'm guessing my art and my sexuality are linked in ways only my therapist could ever understand. I'm sure she shakes her head in dismay about me after every session," she said laughing.

"Fortunately, artists are expected to be screwed up mentally, so I can pretend it's normal."

As Jessica removed the rope barricade, Will walked back to the blue glass piece he'd been exploring when she walked up. It was damn mesmerizing, just like Michael had said. He turned the partial torso piece away from him so that it was lying in a more natural direction, and covered the piece with the palm of his hand.

"These pieces are very sensual. This particular one fits my hand just like it was made specifically for me," Will said, purposely keeping his voice low so only Jessica could hear.

"Too bad. It's already sold, or at least I think it is," Jessica informed him, forcing the words out of her suddenly dry throat. "What is Michael's middle name?"

Jessica watched Will stroking the glass and had to stifle a groan at the sight of his hand moving on it. Her imagination had no problem mentally shifting his touch to her body instead. In fact, she had been thinking about him touching her all day even though she had tried hard not to do so. Adam hadn't proved to be as much of a distraction as she had hoped.

Will didn't feel even a little bit of remorse ratting out his own son to prevent having to tell Jessica about the rest of his life. Tonight he preferred to talk to her about her art while she was in the mood to talk to him. Will decided he would just have to confess later. It wasn't like he was going to have to lie.

"His middle name is William. His full name is Michael William Larson," Will said carefully, running his palm down to cup the bottom of the piece and then back up to the top.

"I was guessing that," Jessica said hoarsely, unable to look away from what Will was doing. "Michael is the high bidder on *Blue Blaze*."

"Not surprising. My eldest son is a somewhat secret patron of the arts and has exceptional taste," Will said softly, liking the pink flush creeping up Jessica's neck and face. "I really like the realism you've put into the pieces. They're irresistible because of it. The only thing that would make them more realistic is if they were heated."

When Will brought his palm up this time, his slipped his middle finger inside the symbolic entrance bored through the center of glass.

"I can't seem to touch the end of this tunnel with my longest finger. How deep does it go?" Will asked, schooling himself to look inquisitive and to keep the grin off his face.

When he finally looked directly at Jessica, Will saw her breathing was erratic. If the woman wasn't about to implode with arousal, he'd eat his new boots.

Jessica started to take two steps toward him, but the math teacher stopped her with a hand on her arm. Grinning at her frustrated look, Will removed his finger and hand from the art and turned it back around to face the general public.

When he looked back, Jessica was scowling at the man who was touching her. Will couldn't have been happier with the situation, especially when he heard the man asking if she was okay and commenting on her face being flushed.

Maybe she should feel more guilty, Jessica thought, looking at Adam, whose face was the picture of concern for her. Then she looked at Will, who had covered his mouth to hide what she knew was a self-satisfied grin. Will had been intentionally trying to seduce her. Hell, he *had* seduced her.

Not only had Adam not even recognized Will, he also hadn't noticed what Will was doing to her art. He was too busy avoiding even looking at the table.

It was the last straw in her relationship with him.

"Adam, never interrupt a woman on the verge of a climax," Jessica said, suddenly tired of being nice to even a good-looking man who was never going to understand her. "Look, I know you're bored silly here. Why don't you go on home? I'll catch a ride with someone."

Will burst out laughing then, drawing both their gazes. "I'll be happy to do it. I've been wanting to give you a ride since I met you."

Jessica looked at Will, a smile twitching at the corners of her mouth. She looked back at a resigned Adam but didn't feel a bit of remorse for what she was about to do. It was way past time to move on.

"Mr. Williams is a neighbor of mine. His son is showing his art here and is the highest bidder on one of my pieces," she said, explaining away Will's innuendo.

Will watched the math teacher sigh in resignation, kiss Jessica's cheek, and walk off dejected. He felt a little sorry for him but couldn't help feeling proud of himself.

"Just so you know, you won't shake me off as easy as your boy-toy," Will warned, smiling at her.

"Just so you know, I lied about the climax to embarrass Adam into leaving," Jessica told Will, turning her expression into a regretful grimace.

"Give me five minutes alone with you, and you'll never lie about a climax with me again," Will promised, narrowing his gaze on the pulse beating madly at her throat.

"Five minutes? That's a little rushed don't you think?" she asked.

"Not after a month of foreplay," Will stated. "But don't worry, once isn't going to be enough. I promise we'll both get there before the evening is over."

Jessica reached into the pocket of her skirt and pulled out the packet she'd carried with her like a talisman. "Fine. It's time to put up or shut up as they say. You better be serious."

Will bit his lip to keep the shout in, took a deep breath, and walked to stand in front of her. "Why is that in your pocket? Were you planning to use it with someone else?"

"No," Jessica told him sincerely. "I was carrying it to remind me of your request. You know, like carrying garlic to ward off vampires. I figured your condom would ward off other men putting a move on me until I could figure out what to do about you."

She reached out her fingers and tucked the condom into the pocket of Will's now very tight jeans. Jessica couldn't help gloating a little over his discomfort and for finally giving him the condom back.

"If you don't put out this time, Everett Williams, I'll probably kill you," Jessica warned.

Will snorted, leaned down, and once again put his mouth firmly over Jessica's to shut her up. He didn't use his hands until Jessica threw her arms around him and clung. When his arms came around her, all his thinking narrowed to just wondering how soon he could be with her.

"I'm ready to find the nearest broom closet or bathroom," Will told her, lifting her to her toes and leaning back with her until she was pressed on him everywhere. "I need to be inside you and I need it now."

"Sorry. *Now* doesn't work for me. I still have two pieces of art to sell. How about my hotel room in three hours?" Jessica asked. "I was never intending to return home with Adam. I planned to rent a car and visit the art museum tomorrow. I was trying not to ruin his evening too early."

"You were right to cut him loose, Jessica. You were never going to be happy with a man so afraid to touch a vagina," Will said on a laugh, which caused her to pull back and almost step out of his arms.

"Aren't you the comedian tonight?" Cocky had never appealed to her. The attitude in Will's words said he was too sure of her giving in to what he wanted, so she gave him a glare.

"Anyone could see the math teacher was never going to appreciate your art. Trust me, you don't want to tie yourself to a relationship like that," Will said, his voice becoming hard and tight, all teasing gone.

Pulling her back into his arms more strongly, Will leaned into her and put his mouth on Jessica's neck, uncaring of the attention they were drawing. He hoped the onlookers were learning a little something watching an older couple make out in public. Will was not letting Jessica go again until she knew for sure how he felt about her. He'd suffered all day and wasn't planning to repeat that mistake.

"I didn't send Adam away because of my art, Will. I sent him away to be with you," Jessica said, accepting at last that there was no reason not to be honest about her desire for him.

"Good. I'll stop teasing and tell you something more serious then. We need to make a stop on the way to your hotel. I meant what I said earlier. One condom is definitely not going to be enough for us," Will whispered in her ear, pulling her hips to his.

"No. It probably won't be, but let me go for now, Will," Jessica whispered back, noticing the immediate cooling in his eyes. She reached out and clasped one of his trembling hands in one of hers, which was shaking as well. "A man with the nerve to wear an earring ought to be confident enough to handle a request for little personal space."

Will sighed and nodded, took a step away, but kept her hand in his.

"Can I play with your vagina to pass the time?" he asked, pleased when her face flushed a deep red at his suggestion.

Jessica stuttered when she tried to talk, and ending up laughing. "If you touch any of my vaginas again, I'm going to scream in frustration. I want you to touch the real thing bad enough as it is. I didn't create them as sex toys. They're a—"

"—*celebration of the feminine*. Yes, they certainly are that, but they're also sensuous and begging by their very nature to be touched, almost as much as the real ones do," Will said on a sigh, not bothering to fight the grin when Jessica crossed her arms again. "You are a cruel woman.

I guess I'll just have to wait until Michael brings *Blue Blaze* home. Then you won't know what I do to it."

Jessica smacked Will in the chest before walking over to talk to someone else looking at her art.

~

By the end of the evening, Jessica ended up selling two of the three pieces she had shown. *Blue Blaze* went to Michael as the highest bidder. *Pink Cloud* was bought by a woman who planned to display it in her guest bathroom to shock her friends.

Normally, Jessica would have been giddy about the success of selling two of only three pieces of art. Instead, she was focused on the man seated next to her, dizzy with the anticipation of being intimate with him.

Will and his new look were more than her willpower could handle resisting, so she pushed her remaining reservations about getting more involved aside. Her daughter Brooke had been right. There was never going to be a man after Will until there had been Will. It was like a scientific fact of their attraction to each other.

"I wondered what you drove other than the bike," Jessica said, smiling at the amount of headroom in the pick-up truck. "I never figured you for a truck guy, but this is as nice as a car inside."

"I realize it's not very efficient or particularly kind to the environment. I'm hoping they make a hybrid big enough for me soon," Will said, steering the truck into the parking lot of the hotel Jessica had indicated. "I just can't drive a compact car. You should see Shane trying to fold himself into his tiny sedan. It fits him like a clown car, but he says he gets great mileage."

Jessica laughed as she imagined the blond giant she met driving a small car. "I admire young people for caring enough to suffer. I used to be that way when I was young. I think I outgrew it when I turned forty. I realized comfort was important to me and that I didn't mind paying for it."

"I hear you," Will said, turning off the truck. "Are we bringing your vagina in with us?"

"Well, I kind of thought you and I would both be going to the room together," she said on a low laugh, "oh—you meant the last art piece."

Will laughed. "You knew damn well what I meant."

"I knew damn well you were teasing me," Jessica countered.

"When was the last time you necked in a truck?" Will asked, laughing. "Because I'd really like to kiss you right now."

"Hmmm. . .that would be never," Jessica commented.

Will flipped up the console between the seats. "Scoot over here, then. I'll give you a little preview of my skills."

"Gee, I don't know, Will. I'm not sure you're the kind of guy I can trust," Jessica said, grinning.

"I am absolutely trustworthy about the important things," Will said seriously. He reached for her and dragged a laughing Jessica across to him. "It's smart of you to worry about the next hour or two, but I'll try to be a gentleman for as long as I can."

"Well, what would be the fun in you doing that?" Jessica protested, turning her knees toward his in the seat.

Will put a hand between her knees and rubbed between them. "Tell me if I do anything you don't like, okay?" He ran his hand up a little higher on one thigh, thrilled when both of her legs loosened to let his hand go even higher.

Jessica groaned at Will's slow exploration. "If I don't scream *stop* at any point, consider you have my blanket permission to keep trying other things."

Will laughed against her mouth, licked her lips and nibbled as he moved his hand higher and higher. He ran his fingers over her underwear, feeling physical evidence of her arousal with a thrill he'd all but forgotten. Damn, he wanted this woman.

"Time to take this indoors, Jessica, unless you want me to investigate the inspiration for your art right now. I already want to pretty damn badly," Will told her, pressing on her damp underwear with a hard knuckle just to make his point. "I want to see the source for your art. And then I want to experience it over and over again."

"Will," Jessica called, her voice hoarse. "I want you to stop now."

"You and your lying," Will chastised softly, the excited look on her face inspiring him. "I warned you about having to suffer the consequences."

His fingers tugged at the top of what he quickly discovered was a fairly small piece of fabric and then delved down to where he could finally slip two fingers inside her. "Much better than *Blue Blaze*—much, much better. I definitely like the original version best."

He pushed two fingers in as deeply as he could, almost undone by her honesty when Jessica shifted to give him greater access.

"How deep does this go, Jessica? My fingers can't reach the end of it."

Will pushed a little farther, a little harder, thrilled when Jessica groaned and closed her thighs around his hand in mild panic. He could feel how close she was to an orgasm. Not forcibly pushing her over the edge was definitely a heroic act of self-control for him.

"I bet you didn't know this is your lucky day, did you lady? I have something that's going to reach all the way inside and fill you completely up. Are you interested?" Will demanded.

"Yes. Damn it, yes," Jessica said, raising herself to meet his mouth with her own. She pulled his tongue inside when he offered it, sucking it to show him what she wanted. "I'm interested now —right now."

"In the parking lot of the hotel or in your room? Your call," Will told her on a laugh, playfully fighting her quivering thighs and pushing his fingers even more firmly inside her. He stroked her until he was delirious with her reaction and the pulsing heat of her.

"Will!" Jessica called out, tensing as the first wave hit.

"You're so damn hot, I can't help it," Will told her, defending his actions as he stroked with the express purpose of making her fly apart for him, because of him. "Go ahead, baby. One of has to have some relief here. I took this too far, but I couldn't help myself. I'll catch up later—I promise. Please just trust me and let go."

"Will," Jessica called his name, thrashing in the seat.

When the orgasm hit full-blown, Will stroked in perfect rhythm to the pulsing in her body. He knew just when to be hard and fast, and just when to slow. It was a couple minutes later before Jessica recovered and came back down to earth. Will's fingers were still inside her but patient now.

God bless older men who knew what they were doing, Jessica thought smugly, feeling a looseness in her limbs that was thoroughly relaxing.

"You are so incredibly beautiful when you let yourself go," Will told her, burying his face in her neck as she throbbed gently around his fingers. "Please do it again for me later. Do it when I'm inside you next time."

"Will," Jessica said with a mildly embarrassed laugh. "Why are we making out in a car like teenagers? I have a perfectly good hotel room reserved inside."

"I couldn't wait," he said, cupping her entire crotch area in his large hand, loathe to remove his fingers from her warmth. He hadn't even gotten around to exploring yet. He wanted everything all at once. "I wish I could find a way to transport us to a bed without having to stop touching you."

"I have to go get a room key. Do you want to come with me or wait?" Jessica asked.

Will laughed and reluctantly pulled his hands away from her. "Is that a rhetorical question?"

Jessica snorted at his innuendo. "Come on. Neither of us has any clothes, so we'll just go get the room together. Leave the vagina in the truck."

"Oh no," Will said, opening the door and climbing out. His body was stiff with longing. He was probably a kid the last time he was this bad off and needing release. "I am not leaving anything that good in the truck unattended. I want it where I can keep my eye on it. I'm just that kind of guy."

"Don't be silly," Jessica said, sliding out her side on wobbly legs. The man had destroyed her. And now he wanted to do it again, probably needed to do it again, she conceded.

When she saw Will cradling her vagina art gently in his arms, Jessica suddenly didn't care how much trouble he was going to be for her. It was nice to be with a man who valued her art and her. It was nice to want someone like that. And it was also nice to be with a man who valued her pleasure as much as his own, Jessica thought, remembering the sheer confidence of his touch.

Looking at Will as they walked to the lobby, Jessica was aware all over again of how good he looked now. She had liked the way he looked before, but he was irresistible with the shaved head and earring, not to mention the long hard body and hazel eyes full of passion.

She smiled at her longing for him and made a quiet decision to ride Everett Williams until he screamed for mercy just as soon as they got to their room. The thought brought on a resurgence of arousal to a level that Jessica had never felt before in her life. Her whole body flooded with heat and she had to work on reigning in her thoughts as they waited their turn to check in.

"That's a pretty wicked look," Will said conversationally, wondering what thoughts had Jessica's face turning several shades of pink. Then he wondered if they were thoughts about him—or about them.

"You offered me a ride earlier. Did you mean it?" Jessica asked casually to Will, even as she turned her attention to the female night clerk. "Reservation for Jessica Daniels, but I need to upgrade that to a double."

"No problem," the female clerk said, smiling and giving Will an appreciative glance.

Jessica smiled at the girl and then looked back at Will.

"Well, did you mean it?" Jessica demanded.

"Anywhere, anytime, and on anything I own," Will said, grinning. "Is that the answer you wanted?"

Jessica laughed and took the two key cards the clerk handed her.

"Yes. Too bad you drove the truck," she joked as they walked through the lobby.

"Give me a few minutes, and I can show you something more fun than my bike," Will said, trailing after her smiling.

Jessica crossed her arms as they waited for the elevator. "I don't know. It may take you longer than five minutes this time. The edge is kind of off for me now. You did a good job earlier."

Will snorted and grinned. "I know what your wicked look meant, lady. You'll be all over me before the elevator gets to our floor."

Jessica snorted herself. "Dream on. There are only three floors total, Mr. Williams."

The elevator doors opened, and they stepped inside as the only occupants. Will set the art piece gently on the floor. When he straightened, he pushed Jessica up against the wall and had his hands up her skirt and on her rear before she could get a whole laugh out of her mouth. His tongue stroked in and out of her mouth several times, and Jessica wrapped herself around him to get closer. It was like they had just left off from this morning.

The ding of the elevator and the doors opening made Will laugh at himself.

"Okay, I was only bluffing," he said, letting Jessica's skirt fall back down and bending to pick up the art on his way out.

Jessica followed him to the room, slid a key card, and opened the door to privacy at last. Her clothes were mostly gone before Will managed to set the art on a bureau. She was pushing him down to the bed, and unfastening his clothes before Will could quite take it in.

His feet were still on the floor, even as his jeans fell around his ankles. The condom was out of his pocket, and he laughed when Jessica ripped it open with her teeth. Then her hands were on him, the condom was on him, and Jessica was sliding down on him before he could really fathom her intentions. Everything she was doing was what he wanted anyway.

Will closed his eyes and prayed he'd last at least a few minutes.

Jessica removed Will's jacket and shirt while she rocked her hips. She ran her hands over the shoulders and chest she had long admired.

Unfortunately, she was having a hard time enjoying the exploration. Just as Will had promised, Jessica rose and fell on an erection that filled her completely. He wasn't the first man like him she'd known, but Will was definitely the most talented with using what he had as he bucked beneath her.

"How close are you?" Will demanded, gritting his teeth and gripping her hips hard.

"Don't worry about me. I'm just taking that ride you promised," Jessica told him with a laugh. "Scream if you want, Will. It's your turn, and I want all of you."

Will opened his eyes wide, his gaze boring into hers. "That's what I want as well," he said honestly. "So give it to me then. Give me everything, Jessica Daniels. Do it while I'm inside you this time."

He pushed up towards her using his elbows, forcing her to change her angle, forcing her to seek her own pleasure while she was working on his. Will could see the moment Jessica went over. He could feel the throbbing inside her begin and it was even better than anything he'd imagined.

"I am absolutely never going to get tired of seeing you do that," Will promised. "Now it really is my turn. I'm dying here."

He grabbed her hips and surged up inside her, thrusting upward over and over until he blasted out of himself and touched the stars that had Jessica's name on them. When she fell weakly across his chest afterward, Will laughed and hugged her exhausted body to his.

"Make sure and tell the math teacher that I kept my promise to give you a ride," Will told her. "In fact, I'll tell him myself if you want."

"Will—stop. I never slept with Adam," Jessica said on a laugh. "I had no intention of it. He was just pleasant, undemanding company."

Will smiled against the top of her head. "Who's on the schedule for tomorrow night? I want to make sure the next guy knows too."

"No one now," Jessica said quietly.

Will lay very still beneath her, laughter dying at her words. He hadn't missed the hesitation in her declaration.

"Is that such a bad thing?" he asked quietly, lifting her hair from her face and fanning it down her back.

"I'll have to think about it later," Jessica told him honestly. "Can we talk about it after we get back home? I really just want to enjoy this time with you."

Will studied the ceiling. If he rushed her, she was going to run from him. That left him with really no choice.

"I could enjoy this a lot more if all my clothes weren't around my ankles," Will said, twisting a strand of Jessica's hair around his finger. "But I have to get dressed again because I left the rest of the condoms in the truck. I'm in a no-win situation with my clothes for a little while. Can we order a pizza while I make the trip out and back? I'm starved."

Jessica laughed against his chest, amused about Will asking permission to order food. What kind of hard-hearted woman did he think she was?

"Sorry, I can't let you order pizza yet. I like to starve my sex slaves. I only let them eat after the third orgasm. You owe me one more, and then I'll feed you," Jessica said sarcastically.

"Fine," Will said, pushing her off him gently and rolling her so she landed on the side of the bed. Then he realized Jessica was still wearing her bra, a very nice white lace bra. How had he missed the lacy underwear? She scrambled his brain, he decided.

"I happen to know a very fast way to give a woman a climax, but I'm not sure you can handle it right now. I know you weren't planning on having the second one so soon," Will said, as proud as any eighteen-year-old who had just scored. It was how Jessica Daniels made him feel.

"I am fine," Jessica said with a yawn, laughing at his bravado. "I can handle anything you can dish out. By the time you get back from the car, I'll be raring to go."

She was teasing, of course, but Jessica wasn't going to let Will out-brag her.

"If you fall asleep, I'm ordering pizza, and then waking you up so I can earn it honestly," he warned.

Jessica laughed as she closed her eyes. The man sure talked a good story, she thought sleepily. Will had had a body-numbing climax with her. She had felt it too because he had been so deeply inside her when it happened. There was no way Will was going to outlast her tonight. No way.

She woke up a few minutes later to Will whispering against her breasts. "Jessica honey, we have to hurry. The pizza is going to be here in twenty minutes."

Jessica laughed, feeling the heat of his mouth on her breasts, and then she realized his fingers were stroking inside her again. Well, at least two of them were. Others were slipping straps from her shoulder and tugging down the edge of her bra. The nipple he tongued rose up to meet him.

"Hello there, gorgeous," Will said to her nipple, making Jessica laugh before he closed his mouth over it. The tugging of his mouth and the rhythm of his fingers were heaven. The man had a master touch when it came to arousing her. It was very nice to just relax and enjoy what he was doing.

When Jessica arched to the tugging of his mouth, Will let go of her to laugh. "If we had more time, I'd let it happen organically, but we have to hurry. Pizza is going to be here soon."

He moved down her body, and covered everything between her legs and above his thrusting fingers with his mouth. Will licked several times, sucked, and then licked some more until Jessica thrashed and throbbed.

"Will! Please," Jessica begged, unsure exactly which wonderful thing she wanted him to do again, but she needed him to do something before she died of being tortured.

"I know it doesn't speak well of my character, but I'm never going to get tired of hearing you beg me for release either. I'll try really hard not to take advantage of it as we go along," Will told her, returning to suck in rhythm with his stroking.

The resulting orgasm from two minutes of that tore through Jessica the way a violent storm shakes a house and everything in it. Will had to hold her down while he absorbed the last of the waves. Jessica couldn't even move when Will finally crawled back up the bed to grin down at her.

"Ten minutes, lady. You were pretty fast," he told her, leaning on one elbow, watching her fight to breathe normally. Jessica looked at him with blank eyes, still dazed from their lovemaking. Will sighed, thinking how much he loved seeing her completely befuddled and knowing he was the reason.

There was knock on the door a minute later, and Will laughed at what a close call it had been with their timing. Rolling off the bed, he flipped one side of the bedspread up and over Jessica to cover her mostly naked body still sprawled in exhaustion.

"Evidently, the pizza didn't take very long either. Wake up and have some with me," Will invited.

Lured by his voice, Jessica sat up in the bed, not fully realizing her bra was still partially off. The flipped-over cover pooled at her waist and she looked down at it, not completely sure how it had come to be there either. She saw Will at the door, but he seemed so far away.

Will glanced back over his shoulder as he counted out bills for the delivery boy. He shook his head at the appealing site Jessica made sitting up in bed all bemused at the world, bra straps off her shoulders, and hair looking like he'd had his hands in it for hours. He sighed, knowing that hadn't happened yet either. She'd messed it up thrashing in her excitement.

"Here," Will said, handing the boy several bills, and shaking his head at the kid's mesmerized gaze. "To satisfy your obvious curiosity, that's what a satisfied woman looks like. It's worth figuring out what to do so you can get one to look that way for you."

"How did you get so good?" the boy asked, sneaking another look at Jessica, who finally tugged up a bra strap and raised the cover to her chest as awareness of her mostly naked condition returned.

"Lots and lots of practice," Will said to him, "but it only works that perfectly with the right woman. She's the best one I've found so far."

"You got me convinced," the kid said, looking in envy at Jessica one last time. "Enjoy your pizza, dude."

Will closed the door and walked back to the bed, setting the spicy pizza in the middle of it.

"Why do you have so much energy?" Jessica asked tiredly. "Why aren't you exhausted?"

"I've been sleeping round the clock for several days," Will said easily. "Don't worry, I'll pass out later and you'll have a hard time waking me in the morning."

Jessica picked up a slice of pizza and took a big bite. "I like pepperoni and mushroom."

Will leaned over to lick pizza sauce from her lip. "I like you, but the pizza is good too."

"Will," Jessica began, but stopped because she was not sure what she intended to say to him. He wasn't acting at all like she thought he would. He also wasn't the type of lover Jessica thought he would be.

Will was dark and brooding at times, intelligent and thoughtful at times, and demanding as hell in bed. Well, not exactly demanding, Jessica thought—more like insistent on having his way. The man had certainly proved he could give her pleasure whether she believed it was possible or not. She'd had three orgasms to his one this evening.

She studied him as she chewed, trying to decide if Will's sexual talent was a good thing or gave him an unfair advantage. She was also wondering how worried she ought to be about the way he made her feel.

Will raised an eyebrow as he started eating his second slice. "Did I miss the question? I don't remember hearing one, but I can all but see the gears in your brain turning."

"I guess I forgot what I was going to say," Jessica said, finishing her slice. "If you have some soda, you're my new best friend."

Will reached to a nightstand and handed her a cold soda. When she looked at it in confusion, he laughed and took it back. He untwisted the cap to open the bottle before handing it to her again.

"My hero," Jessica finally said, laughing softly before taking a drink.

"Hero, I'm not sure about, but I like the idea of being your best friend, Jessica Daniels," Will told her softly. "We'll have to call ourselves best-friends-with-benefits though, since I can't look at you without wanting to be inside you again."

"Will, I don't think. . ." Jessica began, then shushed when Will put two fingers over her mouth.

"I promise you can say when it happens," he said softly. "I just wanted you to know that I still want you."

"I still want you too," Jessica said, sighing and frowning. "You're addictive."

"Are you getting sentimental over sex?" Will joked, looking at his pizza to keep from wondering what it was about them together that was making her frown so much.

"Sentimental? I assure you I am not sentimental. I am practical," Jessica argued, his teasing striking an irritation cord in her. "Stand up and take off your clothes."

"What? Now?" Will asked, laughing. "I'm eating. Besides, I thought you were too tired."

"Take off your clothes," Jessica ordered. "I can't argue with someone who has on more clothes than I do."

Will looked at her state of undress, then stood to drop his pants and underwear on the floor. He sat back down on the bed with nothing but his T-shirt still on. "Okay. We're mostly even now. I don't wear a bra."

Jessica reached behind her and unsnapped her bra. "There. Happy?"

Will's gaze went to her unbound breasts as the lacy bra slid forward and off her arms. He smiled at her perky nipples. "You look damn fine for a forty-year-old woman," he said, peeling off his shirt.

"In three years, I'm going to look damn fine for a fifty-year-old one too," Jessica said with a laugh.

"Fifty? You're going to be the hottest fifty-year-old ever," Will agreed, pleased that the age difference between them wasn't as large as he'd first thought. He liked the idea of them being equals in as many ways as possible.

He tossed the pizza box on the floor, and rolled over to hook an arm around Jessica.

"I'm going to like sleeping naked next to your incredible breasts."

"How in the hell did you wait a year?" Jessica demanded. "Why weren't you doing what every other divorced man does and bedding every available woman you could find?"

"And then what?" Will asked, his belief in his own logic unchanged. "What happens the next day? I made the choice to wait because I didn't want the next day stuff. The day you came to the house and I got mad at my ex for interrupting us, I knew I had been waiting for you. And let me tell you, you sure as hell were worth it, lady."

"Will," Jessica said tightly, closing her eyes to his earnestness. "I'm not the kind of woman men wait on. I'm fickle and unsure. I'm carrying around enough emotional damage for two or three normal women."

"Maybe," Will said quietly. "Maybe you are those things. But you are also a courageous woman and a true artist who puts the conviction of her vision into what she creates. You're the kind of woman who is so painfully honest with the men in your life that you scares most of them off. The math teacher was so intimidated that he didn't even respond to your climax comment."

Will rolled onto her, and used his legs to press between hers. "You're also the type of woman that a man could spend his life exploring and never get to the bottom of no matter how well endowed he is."

Jessica swallowed the tears that threatened and laughed instead, realizing how often she tended to be in that conflicted condition around Will.

"I'm pretty sure I felt you hit the end of the tunnel earlier," she joked.

Will let her make the physical joke because he could see that Jessica was way too far outside her emotional comfort zone.

"Strange, I don't remember being that far inside you," he lied, staring hard into her eyes even as he was smiling. "I'm pretty sure I would have remembered that. Why don't you prove it to me?"

Jessica snorted. "Do you honestly think that line is going to work? You know damn well you wore me out."

"It was worth a shot," Will said. "How about if I beg?"

"You could try, but I'm a hard-hearted woman—just ask my sex slave," Jessica said, fighting not to laugh now.

"How about I tell you you're beautiful? That I love your incredible body," Will told her. He leaned to the side, lifted one of her breasts, and thumbed the end to attention. "Your breasts are more responsive than a woman half your age. Is that just you or is it something I'm doing right?"

"Good question," Jessica admitted. "The girls seemed to really like the way you talked to them earlier. I don't remember that being the case before."

Will laughed. "Well, the feeling is mutual. I like them too," he said, rolling off her and cradling her against him. "I think I'm okay being the current favorite."

"Will," Jessica said his name, her throat tight with anxiety. She was not going to regret her life, not going to regret surviving, not going to feel ashamed for bedding good men before this exceptional one.

"Shh. . .let's sleep now. How can you still be talking about sex? You wore me out," Will said sleepily.

"It wasn't the sex that wore you out. It was all the carbs in the pizza," Jessica said briskly. "Didn't you pay attention in science class?"

"Not even all the time I taught it," Will said, laughing and drifting off to sleep. "Of course, nobody ever thinks social sciences are real sciences anyway."

Jessica looked at Will, puzzled at his last comment. The man got really silly when he was tired. She laughed and pulled the covers from under both of them and climbed in next to him on the sheets.

CHAPTER 12

Will let himself into Michael's house late Sunday evening. He was scruffy and needed a shave but totally happy with the way the weekend had gone. They had spent Saturday getting to know each other, and it had been almost three o'clock Sunday afternoon before he and Jessica had even left the hotel.

It had cut their time at the museum to a couple of hours, but they had only walked around holding hands instead of looking at art anyway. He hadn't been able to stop touching her, and judging by how often she'd leaned her breast against his arm, Jessica hadn't been much better off.

He missed her even now.

"Dad, that's the very best I've seen you look in a long time," Michael said with a laugh. He stood in the kitchen doorway drinking a beer and grinning. "I won the bid on *Blue Blaze*."

Will grinned at his son. "Yes, I know. I spent a lot of time this weekend getting to know the artist."

Michael laughed, feeling only mildly envious. He just wanted someone like her, or more to the point, he wanted the woman he wanted, to be like Jessica. He'd be way okay having Jessica as a stepmother. It was a step in the right direction for the men in his family.

"So when's the wedding?" Michael asked, figuring he'd just plant a seed.

"It was just a weekend, Michael," Will said tersely, running a hand over his head as he walked past his son to retrieve a beer from the refrigerator. It was the first time he had missed his hair in several days.

"Was it?" Michael asked. "You look awfully content for it to have been just sex. You look almost happy, Dad."

Will sat at the table, took a long drink, and rubbed the cold, sweaty bottle across his forehead. "No. I guess it wasn't just a weekend for me, but it was for Jessica. I seduced her and made her want me, but that's not the same thing as her wanting what happened between us."

Will took another long pull on his cold beer. "Jessica doesn't want to be in love with me and is going to fight like hell not to be," he said, his voice rough with the edges of panic he couldn't let himself focus on. "I remind her of her husband. She's not over him yet."

"Her husband? She was married at seventeen for not even a year before he died. How can she still be in love with him after all this time?" Michael asked, sitting across from his father and frowning.

"I don't know, but I know that's the problem. She openly compared me to him several times, and has probably mentally compared me to Nathan Daniels dozens of others. It's what's scaring her away from me—that, and because she suspects I'm in love with her," Will said.

"Is she right?" Michael asked, mentally crossing his fingers.

"Where did you decide to put her art?" Will asked instead, trying to change the subject. He wasn't ready to talk about how committed he already felt to Jessica Daniels.

Michael merely grinned at his father's avoidance of his question, which was its own answer. "I put her art where it will be most appreciated," he said.

Affection between them had always been openly shown, so Michael walked over to the chair, leaned down to hug his father, and kissed his scruffy cheek. "I love you, Dad."

His father automatically reached up to hug back, a reflex action of a lifetime of sincere affection. Love, strong and true, washed over Michael as it always did. He knew not many men felt loved and accepted the way he did by a parent. He never took it for granted, no matter how many other things in his life he didn't handle right.

"Look—whatever you do—don't knock it off the nightstand," Michael said, laughing. "It cost me three thousand dollars."

Will ran a hand over his face, remembering how he used that piece of art to seduce Jessica. He wouldn't be able to look at it without remembering her reaction and her sending Adam away.

"It was worth every cent you paid," Will said. *And not just for its artistic value,* Will thought.

"Of course it was worth it," Michael said with huff. "I have exceptional taste."

"So do I," Will said, finishing his beer and rising. "That's why I had to have the original. Think I'll take a shower and go to bed. I haven't been this tired in a while."

"Yeah, I figured Jessica would be the kind of woman to wear a man out," Michael said irreverently, heading out of the kitchen only a couple steps in front of his father.

Will reached out and smacked Michael on the back of his head as he followed him down the hall. "You are not allowed to think of Jessica that way."

Michael laughed. "Damn. I put *Blue Blaze* in your room. What more do you want from me?"

"Jessica's mine, boy. Get your mind off her and go find a younger model," Will ordered.

"Fine. What about her daughter?" Michael asked, laughing and teasing.

"She's a teacher," Will said. "A college professor—Philosophy, I think."

Michael mocked shivered. "No—not for me. Way too brainy. I guess I'll have to take some of those leggy blondes Shane offered."

"What about Carrie?" Will asked. "You giving up on her?"

Michael frowned. He was never going to be able to completely give up on Carrie Addison, but he wasn't going to stand by and watch her marry the third wrong guy either.

"She's engaged again, and I am tired of being the moth to her flame. It's painfully obvious I'm not what she wants," Michael said softly.

"Is she afraid of you for some reason?" Will asked. "I never thought to ask that question before, but Jessica has certainly shown me that sometimes women are afraid to get emotionally involved, even with trustworthy men."

Michael remembered their one extraordinary night together several weeks ago. She had stood in his largest art piece, looking up at the twisted metal, and then looked at Michael with tears in her eyes. Her tears had seduced him, and he had kissed her with his heart open. She had even taken him home. Defenses down for the first time since he'd known her, Carrie had given Michael everything she had as a woman that night. In his mind, it had been the most perfect first time with a woman he'd ever had.

The next morning, Carrie wouldn't even look at him and had hidden in the bathroom until he'd gone. Michael still had no clue what had happened, but he sure as hell couldn't ask for an explanation from a woman who was so obviously ashamed of having been with him. He dreamed of their time together daily and hadn't been able to touch a woman since. He for damn sure couldn't believe Carrie had gotten engaged already. It hadn't even been a month yet.

Michael ran an agitated hand through his hair. "I'm done. I have to be. I gave it my best shot, and that's all you can do. She's engaged to another guy again, and I'm tired of competing."

Will nodded, thinking about his weekend with Jessica and how he had tried to give her all he had, to take all she was willing to give him.

"Yes," he said, agreeing with his eldest. "That's all you can do."

~

THREE DAYS LATER MICHAEL STOOD AT THE PATIO DOOR LOOKING OUT into the courtyard watching his father chiseling away at the statue that was close to being a full figure now. Another David was fully emerging, he thought, only half listening to Shane's argument in his ear.

"I can't take mom in right now. I have to finish the initial drawings by the weekend. Let's put her in a hotel room. I'll even pay," Shane said. "It will also keep me from having to hire a cleaning service to dig me out of my chaos here."

"We can't do that. She's making me feel guilty because I took Dad in, and her feelings will be hurt if one of us doesn't take her," Michael told his brother.

"Of course she's making you feel guilty, that's how Mom gets her way. I love her, but no one wants to live with someone constantly critiquing them," Shane said, frustrated as any kid was at having to deal with divorced parents. "It's kind of interesting that Luke forced her out of the house this time. He never did that before."

"Everybody has a line of no return," Michael said, thinking of how he currently felt about Carrie.

"Can Dad stay with Jessica?" Shane asked, the logic of the solution seeming pretty obvious to him.

Michael was silent for a couple of heartbeats. "Shane, Mom's not wanting me to ask him to leave. She just wants to stay here, too. I think she wants Dad back."

"No way," Shane denied. "Why do you think that?"

"Because she told me—you know she tells me fucking everything like I'm her best girlfriend or something. And for the record, I want a share of the profits if you put that shit in your book," Michael demanded, his laugh sardonic. "Mom said she misses the way Dad made her feel protected and cared for like she was a special person. She said she might have made a mistake leaving him for Luke."

"Has she seen Dad since he was with Jessica?" Shane asked.

"No," Michael said. "She would not be pleased with how contented he looks. But the other problem is Dad hasn't seen Jessica all week. He's been carving pretty much until he drops, then he sleeps, gets up, and spends another twelve hours on it. Jessica's avoiding him. Dad thinks she's still in love with her dead husband."

Shane's deep sigh reached all the way through the phone.

"Aren't things supposed to get better as you age? Where the hell is all that wisdom people keep talking about? And why can't our parents find any of it?" Shane demanded.

"Beats the hell out of me," Michael said, laughing. "So what am I going to do? I have the extra room. I don't think Dad would care all that much, but my instincts are warning me Mom will take advantage of the situation."

"Talk to Dad about it," Shane advised. "There's really no other choice. I need two days, and then I can take whichever one you don't want to deal with."

"I guess I could have them both here for two days. Maybe it might force Dad into tracking Jessica down and seeing what's up with her," Michael said. "He's giving her too much space."

"I definitely am going to owe you for some of my book content. Most children of divorced parents want them to reconcile. Why don't you?" Shane asked. "I mean—I don't either, but what's your reason?"

"Jessica gets him. Jessica gets his art. Mom will clean my kitchen, scour my pots and pans, and my refrigerator will be full of great food.

She will also complain about the metal in the courtyard and tell me I need curtains on the patio door to block the view," Michael said. "I want Mom to go back to Luke. She was happier with him. What's your reason?"

"I agree with you about Mom and Luke. I got okay with them pretty fast as a couple because anyone can see they want the same things in life. Mom always wanted things Dad didn't want," Shane explained. "I miss the family unit, but not the constant struggle. My awareness is why I chose psychology as a field of study."

"You always took college way too seriously. In the future, try drinking and sleeping around," Michael advised. "It's less work than becoming a renowned psychologist, and a lot more fun."

"Call me back later and let me know what happens," Shane said, ignoring Michael's other comments.

"Sure," Michael said, clicking off his cell phone.

He rolled his eyes to the ceiling, and then brought them back to the man at the end of his courtyard wearing a breathing mask and covered in enough marble dust to look like a ghost. The smoothing phase was always the messiest.

"No problem. I'll just tell Dad that Mom is moving in for two days. It's not like my life isn't insane enough as it is," Michael complained to the walls.

~

THE FIRST DAY ALL THREE OF THEM WERE IN THE HOUSE, ELLEN COULDN'T help noticing the men avoided her by staying out in the courtyard all day. Michael was using a fire pit to bend metal into circles. A pile of at least thirty rusty rings was now heaped up near the patio door.

Ellen Larson Cannon couldn't help wondering what her son had against curtains that would shield the mess from the house. She toyed with the idea of buying and hanging some for him anyway, but Michael was already impatient with her. She didn't want to risk him getting more upset.

Not that Will was much better. He certainly hadn't spent any time with her since she arrived. The shaved head and the earring were a shocker, but the distant look in his eyes was the most disappointing. They had always been close. Even when she'd been dating Luke, Will had always listened with a sympathetic ear. Losing his concern for her happiness had bothered her more than she thought it would. In fact, it almost bothered her more than Luke's ultimatums about their marriage.

Barely forty and in the upswing of his career at a law firm, her younger husband wanted her to be all about his work and his life. Truthfully, most of the time she was happy to entertain his clients and coworkers at the cabin. He also had some nice friends, and they did many fun things as a group. Lately though she was tired of feeling like nothing more than a servant in her own home. She didn't like being taken for granted. Her ex-husband and sons had been much more appreciative of her.

Comparing her one-year marriage to Luke Cannon to the thirty-plus-year marriage to William Larson had become a habit lately. If she'd only acted on her remorse sooner, Will might not be so enamored with the Daniels woman. She couldn't be that much fun in bed, Ellen reasoned. Her friend that was raped could barely stand sex anymore, and her husband had given up after a couple of years and filed for a divorce. Ellen knew Will wasn't going to be able to live very long with a woman who wasn't as passionate as he was. His libido had not diminished much with age.

It was the idea that Will was finally moving on from their divorce that bothered Ellen the most. For the hundredth time in just the last month, Ellen wondered whether she had made a mistake in leaving Will and the security he had given her. Her ex-husband was great in bed, but Ellen preferred Luke's elegant lovemaking to Will's more earthy approach. Still, both men were enthusiastic lovers and she had never lacked for physical satisfaction with either of them.

If it wasn't for the adolescent motorcycle habit and the naked statues, William Larson might have been the perfect man and she would still be with him. Well, and maybe it would have been nice if Will's idea of a good time wasn't going to art museums or walking through gardens. Normal pastimes like sports and watching television were foreign concepts to Will for relaxation. Not that Will ever relaxed really, the man could work on his naked statues from dawn until dusk, and often did.

No, Will hadn't been perfect for her, but he had been a good man. And in all the time she'd been with him, he had always been appreciative of her. She just hadn't realized it until lately.

Ellen sighed and wondered if cooking dinner would warm

Michael and Will up to her presence. When the doorbell range, she went automatically to answer it.

"Ms. Daniels," Ellen said with a frown, not liking that she had to look up a good six inches at the woman standing on Michael's stoop. "Please come in."

Jessica was equally surprised to see Will's ex-wife standing in the house looking like she belonged there. She cursed the urge that had brought her over here in the first place, but since she was already crossing the threshold, she figured she might as well do what she came to do.

"I came to see Will," Jessica said at last. However, her resolve about having a heart-to-heart about her apprehension of their relationship simply fled in the face of her annoyance over the woman's presence in the house.

"Yes. I figured you were here for him," Ellen said dryly, closing the door behind her. "Will is working in the courtyard. He's been there practically non-stop since I got here yesterday."

"I see," Jessica said, not really seeing. But how did you respond to that sort of comment from your lover's ex-wife? All Jessica could think about was that the woman had been there overnight. Maybe she'd waited one day too long to come talk to Will.

Ellen motioned out the patio door. "You're welcome to go on out if you don't mind the chaos going on out there. Michael is throwing metal everywhere."

"It's interesting to see Michael work. What's his new piece going to be like?" Jessica asked, trying to make polite conversation.

"Rusty, bent metal just like his other pieces I imagine," Ellen said in response. "I'm afraid I'm not a fan of my son's art. His high concept symbolism is lost on a lowly math teacher."

Math teacher? Mentally rolling her eyes, Jessica filed that little tidbit away for the next time Will teased her about Adam.

"I saw Michael's giant metal man at the Louisville Fairgrounds. It made me his fan for life," Jessica told her, giving the woman a tight smile. "I also saw some of his other work in Cincinnati last year. That smaller piece he did for the city park has the most beautiful color treatment on it. Michael said it was rust-proofing, but the blood-red dripping finish makes an impression."

"Your artistic observations are lost on me," Ellen said with a laugh.

"I do appreciate there seems to be an audience of some sort for his work."

"Well, being an art teacher, I guess I'm a fan of all art. Will took me to see his work at the art center in Berea on our first date," Jessica said, tired of hearing the woman's dismissal of Michael's work. "His David statue there was so realistic I couldn't stop myself from the touching it. I think I might have embarrassed Will with my reaction."

"Doubtful," Ellen said, smirking. "Almost every woman does something crude to the man parts on his marble men. Will used to grin like an idiot when he caught a woman sneaking a feel. I would have been jealous, but Will isn't the kind of man to shift his attention randomly from woman to woman."

Jessica nodded, offering a tight smile. "Will told me he was a one-woman kind of guy. Still, it's good to hear it from a woman he was once committed to."

"Ms. Daniels, I think it's only fair to warn you that I'd like to be that one woman in Will's life again. I've decided I made a mistake divorcing my husband," Ellen said firmly, watching for emotion in Jessica's eyes.

Jessica had run into her share of jealous ex-wives and girlfriends over the years, so Ellen Cannon's declaration did not bother her. The only thing she wondered about was whether Will had any feelings left for the woman. Since she considered her relationship to Will temporary anyway, she decided in that moment of holding the woman's gaze to keep him for the duration. Will's ex-wife would just have to wait for her second chance.

"I'm afraid you're one weekend late wanting Will back. Now you're going to have to wait until he gets tired of me first. That may take a while," Jessica warned softly but just as firmly.

Ellen watched Jessica Daniels slide open the glass patio door and step out.

So that was the reason for Will's emotional distance, Ellen thought. He was sleeping with the Daniels woman. Fortunately the relationship was still new, and not running smoothly if Jessica's face was telling the truth. Not once had the woman smiled or looked happy about her relationship with Will.

She needed to work quickly, Ellen decided. She needed to make sure Will knew her intentions before he spent any more time with the Daniels woman.

CHAPTER 13

"Hey," Michael said, watching Jessica halt and smile at the metal across the fire pit.

"Do you enjoy pounding the metal into compliance? A furnace would be more practical for that much effort," Jessica said, smiling. "The metal would bend like a cooked egg noodle."

"It would also be more expensive," Michael said with a grin. "I did learn to pound with both hands so I wouldn't end up with one super-sized arm."

He made a sign to indicate how much larger his right bicep could be.

Jessica laughed. "What are you working on?"

Michael looked at the rings in a pile. "Wedding present," he said coldly. "I wanted to make sure the love of my life has something to remember me by this time around when she marries the wrong damn man again."

Jessica raised an eyebrow at both his anger and his passionate resentment.

"Sorry," Michael said. "I've been interested in my events planner for a few years now. We got close a few weeks ago, but she dumped me without saying what went wrong. Now I hear she's getting married again. This is marriage number three for her."

Jessica looked at the pile of metal rings and back at Michael. His need to personally pound that large pile of symbolic wedding bands suddenly made a lot of sense.

"Rust-treat the finished piece like you did the one in Cincinnati. Make it so it looks like you bled all over it. It will make a stronger point," she advised.

Michael smiled and sighed at the great suggestion. "Go kiss my father and make him look like he did when he came home Sunday. He's been sleeping with your vagina and trying to give you space."

Jessica sighed and shook her head negatively. "I'm sure glad my daughter lives in Ohio. I don't think I could handle my own adult child interfering in my dating life. You and your brother are bad enough."

"I guess you saw Mom," Michael said, ignoring her comment about interfering. He was safeguarding, even if Jessica didn't know it.

She nodded and looked down, not really having anything remotely nice to say about Michael's mother.

"Don't let Mom bother you. She mostly a good woman, but she can be more melodramatic than an angry artist," Michael said, frowning. "Her husband kicked her out. Shane is taking her this weekend."

Jessica nodded again, saying nothing in return. She couldn't tell a son—even an adult one—that his mother wanted his father back. It was every divorced kid's dream. She also couldn't tell Michael that she was still intending to break up with his father eventually, but that his mother's comments had changed her mind about doing it today. Ellen Cannon's warning had shown Jessica the reality of what Will might end up doing after her. Up until today, it had been theoretical. She'd be a fool not to wonder if Will had at some point just been waiting for his wife to come around.

Jessica sighed at her thoughts and chastised herself for worrying about it. She had learned over the years to be selfish about taking what she wanted because most of her relationships never lasted long anyway.

Granted, she was more conflicted about Will than the typical man she dated.

Panicked as she was about staying involved with him, while facing down Ellen, she had become equally panicked about never having him again. Knowing Will might decide to go back to the woman, all Jessica wanted now was more time. She wanted at least a few more nights, a few more memories. If Will wanted to give them to her, Jessica was going to be selfish enough to take them. His ex was just going to have to wait her turn, and Jessica was not sorry about letting the woman know she considered Will hers for the moment.

Jessica walked resolutely to stand in Will's line of sight, waiting for him to see her.

Still absorbed in his task of sanding away the chisel marks on the statue's chin, it was a few moments until Will saw Jessica standing there quietly watching him. He walked to his tools table and put his equipment all down. He brushed himself off as best he could, removing his breathing mask as part of the process.

"It took you long enough to come see me," Will said, stepping in close to her. She reached out and touched his earring and then ran a hand over his shoulder.

"I—I needed some time to think about the change in our relationship," Jessica said.

"Come to any conclusions yet?" Will asked, reaching around her and tugging her hips flush to his to remind her of just how much things had changed.

"None at all," Jessica replied, sighing. "I ran out of patience with myself and came to see you anyway."

"I swear I didn't plant my ex-wife in the house to make it harder or to punish you for making me wait," Will said, grinning even when his eyes were serious.

"Good to know," Jessica said, trying for a teasing smile and not really getting there.

"Hey," Will said, seeing her doubts as clearly as if she had voiced the words. "You know how it is between us. We talked about this."

"Well, I thought I did. Now I'm not so sure. I'm having a hell of time figuring it out after seeing your ex here. Got some way to convince me?" Jessica asked, not really teasing at all.

"Not with Michael and Ellen watching, but if you take me home with you, I think I can put all your fears to rest. Mine, too. Have you had any dates this week I need to worry about?" Will asked, seeing the answer flash in her gaze even before she tilted her chin.

He laughed at her irritation and pulled her closer. "Good to know we're both being monogamous," he said, tilting her back over his arm. "I've worked too hard today to do any competing."

Will put his eager mouth on hers, and her groan of satisfaction vibrated both of them. When he pulled away, Will moved them both from the line of sight of Michael and the patio door just in case Ellen was spying. He pressed Jessica against his statue, which in turn pressed David 17's marble penis into the small of her back.

"Touch me," he whispered. "Show me you want me so I can get through the next few hours without being inside you."

"Will? Do you realize what you've backed me into?" Jessica demanded, putting her hand on his dusty jeans and feeling him come instantly alive for her. As she stroked Will, she could feel the hard marble pressing against her back. She much preferred the real one, Jessica thought, stroking more firmly.

Will laughed and leaned into her hand to enjoy the moment.

"Yes. I only wish I could be that hard with you," he joked.

"If you get any harder, we're going to end up shocking your son," Jessica said, pressing her face against his dusty neck.

"Okay, maybe you're right," Will said laughing. He couldn't help noticing she didn't mention caring if Ellen saw, but he was wise enough not to gloat about it. "Maybe you're right about shocking Michael. Let go of me, woman."

"No, not yet. You started this. I need a little something for me now," Jessica told him, sliding hands from the front of him to put them behind his hips and arch herself against him to rub until the arousal spread through her. "Yes, I definitely need you to come home with me. Clean up and meet me there in an hour."

Feeling her heat even through all the denim between them, Will rocked against Jessica. There was great relief to be in her arms again and to know she still wanted to be with him. Each day that passed without hearing from her, he had grown more afraid Jessica had opted to be in denial about it.

"Can I come back tomorrow night too?" Will asked. "I don't want to be here right now. The house is too crowded, if you know what I mean."

"Bring the bike and stay for the weekend," Jessica said, pushing him away with her hands. "We'll go for a ride Sunday and find someplace to have breakfast."

Will smiled at her willingness to take another bike ride with him and met her gaze levelly. He could already feel her wrapped around him, feel her sigh of pleasure against his back. It was the happiest thought he'd experienced in years. He fell the rest of the way in love with Jessica Daniels without any regret.

"Better get ready to hear how I feel about you," he warned her. "I've been looking all my life for a woman who liked to ride me *and* my bike."

Jessica was already shaking her head at his teasing. "Don't push me, Will. I had a hard enough time coming over here. I still have the urge to run like hell from what you make me feel. Dealing with your ex did not make me feel better about things."

"You have no competition and I'll see you in a hour," he called after her, smiling at the white marks on the back of her jeans as she walked away.

After Jessica had exited through the patio door, Michael leaned around his work and looked at his dad, who was grinning again—thank God. As the eldest son, he didn't care if he was being disrespectful or not, he just had to know if it was intentional.

"Did you do that on purpose just now?" Michael asked.

"Is there an answer to that question that you won't harass me about?" Will asked in return, hurrying back to his table to put away his tools with the sound of Michael's laughter echoing through the courtyard.

He hadn't put handprints on Jessica on purpose, Will thought, but he wasn't sorry about them either. He hoped Ellen saw them and knew what they meant. He didn't want to have to explain it to his ex-wife, but he would if he had to.

~

LATER, WILL WAS IN SUCH A RUSH TO GET SHOWERED, PACKED, AND OVER to Jessica's that he momentarily forgot Ellen was there. He walked from the bathroom to his bedroom with only a towel wrapped around him, an easy habit he had gotten into when there had been just Michael and him in the house.

When he walked into the bedroom, he was suddenly wishing like hell he had gotten dressed in the bathroom. Ellen was sitting on the bed with *Blue Blaze* in her hands, turning it around as if it was puzzle she was trying to figure out.

"Is this what she's making for art now?" Ellen said, mildly disgusted. She put it on the bed beside her. "I guess it's better than the rape art. Though I've got to say it looks too much like a woman's private area. I suppose the colors are nice enough."

"It's called a vagina, Ellen," Will said. "You have a college degree. You're allowed to use the right anatomical terms."

Angry at himself for engaging yet another time in an argument about art so similar to the other thousand they'd had over the years, Will turned his back to her. He went to his dresser and pulled out clothes to toss on the bed.

"What are you doing in my room?" he asked fiercely, delving into another drawer for more clothes. He walked back to the bed and found Ellen sitting next to his clothes with one hand on top of them.

"William, don't go to her. You're not making the woman happy. Haven't you noticed the anxiety on her face when you're around?" Ellen implored.

Using an assertive move vastly familiar to both of them, she put her hand on Will's hip and ran it down his thigh, sneaking it through the towel flap at the last minute. She stroked him and made sure he felt her polished nails lightly scoring his abdomen with every motion. A few seconds later she got the reaction she had hoped for and was accustomed to with Will. Her heart leapt at the thought of what it meant and she squeezed harder to reward him.

"Nice move," Will said coldly, staring into the surprised gaze of a woman he'd once thought he'd spend his life with until he died. "Now go back to Luke and use it with him. I'm not your husband anymore."

When her hand dropped away, Will immediately moved out of her reach. Uncaring any longer what she thought, he pulled off the towel and pulled on briefs while she watched. He tucked his now withering erection into place with no thought of sparing Ellen the embarrassment of his rejection.

"I'm leaving Luke," Ellen said softly. "He doesn't appreciate me like you did."

"That's your problem to work out with him," Will said, not inclined to be supportive or caring in any way at all. In fact, he might never be supportive of Ellen again.

He was stirred up and frustrated with her for trying to seduce him. He was angry with himself for letting Ellen get as far as she did, even if it was just a Pavlov's dog kind of response brought on by thirty-three years of marriage. Will hadn't done anything he regretted in a long time, and now he felt ashamed of himself. He'd asked Jessica not to date, but then he'd let Ellen touch him, stroke him for pity's sake. Why hadn't he just smacked her hand away? He might have to shower again now to get over the feel of her hands on him.

Will pulled on jeans and a blue T-shirt Michael had given him that said *A Sculptor's Life Is Carved In Stone* on it. It was one of his favorite possessions. Not that he cared much about what he was wearing, his main priority at the moment was just to be dressed enough to go out in public. He needed to get out of the house and as far away from Ellen as possible.

"Will, that woman can't be better in bed than me. You and I can have all we had, and maybe even more because I would be more appreciative this time around," Ellen said quietly. "At least think about us."

"No thanks, I'm just not interested," Will said, meaning it. "I tried to reconcile with you after we separated—before you ever married. I might have been able to forgive you for Luke then, but not now. You're a married woman, Ellen. You need to act like one and work things out with your husband."

"William," Ellen said, her voice rising with her agitation. "Stop thinking like a man for a minute and at least try to be logical. Being a rape survivor, Jessica Daniels probably has a mile-long list of things she's unwilling to do with you in bed. My friend Susan's husband left her because she just couldn't get past the other men abusing her. You'll be bored with the Daniels woman before a year is done."

"No, I won't be bored. If Jessica and I ever had a problem, I'd go to therapy with her to try to work it out. If that was ever the case—which it is definitely not at the moment. You never did understand the healing power of art, Ellen. You didn't get it for the whole thirty-three years we were together," Will told her sadly. "But it would be damn helpful to both your sons if you could just open your mind and try to get it—even a little bit. Your sons are artists. You need to start accepting that art is both their career and their life, even if you never accepted that it was mine."

Will pushed all his clothes into a backpack. Then at the last minute, he scooped up Jessica's art piece.

"See this? Jessica's art has gone from rape scenes to a celebration of what is wonderfully feminine. Jessica Daniels healed herself long before I came along. In thirty years of relationships with men on her terms, she's had more lovers than I can bear thinking about. Frankly, I had to stand in line to get a damn date with her. Even this weekend, I had to literally chase off a man ten years younger than me," Will said, liking the shocked look on Ellen's face. "That's how much I wanted that woman, and I still do. Now that I have my chance with her, I'm putting everything I am into making it work."

Will added the art piece to the contents of his backpack, afraid to leave anything of Jessica's in the house while Ellen was there. He zipped the pack shut and clipped the security fasteners he almost never used. The extra precaution just seemed necessary.

Then he walked out and left Ellen sitting on the bed.

At the end of the hallway, Michael was coming out of the kitchen with a glass of water.

"*Blue Blaze* is coming with me until your mother moves out," Will told him. "I don't want her turning it into a door stop while I'm gone."

Michael raised his eyebrows. It was a reference to his mother's typical reaction to receiving a piece of art from her sons. And it was an ancient argument between his parents.

"It's not insured yet," Michael warned, not worrying about its safety so much as he was his dad's state of mind. "Don't go wrecking your bike today."

"Trust me," Will said loudly, looking back down the hall and seeing Ellen walk out of his room. "Jessica Daniels' vagina is always going to be safe in my hands."

Michael sputtered and coughed as the water went down wrong. His mother rolled her eyes and shook her head as Will slammed the front door after him.

CHAPTER 14

Will coasted the bike to a stop on the street in front of Jessica's house. When he got his helmet off, he saw her sitting on her window ledge, leaning out and smiling down at him.

"Pull the bike into the driveway," she directed. "I'll be right down to let you in."

Will backed up the Harley and rode it into the driveway just as Jessica came out of the house. She was smiling hard and almost laughing, reminding him of what she had been like the first time they went out. He had wondered if he was ever going to see that level of happiness in her again.

"You look good on that black monster," Jessica told him. "Cars never did it for me, but I get a flutter just thinking about riding around with you on the bike."

"You know, my son Shane told me to shave my head, get an earring, and ride around on the bike to pick up women. I guess you're proof that it works," Will said, reaching out to tug her to him by the front of her shirt.

Then Will turned her sideways and maneuvered her to sit in front of him on the ample seat. "Kiss me, Jessica. You have no idea how much I need it right now."

"Kiss you in broad daylight in my driveway?" Jessica asked, amusement lifting the corners of her mouth.

She felt lighter suddenly, lighter and happier now that Will was with her.

She felt lighter still when she realized Will had forgotten again to be careful with her. One hand was in her hair tugging her head back for a soul-stealing kiss. The other unerringly found her breast to squeeze and lift it, effectively making her groan into his mouth at the pleasure of his touch.

Realizing where they were, and how fast things were getting away from his control, Will moved his hand from her breast to her back where he could slide her hips more intimately between his legs.

"You know," Jessica said, pulling her mouth from his. "I have a perfectly good house with a king size bed. We could take this inside."

"I thought you'd never ask," Will said, boosting her up to standing with a hand under her rear.

"You're a very physical man, aren't you?" Jessica said on a laugh. "Though I have to say you seem to have turned manhandling into an art form."

Will climbed off the bike and looked at her with concern. "Do I scare you?"

"No," Jessica denied irritably, walking off and leaving him to follow her up the sidewalk. "It scares me that I'm starting to like your macho side. I've spent most of my life avoiding the kind of man you are."

Will frowned, thinking about that a moment. "What kind of man is that?"

Jessica looked at him and shrugged as they stepped through her door. "The kind of man who's big enough and strong enough to do pretty much anything he wants. I learned that early on with you, remember? I almost had to hurt you to break your hold on me."

"Have I done anything since then to make you feel that way again?" Will asked, setting his bike helmet on a well-used wooden bench in the hallway with several pairs of shoes lined up under it. He put his backpack next to the helmet and unzipped his jacket.

Jessica opened a closet and took out a hanger. "Hang your jacket on the pegs above the bench. Leave it there. I like the way it looks next to the helmet."

She waited until Will was hanging up the jacket to answer his question. "I don't know," she said flatly.

"What?" Will asked, his face a puzzled frown.

"I don't know if you've done anything that has bothered me as much. I can't think of anything, but you definitely make me feel nervous and a bit on edge," Jessica said honestly.

"Do I make you anxious?" Will asked.

Jessica waited a few heartbeats. "I guess that's a fair description."

Damn Ellen for being right, Will thought. Damn her for planting doubts in his head.

Jessica walked up to Will and ran her fingers over his lips. "That doesn't mean I want you to change anything you're doing. If you stop being yourself, I will never figure it out. Then we both lose by not knowing how it is between us. I'm being honest with you because I've taught myself not to put up fronts. Now kiss me so I can lure you to bed."

Will picked up his backpack and took the one giant step into her that covered the remaining empty space between them. He didn't touch her other than to press his lips to hers. It was Jessica who groaned, grabbed his T-shirt with two hands, and deepened their kiss.

Will ended up laughing against her mouth when he got his tongue back.

"You know, I'm not the only aggressive one in our relationship. You do your own share of grabbing, lady. Don't forget to factor that into your thinking," Will told Jessica, putting his mouth back on hers with a little more aggression this time.

Jessica pulled free and tugged on his hand. "House tour later," she said. "Bedroom is upstairs. Come with me."

"Best offer I've had all day," Will said, laughing, letting Jessica tug him along behind her.

Will followed Jessica up a set of antique wooden stairs and into a room with airy curtains and layers of covers on the bed along with pillows of every size. Most of the furniture was worn and fragile, too feminine for Will to feel completely at ease. Fortunately, the bed seemed like the sturdiest piece in the room and it was the only one he cared about at the moment.

"You're way more girly than you look," Will said softly, setting his backpack down. He unzipped a side pocket and pulled three condoms out. "Now the lacy lingerie makes complete sense."

Grinning at the condoms and his comment, Jessica pulled her shirt over her head revealing a pink lace demi-bra that barely restrained her breasts.

"Do you ever wear plain cotton?" Will asked, tossing the condoms on the bed and walking to her.

"Not if I can help it," Jessica said, closing her eyes and leaning into Will's hands when he lifted her breasts and brushed the ends with his thumbs.

They stood like that at the foot of Jessica's bed, weaving with the arousal building between them. Jessica had her eyes closed in bliss, and Will couldn't look away from her face.

"Jessica, I know what I want. Tell me what you want," Will entreated softly. "I really, really want to give you what you want."

Jessica reached behind her and unhooked her bra. It fell easily from her shoulders and across Will's hands still on her breasts. "Okay. I want to feel your hands on me for real."

Will flung the bra across the room and it landed in a chair. He touched her breasts again, caressing their fullness and the tight buds that beckoned him to do more.

"I saw your blue lacy bra and a preview of these when you flirted with me at the café. I wanted to do this then. I wanted to do more. I wanted to lift you into my lap on one of those bar stools and show you just how incredibly sexy I thought you were," Will told her, his voice so husky with desire he could barely speak.

"Oh, I remember. I showed you my bra on purpose. I asked you for a ride then, but you turned me down," Jessica said, laughing as Will sat on the bed and pulled her across his lap with one of her knees on each side of his legs.

"I was being a big chicken, but I have since gotten over it. Jessica Daniels, you can ride anything of mine you want," Will said, lifting under her arms until her breasts were level with his mouth.

He took one pretty pink bud between his teeth and twirled his tongue around it until Jessica called out his name. She put a hand behind his head to hold him in place, but Will just shook his head against her and laughed softly. He eased her back into his lap before transferring his attention to the other side. She bent backward in ecstasy, raising her breasts higher to him.

Will laughed softly as Jessica moaned, and then he had to catch her when she almost fell backward off his lap.

"I'm not trying to torture you," he promised, hearing the rough edge of desire in his voice. "I just like seeing you wearing passion and not much else. I still can't get over how much better sex is with you."

Now that comment had her opening her eyes and meeting Will's gaze with her own.

"What do you mean?" Jessica asked. "I thought you had a good marriage."

"It was good in many ways. And I was faithful, but the last year or two the sex was practically non-existent. Ellen was already seeing Luke during the last six months we were married, but I didn't know it for a long time," Will told her. "She had pulled away from me totally by then, and I couldn't do much about it. We weren't really lovers any more, but by that point I was losing so little I couldn't care either."

Will pulled her hair to the front over her shoulder. He combed it with his fingers and let them drift over her breasts while she watched.

"I can hardly believe you're real—the way you respond, the way you kiss, the way you close your eyes and just let me enjoy you. You're the woman men think about, but mostly think they will never find," Will said.

His praise swelled her heart to bursting, but it also embarrassed her.

"There are a lot of women like me looking for men like you," Jessica said sincerely. "Now you wouldn't even have to pay attention to see them. You look so good, they'll fall at your feet."

"I think you have me confused with my son, Shane," Will said on a laugh.

"No—I know exactly who you are," Jessica said. "You're a great father, a good friend, a nice man, a very talented sculptor, and the most patient, thorough, enthusiastic lover I've ever had."

Jessica smiled and traced his lips with her fingers and then felt his smoothly shaven face. He had shaved in his shower. He had shaved for her. Mating rituals, Jessica thought, stroking the line of his jaw and down his neck. She had always appreciated them.

"I like your shirt. You can wear it again tomorrow," Jessica said, pulling it up and over his head before running her fingers through the smattering of black and silver curls that lightly covered his chest. She pressed her breasts into Will's chest, her nipples peaking against the friction of being that close to him.

"I've thought about being with you all week. I kept telling myself it couldn't have been as good as I remembered," Jessica whispered. "Now show me how nice it can be Will, but don't be so nice I can't remember it clearly tomorrow."

"Just promise me you'll tell me if I do anything you don't like," Will requested.

"Okay. I don't like this—I don't like the constant worry you have. You're making me apprehensive when two minutes ago I just wanted your mouth on me," she complained.

Then she sighed in approval when Will lightly pinched and stroked her nipples until she was aroused again.

"That's much better," Jessica said sincerely, looking at him through mostly closed eyes.

Will growled in response to her praise, lay back on the bed, and then lifted her hips to literally throw her over his head.

Jessica landed face down just below her pillows and was still laughing when Will crawled up on the back of her and slid his hands under her to cup her breasts again. He nudged her hips with his, and she spread her legs in both reaction and anticipation.

"You have definitely got some great moves," Jessica told Will, enjoying the way he made her feel so completely female and completely wanted.

"Me? If you keep bending your knees and backing into me, I'm going to go insane. Next time, I'm getting us both completely naked before we ever hit a bed," Will declared, removing his hands from her breasts and easing himself off of her to kneel behind her.

He lifted and pulled her hips backward as he surged against her, already imagining just how it would be to thrust in and out of her in this position.

"Can we please—for the love of God—lose our clothes, Jessica?" he pleaded roughly, all but insane with lust.

Her muffled laughter against the bedclothes captured Will's attention.

"What's so damn funny?" he asked, letting her go, and rolling her over so he could peer into her smiling face.

"You don't have to beg, Will. Just let me go long enough to undress," Jessica said, laughing. "I'm just as bad off as you are. I want you even though you're a crazy man in bed."

Will rose to his knees again and pulled Jessica to hers. He unsnapped and unzipped her jeans and let her do the same to his. He pushed her jeans off her hips, but stopped at her thighs when she took his now aching erection in her hand.

"I honestly have never wanted a man so much in my entire life,"

Jessica whispered. "It's shocking to me that it's always like this with you."

Will leaned his head weakly on Jessica's shoulder as she stroked him to a level of arousal he hadn't had in years. Her hands were blissful. And this woman, Will thought, this was the right one to be touching him.

"Okay. On the count of three we're going to let each other go, fall to our backs, get the rest of our clothes off, and then find the damn condoms I threw somewhere over here earlier," Will ordered.

"Fine," Jessica said, turning loose of him reluctantly, running fingertips along what she had created. "One. Two. Three."

They moved apart, lay down, and shed their jeans at the same time, throwing them off the side of the bed to the floor. Then they were both on their knees again looking for the condoms.

"I swear I tossed three over here earlier," Will vowed.

"I know you did. I saw them hit the bed," Jessica agreed.

"Damn it," Will said, when they were nowhere to be found.

"Look, I can't get pregnant," Jessica said at last. "If you don't mind my past, I certainly don't mind yours. I don't usually do this without protection, but I'm willing to make an exception with you, Will."

"Jessica," Will whispered, crawling over and pushing her to her back. She let her legs fall open in welcome and Will accepted the invitation with gratitude, sliding into her welcoming wetness with incredible relief. "I wanted this level of intimacy all along. I'm falling in love with you. I know you don't want to hear it yet, but you're going to feel it every time we do this anyway."

"Will," Jessica said brokenly, arching up and straining against his hardness, all the while struggling to put aside his confession. "God it feels amazing to have you inside me. Less talking, more moving."

Will laughed at her demand. After what he'd just admitted, he was grateful Jessica wasn't asking him stop, because he couldn't have. Like her, he could feel everything so much more without the condom and was lost in the wonder of it.

When Jessica brought her knees up alongside his hips and raised herself up to him to wrap arms around his chest, he felt himself hit the bottom of her with a possessive thrill that shocked him. It was like finding the place he belonged at last.

They moved together, and then took turns moving around each other as they enjoyed the smooth slip and slide of their bodies with nothing but skin against skin. Their movements were slow and sure in the late afternoon light as they watched each other climb and climb.

And just as Will feared Jessica wasn't going to get there before he did, he felt the throbbing inside her begin. He let himself follow her over the edge and rocked against her until the waves had passed for both of them.

"We'll try a new position next time," Will said, kissing his way across her cheek and down her neck. "I just couldn't wait any longer."

"Neither could I," Jessica said breathlessly, running her hands over Will's hips. "Neither could I."

CHAPTER 15

A couple hours later, they ordered Chinese food and ate in Jessica's large kitchen with its ancient but sturdy farm table and six less sturdy mismatched chairs.

Will couldn't stop looking at her. Jessica had put on cropped leggings falling just below her knees and the white gauzy shirt she'd worn to the art show last weekend. She'd left the bra off and her breasts swayed gently with every movement. She was so utterly sexy and feminine, it was all Will could do to be civilized and keep his hands to himself while they ate.

"So do you own this house?" Will asked, forking in bites of sweet and sour pork, and trying to distract himself from watching Jessica's breasts.

"No," Jessica admitted. "I rent. I've thought about buying but just couldn't bring myself to buy a house I barely like. I mean—it's a nice house, just not my dream home."

"No offense, but this house doesn't seem very supportive for your art. Where do you do your work?" Will asked, truly wanting to know.

"I have a friend who owns a glass blowing business in Richmond. I borrow his work area when the mood hits," Jessica said with a shrug. "I've been apathetic lately about my work and don't have a strong enough desire to create anything. I've only managed one art piece every six months."

She stopped eating her cashew chicken and sighed. "My life feels stagnant. I have enough time served in the school system to retire, but what would I do then?" she asked, shrugging her shoulders. "I'm not making a living from my art the way you or your sons do. Glass vaginas are not exactly in great demand, no matter how pretty or sensual."

"I like your vagina art. Keep doing it," Will ordered, laughing. "I also like what you did for Melanie and Brent. The café has been hopping busy since you put up art there. I bet other businesses would pay you for similar efforts."

"Yeah, that was really fun. Do you know I'm afraid to go to the cafe now for fear they'll put me to work again? They keep threatening to hire me when I retire," Jessica said on a laugh. "Somehow slinging chicken salads and pouring gallons of iced tea every day just doesn't appeal to me as a job. I'm waiting until Brent and Melanie hire real help before I visit again."

Will laughed. "They miss you. I know this for a fact because they ask about you every time I go there."

"I miss them too," Jessica said, smiling.

"Would you still have to work if you retired?" Will asked, trying to dance around the bigger financial questions, but he wanted to know her situation because he cared about her.

If he went by the furnishings of her house, Will would guess the answer was yes to his question. Jessica was straining the meaning of "shabby chic" in just about everything he'd seen except the bed and kitchen table. At his size and weight, pretty much everything else in her house was at risk around him. He was surprised it wasn't around her.

"No—I guess I wouldn't have to work. I could live okay on my retirement. I also have some investments left from my early artwork even after I paid for Brooke's college education with a large chunk of them. She's done the last four years on assistantships and awards, and she worked part-time. I don't have champagne tastes in much of anything, so I've found it easy to live within my means," Jessica said with a shrug. "I worry more about boredom than anything else. I like to keep busy."

"I hear you. When I'm working on a piece, I get physically tired long before I lose the desire to stop carving. I'm also getting slower as I get older," he said, laughing. "I pad my contracts with an extra month now just in case something takes me longer than it used to."

"Well, your work is worth the wait. I'm sure you hear that all the time," Jessica said with a smile. "And your ex-wife told me about the perk you get watching women cop a feel of your statues' assets. I know I couldn't keep my hands off the first time I saw how realistic the anatomy was on the statue in Berea."

Damn Ellen and her mouth, Will thought. He had all but forgotten Jessica had talked to her. Now Will had to admit that if his ex-wife had told Jessica about him laughing over the women, Ellen probably wouldn't hesitate to brag to Jessica about what happened in the bedroom today. It made him mad at himself all over again for responding at all.

Will frowned and put down his fork.

"Well, it was always fun for me to see the delight on their faces as they touched a statue's marble penis with reverence, but I never took advantage of anyone's innocent pleasure," he told her sincerely.

Jessica stopped eating as she realized Will's tone was much less relaxed now. She picked up her soda and sipped as she watched him look for words.

Will hated that he was going to have to risk the easy camaraderie between Jessica and him so soon, but this kind of secret was far more significant than simply not telling her about a previous job. "This discussion reminds me of something more serious I guess I need to share with you."

"Well, the expression on your face is more scary than anything you could tell me. Just say it quickly," Jessica suggested. "Be honest and brave. That's all we can be with each other. Trust me, I know. I've in been therapy for thirty years."

"First, let me just say that nothing of any significance happened," Will said, holding her gaze.

Jessica lifted an eyebrow and tilted her head. "The old *nothing really happened* story, huh? That's ominous, but let me guess. Did Ellen try to seduce you?"

"Why in the world would you guess that?" Will asked, shocked at how fast Jessica had guessed.

Jessica sighed and went back to her cashew chicken. "Oh, I'm not guessing. Your ex-wife warned me this afternoon she was going to try and get you back. What did she do? Wait for you and try to cop a feel when you got out of the shower?"

"Did you have a damn camera installed in my bedroom the night you spent with me?" Will asked, looking pained and upset at her accuracy. "Yes. I forgot she was there and she was waiting in my bedroom after I showered. My brief response to her hands on me was just an old habit that came back to haunt me momentarily. I shook her off and came over here to you."

"Good," Jessica said, licking her fork and favoring Will with a lusty gaze. "I'm not done with you yet. Ellen had her turn. Now you're mine for a while. I told her that this afternoon."

"I guess now I understand how freaked out you were when I talk to Steve Lipton," Will said, surprised when Jessica only laughed. He studied her for a few moments, amazed when Jessica resumed eating as if nothing shocking had been discussed.

"You don't seem very upset about it. Why are you not wanting to kill me—or her for that matter?" Will asked, wondering if he'd been wrong about how much Jessica liked him.

"I don't like drama, and I haven't been jealous since high school. If you genuinely wanted your ex, you'd be with her and not with me. If you were doing us both, Ellen would have followed you over here because I can tell your ex-wife would hate sharing," Jessica said, taking another bite before finishing. "Since I don't believe either of those is the case, I see no reason to be in a killing mood. Now, if the woman tries to brag to me about making you get it up, just know I'm going to thank her for sending you to me already primed and tell her everything we did in great detail."

Jessica's words were terse, but Will clearly heard the truth of her intentions in her voice. It would be mildly satisfying to see Ellen get that embarrassed, he thought. Then what Jessica had said finally hit his brain.

"Ellen did not prime me, damn it. If anything, she made me ashamed of myself. She's a married woman and she's not the one for me any longer. It was old habit and it lasted all of five seconds. I shook her off," he said firmly, taking another bite of his food and chewing forcibly.

"Will, you don't have to be upset. I believe you're the innocent in this," Jessica protested with a short laugh.

"Don't you even care that I let her touch me?" Will asked. "If Adam had touched you intimately at the art show, I'd have at least wanted to break his damn arm."

"Let me get this straight. You actually want me to make you feel worse about what happened than you already do?" Jessica asked in return. "You want me to do this even though I know full well Ellen was the villainess in what occurred?"

"Yes," Will began, then changed his mind after hearing how ridiculous it sounded. "No. I'm not sure. What would you have done if I had given in to her?"

That got a full belly laugh out of Jessica. She could see it had taken a lot of nerve for Will to tell her what happened with his ex-wife. The least she could do was stroke his ego about it, she thought wickedly.

"If you had given in to your ex, I'd have had to kill you both, and then coerce an old lover to help me bury your bodies in my back yard. I'm really glad you didn't let that happen," Jessica said, blowing him a kiss across the table. "I like what you did do much, much better. Today was extraordinary. I have to admit it was much better without the condom. I haven't let a man know the real me in years."

"Damn it, Jessica," Will said, his face flushing with arousal because he wanted badly to be inside her that way again. "You are certainly not like other women."

"No, I'm not," she agreed. "I've been telling you that all along."

Jessica got up from her chair and walked to his. Surprising him, she grabbed the bottom of his ladder-back chair and turned it sideways so she could straddle his lap. Pulling the gauzy shirt over her head and from her body, she let it drop to the floor until she was happily naked from the waist up. "I'm too honest to be like other women, but there are advantages to being with a woman like me. Want to hear me tell you in detail what I want next from you?"

"You have no idea how much," Will said, cupping her breasts in his hands, closing his eyes with how good it felt.

Okay, Will decided, his hands happily full of the moaning, aroused woman of his dreams. He was done being a regular guy. He just wanted to be Jessica's guy, whatever the hell that meant. Eyelids drooping, Jessica leaned into his hands, humming with pleasure as he cradled and massaged her breasts. He was infinitely grateful that what he did seemed to please her.

"What do you want?" Will asked in a rough whisper, squeezing firmly until her eyes opened and held his.

"First, I want to fill up the gigantic clawfoot tub that lured me into renting this old creaking house and soak with you until we relax. Then I'm going to wash away the memory of your ex's hands on you and replace them with a much better version of mine doing wonderful things to get you in the proper mood. Then I'm going to bend over that cast iron tub which is bolted to the floor and let you do what we didn't get to do today because we were too damn anxious," Jessica said, putting her hands over Will's as he massaged. "I'm tired of just thinking about how great it's going to be."

"I swear you make me harder than the stone I carve," Will said, letting go of her breasts and pulling her tightly against him. He reached sideways to the floor and picked up her shirt. "Look—put this back on and let's finish dinner first. I can wait a little longer. It's a perk of being my age."

"*Your age?* Don't kid yourself," Jessica said, sliding off Will's lap and standing. "You make love with ten times more enthusiasm than any man I've ever known of any age. I find myself daydreaming all the time about what you're going to do me next."

"Okay, that's the official limit of my patience. Damn it, Jessica," Will said, laughing and grabbing her hand. "Being with you is already like being a kid again, and I guess I'm still making up for a year of nothing. Come on, let's go take that bath. We'll warm up food later."

He tugged her along behind him and led her up the stairs to the bathroom.

~

AN HOUR LATER, WITH ONLY HER KNEES NOW SUBMERSED IN THE WARM water, Jessica gripped the rounded edges of the cast iron tub to brace herself as Will thrust steadily and firmly from behind her. Her arms began to shake with the effort of holding her body up as she felt the first wave of a devastating climax roll through her.

"Harder," she demanded, her voice echoing off the bathroom walls. Will laughed roughly, but still responded to the authority in her request, surging against her hips to meet her demand.

"Jessica," Will said, sliding his hands around her thighs and up the inside of them to cup her. "I can feel you going over. Let go now, baby. Please let go. I need you to—oh God—yes. That's it."

Her scream of release bounced around the room and Will shook violently as he found his own release at the same time. He was trapped inside Jessica, held there by the sheer animal force of their joining. It was unquestionably the best sex he had ever experienced, and the pleasure lasted longer than he'd even known was possible for a man. When it was done, he was dizzy.

"Are you okay?" Will asked finally, wrapping himself completely around Jessica from behind, pulling her upright and back against him. He pulled her hair to one side, and lovingly kissed her neck. He palmed a breast with one hand and held her stomach with his other. "I've never—my God, I have no words for how much I like what we just did. It was truly a spiritual experience."

"I've certainly never had an orgasm last that long." Jessica said, relaxing against Will as he held her, her hands on his arms. He made her feel so feminine, so yin to his yang.

"Glad to hear the pleasure was mutual. I was just thinking the same thing myself," Will said, laughing and vibrating them both. He'd always heard about two people becoming one, but he'd never come close until this moment. "The plus of aging for me has been longer orgasms, but I've never had one last a full minute before. I also don't think I've ever felt so physically connected to a woman."

"Well, I've never done this position before," Jessica confessed. "It takes a lot of trust to turn away from a lover's face, to trust someone behind you. I was never willing before you. I have to admit you are the most amazing lover I've ever had, Will."

Will tightened his embrace, kissing her neck and leaving his mouth on her skin. "If we're good together, it's because I'm in love with you, Jessica Daniels."

Jessica leaned back in his arms and closed her eyes. "All I can promise you is that I will be faithful until you get tired of me and send me away."

"Then you're going to be mine for the rest of your life because I am never sending you away," Will warned.

CHAPTER 16

When his mother drove away to go to his brother's house, Michael Larson was happy to be alone at last. His father was at Jessica's still and likely wouldn't be home until late Sunday. That left all Saturday evening and the whole next day for Michael to enjoy the peace and quiet of having his house all to himself. He loved his parents and was glad he was able to help them, but it was damn nice to be alone again even if was just for a couple of days.

In fact, Michael was happy enough not to feel bad for not having a date.

When he was three beers and most of a pizza even happier still, Michael was thinking he'd have an early night. The doorbell ringing jarred him from his relaxation but fortunately didn't erase it. He looked at the clock, wondering who could possibly be visiting at eight-thirty on a Saturday night.

When he opened the door, he was shocked to see a very ill-looking Carrie Addison standing on his doorstep. It was all he could do not to catch her up in his arms.

"Michael," she said in greeting. "I'm sorry I didn't call. I didn't know what to say—so I just decided to come see you instead. Can I come in and talk to you?"

Michael couldn't help noticing the polite smile on her lips never quite reached her eyes.

"Sure," Michael said. "You look wiped out, Carrie. What's up?"

"Do you mind if we sit? I'm not feeling well, and standing for too long makes it worse," she told him.

"Sure. Come on in," he said. He led her to the kitchen and turned on a light. "Is this okay?"

She sat in a kitchen chair without waiting for an invitation. "I looked up your personal information to get your address in case you're wondering how I knew where you lived. I normally would never do such a thing, but I needed to contact you outside of working hours."

"I don't have a problem with you knowing where I live or with you contacting me outside of business hours," Michael said dryly, taking a chair across from her. "You look seriously sick. What's wrong?"

"Nothing that won't be fixed in a few months," Carrie said, looking at the darkened patio and seeing the shadow outlines of metal and the tools she guessed Michael used in his work.

She closed her eyes to keep from getting dizzy. The nervous anxiety she felt was making the nausea worse. When she opened her eyes again, it was to see Michael staring at her in concern.

Carrie could imagine this was what Michael had looked like standing outside her bathroom door the morning after while she had sobbed with regret for spending the night with him. A tear escaped one eye and then the other. She watched Michael stand up to come to her, but she shook her head and motioned for him to sit back down. Reaching into the napkin holder on the table, she pulled out a paper napkin and wiped away the tears.

"I'm pregnant," Carrie said flatly. "And it's your child. I hadn't been with anyone for three months before you. There hasn't been anyone after."

"But you're engaged," Michael said in partial denial, the shock too great to take in. Carrie was having a child? His child? His eyes went to her stomach area, but of course she was as slim as ever.

"I was engaged. I'm not any more," Carrie said quietly, another tear escaping. "I couldn't marry one man when I was pregnant with another man's child. And for the record, I'm not having an abortion. Tom asked, but I said no."

"Carrie, we used protection every time," Michael said. "Didn't we?"

Carrie closed her eyes and nodded. "As far I can remember, yes. I recall we used a condom every time," she agreed. "Michael, I don't think you did this to me on purpose. I hope you know I certainly didn't intend to get this way. As a habit, I stay on birth control and use condoms. Women using my type of prevention usually take months to conceive. I can't explain how this happened. The test at the doctor's office was positive and the reality of it is making me very sick. I'm just a little over five weeks along."

"Can I get you something? Some water or a soda?" Michael asked, needing to stall and give himself a moment or two to absorb the shock that he'd somehow gotten Carrie pregnant.

"Ice water please," she said softly.

He got up to get a glass from the cabinet and walked to the refrigerator in a trance.

"Look, Michael, I know it might be hard to believe you've been the only one for several months, but I hoped you might give me the benefit of the doubt because of our working relationship," she said seriously. "I wouldn't lie to you about something this important."

He brought the ice water back to the table and sat back down across from her. "You can completely stop worrying about that. I believe you."

Carrie stared at him in shock. "I—I know my behavior after we were together must have seemed insane to you."

Michael nodded. "It did, but frankly you getting engaged again seemed more insane to me," he said. "I couldn't understand what I did so wrong that you wouldn't even discuss what happened with me."

"I was already engaged to Tom when were together. Tom and I were not—well, we were—waiting," she finished lamely. "What I did with you was just truly a moment of weakness on my part. It was that damn piece of art, *Anguish*. Your art seduced me."

"Well, I'm glad because nothing else had worked up to then," Michael said harshly.

He felt chastised for his comment and his tone when Carrie turned her face away from him and two more tears ran down her face.

"Sorry. I wasn't trying to be a smart-ass. Being with you was the most amazing first time I've ever had in my life. I haven't been able to touch another woman since," Michael said. "What did I do that night that was so horribly wrong?"

She wiped her eyes and lifted her chin, not yet meeting his gaze.

Just tell him, she ordered herself. Tell Michael Larson the truth, and tell him why you told him about the baby. You are not going to be able to do this alone.

"I'll tell you if you still want to know after I ask the question I came here to ask you," Carrie said quietly.

"Okay," Michael said, leaning back in his chair. "Ask."

"I want to know if you want our child to raise, because I don't want it. I'm not a bad person, but I've gone through enough in my life, and I can't do this. So if you don't want the baby, you don't have to give it another thought. I'll arrange for an adoption and never tell anyone it's yours. I didn't even tell Tom who the father was."

Michael all but knocked his chair over standing up. Carrie didn't want his child. Hearing it from her was like being struck across the face with a sledgehammer.

He walked to the patio door in a daze and stared out into the darkness. Pressing his forehead to the cool glass of the door, he let himself think of the attraction between Carrie and him. After waiting for several years to be with her, he had been inside her more than out of her for the entirety of the night. The fire between them had burned hot, and Michael still felt that same level of longing for her. If that fire had melted Carrie and him together to create a child, he reasoned, that child was a creation of his every bit as much as any piece of art he'd made with his hands.

Michael raised his forehead from the glass and turned back to the woman sitting quietly in the chair. He had seen her ordering and commanding an army of people in her events business with a precision any military general would appreciate. Tonight, she looked vulnerable and defeated. His heart hurt to realize he and his unwanted child were the cause of her distress.

"Yes. I want our child," he said firmly, walking back to the table and forcing himself to sit for a third time. "Whatever you need from me, you have it. I'm glad you didn't get an abortion and marry Tom. I'm glad you looked me up and told me about the pregnancy. As far as I'm concerned, you did all the right things."

"Are you sure?" Carrie asked him, though she saw the resolution in his face. She just wanted to hear him once more say he would take care of their baby before she laid the rest of her sins at Michael Larson's feet.

"Let me put it this way. I want any child I created with you under any conditions," Michael said emphatically. "I don't have any idea how to make you believe me other than to show you over time."

"Okay," Carrie said. Nausea threatened to overwhelm her again, but she pushed it down. "I'm going to believe you."

"Now tell me what went wrong between us," Michael demanded quietly, keeping his tone as soft as he could. Whatever it was, he intended to fix it.

Carrie looked at her hands and then back into Michael's determined gaze. He's not the careless boy he was, she thought, but it didn't change the bigger things.

"When I was a sophomore in college, I was crazy about this guy who was a senior. One night I went to a party and ended up in bed with him. We had both been drinking, but I was stupid enough not to care. It was my first time to have sex with anyone. I got up afterward to go to the bathroom. When I came back to the bed we had been using, the boy was already gone. I got dressed and went back to the party where I found him holding one blonde on his lap while another clone of her leaned on the arm of his chair. I don't even think he realized he'd just taken my virginity and discarded me six seconds later. Young women can be stupid and naïve about such things. I was both. It was obvious being with me had meant virtually nothing to him."

Michael closed his eyes at the amount of pain in her expression. After watching Carrie marry and divorce twice, he was empathetic about how much it hurt to see the person you wanted be with someone else.

"I'm sorry you were hurt. The guy was a jerk for what he did to you, but I was just as careless at his age. I drank and partied pretty hard in college. I eventually got over it, or whatever it is that young men do to finally grow up," Michael said.

Carrie shook her head. "That's a great rationalization if you're a young guy sowing wild oats, and not so great for the young woman who ends up being the field he's plowing."

Michael said nothing in response to her comment. At this point, he knew better than to laugh. Instinct told him Carrie wasn't trying to make a joke. He watched her clear her throat and take in a deep breath before she continued her story.

"A month after I'd been with the guy, I found out I was pregnant with his child. Since I didn't want the baby of a man who couldn't tell one woman from the other, I had an abortion and never said anything about it to anyone. I didn't tell my parents, my sisters, or confess to my minister. You're the first person I have ever told. Regardless of why the guy behaved as he did, I'll never be able to forget him or what I did as a result of what happened between us."

"*Carrie,*" Michael said, his heart breaking for the pain she had held inside all these years.

It would have been awful to go through that experience alone. Michael reached out a hand to pick up one of hers. It was limp and cold in his, no life to it at all. He felt a sudden need to infuse her with his energy, but Carrie went on talking, giving him no choice but to listen.

"Getting an abortion is a terrible experience, Michael. Since I had genuinely cared about the guy, I was devastated afterward when I realized I had willingly killed a part of both of us. I grieved for months. When I finally came to terms with myself, I vowed I would never have an abortion again, no matter what the circumstances."

Carried looked at him, held his gaze and saw the concern he felt for her now. There was a flicker inside her, and then she remembered how much pain he had caused her. She pushed the flicker away.

"So here I am in your kitchen trying to keep that promise to myself even though I was careless enough to end up getting pregnant by you for a second time in my life," she said, watching the horror come into his face.

Michael pulled his hand away from her. "You're saying it was me? You're saying I was the guy in college who took your virginity and got your pregnant?"

"Yes," Carrie said, standing, preparing to run if she needed to. "It was you. It was you back then, and God help me, it's you again now. I thought in a town the size of Lexington that I would never have to be around you ever again after college, but the universe seemed to have other plans for me."

"You've been staying away from me on purpose?" Michael asked, the question all but choking him. All the time he'd chased her and she'd been running like hell in the other direction.

"Yes. I stayed away in every way I could. It worked for a number of years. In my original projects, I refused to plan art events. Then three years ago, I suddenly couldn't talk my boss out of assigning me to you because he wanted us to work together. What the hell could I say? How could I refuse without looking unprofessional? I was the best at what I did, and Paul wanted me to work with you. Then to my surprise your art events accelerated my career, so I resolved to find a way to live with our business relationship despite the past," she explained.

"I was attracted to you the first time Paul introduced us three years ago," Michael said, his innate honesty ruling his tongue. "You've been married and unavailable twice in two years. The women I dated other than you never really mattered to me. Every time you were single, I tried to be with you. You know that."

"Yes, but now you can understand why I didn't—and still don't—want to be involved with you. Staying away seemed the only choice to me, but I hear crazy people never think they're crazy, only other people do," she said, sighing and looking away from him.

"Carrie, all I have wanted in the last three years is a chance to get to know you," Michael declared. "How are those women I dated any different than the men you married? If you had dated me, you wouldn't have married them."

"I don't think you're hearing me, Michael. How can I make this clear to you? When I decide to spend the rest of my life with a man and have his children, it's going to be with a man I can fall in love with and trust completely. That will never be you," Carrie said firmly. "Every time I look at you, I only see the boy that hurt me. I don't like the way you are with women."

Michael stood and walked away from her, too horrified by what she was saying to be able to think about all it meant. All this time he had loved her, chased her, and she had hated, feared, and loathed him for the mistakes of their past. Instead of him being a moth to her flame, it looked like it had been the other way around. Or maybe it was both. God help him, even after all she'd said he still wanted her.

"So you're probably wondering, if I hated you so much all this time, then why did I crawl into bed with you a month ago?" Carrie asked the obvious.

Michael turned around to look at her, his own pain finding its way into his words as he answered. "Let me guess, you were planning to sleep with me and dump me? Or did you just intend to embarrass me with your rejection the next morning and hope I would spend all the weeks that followed being mentally tortured trying to figure out what I had done wrong?"

"No. It was actually nothing like that at all. At the art show last month, I stood under all that twisted metal in *Anguish* and wondered how you couldn't see that you had created a replica of the pain that was inside me for you all this time. When you kissed me while I was crying, I simply broke. When you were inside me all night, I was like a drug addict wanting fix after fix. But the next morning—the next morning I hated myself for my weakness. Because it was wonderful, I hated you even more for not remembering that you had once been inside me all those years ago."

Carrie picked up the ice water where she stood, drank half and put the glass back on the table. She put a shaking hand on the chair for support.

"I didn't tell you my story to make you feel bad about college or what we did a month ago. I just want you to know why I really can't spend the rest of my life letting you destroy me over and over. For the record, I don't hold you any more accountable for the college stuff than I hold myself. It was my fault for having unprotected sex with a drunken guy. I considered that the end of our short, pathetic story back then," she said. "What happened between us a month ago, I can't explain completely, not even to myself."

"Carrie—I'm sorry about what happened when we were in college," Michael said, his voice barely a whisper. "All I remember is some generic two years of an emptiness I finally got tired of and outgrew."

"I guess that's my point, Michael. You don't remember it, but I will never be able to forget," Carrie said. "What happened the first time is the reason I'm making myself come tell you now. Otherwise, I might have done as Tom asked and started over with him."

"Or you might have dated me when I asked you the first time," Michael told her.

"I would never have dated you because you have poor taste in bed partners. Among the other women you were seeing when we met, you were dating Erin then, remember?" Carrie said lightly. "She made a special point of telling everyone in the office all the things you liked to do to her in bed."

"Well, shit," Michael spat. "It's not my fault she was indiscreet."

"How about Angela or Daphne?" Carrie asked. "And I seem to recall several others besides them. The two blondes you were with at the party were from my sorority. I got to hear in great detail how they competed in bed for you—together. So how much have you really changed since college, Michael? My actions seem to indicate I'm still just as stupid as I was then. I'm not sure people ever grow up. I don't believe you have when it comes to women."

She turned as if to leave but stopped and looked at the floor as she finished.

"I would rather have nothing more to do with you, but I simply can't do the wrong thing again. Killing one of our children was all the evil I had in me for a lifetime. Now I just want to find a solution I can live with and try to go on. I can't raise a child when I don't even like the father. So if you want our baby, you can have it. You seem to have grown into a mostly decent man despite your womanizing," Carrie said.

Michael wanted to find words to explain to her how empty it was to fill your hours with women other than the one you wanted, but he couldn't. All he found inside was the same level of desire for Carrie Addison that he always seemed to have when he was near her. He wanted her in his life, wanted to get to know her. Something about her called to every instinct he had.

"Carrie," Michael said quietly, "you are the ideal for me. I've regretted many of the women I've known, but I am not sorry for being with you a few weeks ago. That's a night I will never forget. I didn't mean to get you pregnant, but I will do the right thing for you and our child. You have my word."

She walked to the kitchen doorway. "Don't answer me now. Think about it for a few days, and then you can let me know for sure."

"I can tell you that answer already because I know what I want. I won't change my mind about you or the baby," Michael said, meaning it even when he had no idea how he was going to making it work.

"Well, be sure about the baby," Carrie advised softly. "I've learned the hard way that the consequences of some bad decisions last a long time."

Michael heard the front door click and knew she had gone. He had known better than to try to stop her. It was obvious Carrie couldn't wait to be away from him after what she'd shared. He got a beer out of the refrigerator, sat at the table, and drank it while he stared at the half glass of water she'd left behind.

He thought of his father curled up in the bed upset over wrongs he'd imagined he done to a woman he cared about. His sympathy to that situation grew a hundred-fold.

Certainly his reaction to Carrie getting married each time had not been good, and he'd gone a little overboard with dating to forget her each time. But no one he'd dated over the last three years had meant anything to him. His fondness for Erin, who until tonight he had considered a good friend, had now dimmed as well with finding out she'd been so indiscreet.

Only being with Carrie had ever felt right to him. She was the woman he ached for, as his dad would say. At least he now knew there was a fire in Carrie Addison that burned just as hotly for him. Two husbands and a potential third hadn't been able to keep her out of his arms a month ago. Michael intended to find out what it was that drew them together over and over no matter what they did.

Maybe he couldn't change the past, Michael decided, but he could definitely bend and shape the present. One way or another, he was going to be Carrie Addison's next husband, even if only for the next seven or eight months. During that time, Michael would try to balance his karmic debt to her with kindness and support. Then after the baby was born, if she still wanted to leave, Michael would find the courage to give her a divorce and help her find whatever life she wanted without him and the baby.

As Michael drank the rest of his beer, he thought of the pile of metal rings in the courtyard. It was ironic that he had been creating the four-foot-tall sculpture of multiple wedding bands to remind Carrie of her multiple marriages.

Now Michael was putting himself next in line to become one of her husbands, and it wasn't so damn amusing anymore. His arrogance had burned to ashes in the same fire source that created his child.

So instead of having the lazy day he'd intended tomorrow, Michael decided he was going to buy the purest gold he could find and make a set of matching wedding rings. In the metal he would etch the truth and hope Carrie would be seduced by his art one more time.

CHAPTER 17

Will woke in the dark and heard someone calling out in panic. It took a couple moments for him to realize that what had awakened him was Jessica tossing and turning in the bed beside him. She was having a dream and calling out in distress.

"No. Please. Don't do this. I'm married. Nathan—Nathan," she called, finally lapsing into gut-wrenching tears.

Will put one arm over her for comfort, trying to avoid restraining her.

"Jessica," he called loudly, scared and hurting for the torment she was in. "Jessica, wake up. Honey, you're dreaming."

Jessica opened her eyes and flinched away from Will, then relaxed again as her vision cleared and focused on him.

"Oh, God. That was awful," she said, patting Will's arm across her. "That hasn't happened to me in a really long time. Thank you for waking me up."

Will cradled her in his arms, holding her as tightly to him as he dared. "You were calling for your husband," he said.

"Yes," Jessica agreed hoarsely. "It's a dream I've had many times before. It's just been a while since the last time."

"You tried to think of Nathan during the rape?" Will asked softly, lifting his arm from her stomach, to let his hand stroke back her hair.

Jessica waited a long time before answering. "Yes. But it didn't make any difference. They wouldn't stop. One of them knew Nathan was dead."

Will fought back the surge of anger he felt. This was not the time to express it. Jessica needed relief, not to be worried about him.

"Well, I can see why you would call for Nathan," Will said, softly rubbing her arms and tucking the cover over her bare shoulders. "I'm sure your husband would have stopped it from happening if he could have. I'm sure he's been grateful for every good man you've known since. In fact, I am absolutely, positively sure of that because I feel the same way now. I'm not jealous of your past anymore."

Tears ran down both sides of Jessica's face and into her hair. Will's words were a soothing salve to the newly reopened wound in her.

"I thought all the remembering was behind me. I haven't thought about the rape or Nathan in years. It's just that you—," Jessica stopped herself from the comparison.

"It's okay. You can say it—I remind you of your husband," Will finished.

"Yes," Jessica said, tears making her voice thick. Her heart hurt for being unfair to Will.

Will looked at her tears, and they called to him for a solution. So he opened his mind and found one. He could listen and be her friend.

"Tell me about what it was like to be with your husband," Will whispered, kissing her shoulder in the dark.

"I can't do that," Jessica protested. "It's not fair to you, and I just—can't."

"What happened wasn't fair to you or Nathan. Screw fair," Will told her. "I'm not going to be jealous of a good woman who loved a good man. And you have a right to those memories. Tell me how he made love to you, Jessica. What did your husband do?"

"I'm not going to talk to you about this. Besides, I don't remember anymore," Jessica denied, tears burning and flowing. It was even partly true. She and Nathan had been barely more than children when they were married.

"Let's start with little things," Will coaxed. "How did Nathan kiss you?" Jessica was quiet for so long, Will thought she might have fallen back to sleep. He stroked her hair again. "Tell me, honey. How did your husband kiss you?"

"He kissed me like he had to or go crazy," Jessica replied at last, the words burning her throat.

"Okay. That makes perfect sense. Now tell me the favorite move he did with you," Will encouraged, rubbing her arms.

"I can't," Jessica said, shaking her head. "I can't talk to you about what I've done with other men."

"It's okay. I wouldn't want to know about what you did with Steve Lipton, but I absolutely want to hear about Nathan Daniels. It's a contextual interest. Dip into that honesty you're always bragging about and tell me," Will said firmly, his hands on her more insistent than before to keep her from turning away.

Jessica closed her eyes and let the ragged sigh she'd been holding back escape.

"Nathan would hold my breast and thumb the nipple to make it hard while he French-kissed me," Jessica said, feeling evidence of Will's arousal pressing against her leg and his chuckle in her ear. She sighed wistfully at how simple it all sounded and how comforted she felt in Will's embrace. "We weren't very advanced then."

"It's still a great move," Will said frankly, his hand finding her breast and cupping it lightly. "Anything else?"

Her silence told him there was, so he pressed.

"How aggressive was he in getting inside you?" Will whispered the question.

"He—he wasn't as careful as—he usually just made sure I was really ready and then slid inside in one move," Jessica admitted.

Will laughed softly. "Damn impatient young men."

Jessica laughed and sniffled in return. "It had its charms at the time."

Will kissed Jessica's teary eyes. "The joys of youth, right? What did your husband call you in bed, Jessica?"

"I can't tell you that—besides, it's embarrassing," she said, her voice breaking in shame.

"*Jessica,*" Will said firmly, in a tone that normally got compliance from most people. "Answer my question."

"*Luscious,*" Jessica admitted softly. "Nathan called me that because he said he liked the way I tasted."

"Well damn—no wonder you get us confused, it's uncanny how much he and I are alike," Will commented, making Jessica laugh.

"Yes, and you both talk way too much during sex," Jessica said hoarsely, half-laughing, half-crying. "I can't believe I'm telling you this."

Will bit his lip to keep from sighing. Despite what he promised, he was now officially jealous of a dead man. "You are a very sexy and amazing woman, Jessica Daniels. Nathan was a lucky man to have a wife who loved him as much as you did. I bet you loved him back just as much."

"Yes," Jessica said, voice choking with the tears she couldn't stop. "I loved him. I truly loved him."

"Of course you did," Will said quietly, holding her as she cried and grieved.

Unfortunately, the heartfelt declaration of love wasn't something Will had been expecting to hear her say about any other man but him. Jessica had told Will she had never loved any man since her husband, but it was still damn hard to hear how easily Jessica had said those words about Nathan Daniels. Having insisted on the conversation, Will had no one to blame but himself for how disappointed it made him feel.

Jessica cried herself softly to sleep while Will held her close in the dark. He wondered what his chances for a future were with a woman who was still very much another man's wife in her heart.

~

THEY WENT FOR A LONG BIKE RIDE THROUGH THE HORSE FARMS ON THE way to eat breakfast Sunday morning. Will enjoyed having Jessica pressed intimately along the back of him, so he let his sense of contentment override his other concerns.

He had awakened to a fully dressed Jessica kissing his jaw line and teasing him about sleeping his life away. Seeing her smiling but still anxious expression, he'd quickly decided to put aside what happened in the night, telling himself he would think about it later. Jessica looked and acted mostly okay, and that was the most important thing, even if she still wasn't her typical carefree and happy self.

Until the anxiety left her, he wasn't going to discuss what had been said in the dark. He wasn't sure he was ready to hear how Jessica felt about her dead husband, especially if she still longed for him. Instead, Will decided to focus only on enjoying the bike ride and just being with her.

They pulled into a local organic restaurant in Midway known for its great food and fun atmosphere. When Will turned off the bike,

Jessica climbed off and removed her helmet, shaking her hair loose. She bent to the mirror to check her appearance and grimaced at what she saw. Will grinned and pulled the ink pen from his pocket that she had used before to secure her hair. The beaming smile Jessica gave him was all the reward he could have asked for.

"My hero," Jessica said, taking the ink pen from Will and grinning.

"It hasn't been out of my pocket since you gave it back. I hope you know it was really hard to ride away from you that day knowing you were upset with me," Will told her.

She twirled her hair up and leaned into Will for a thank-you kiss as she slid the ink pen into her hair.

"Resourceful men on sexy black bikes are impossible to resist for long," she told him, clutching his shirtfront for a moment. "Especially tall, handsome ones offering to pay for breakfast."

"Speaking of breakfast, I smell something with bacon," Will said, his stomach growling. "Or is that a new perfume you're wearing?"

"No way. If I bought something to wear here, it would smell like a giant blueberry muffin—split, buttered, and grilled," Jessica informed him, "and probably would have strong fragrance notes of some sort of flavored coffee."

Will laughed and took her hand as they went inside. They talked and laughed over breakfast and joked with other restaurant patrons who couldn't help staring at the striking, tall, older couple dressed in motorcycle gear.

"So how long you two been married?"

Jessica paused mid-bite of her muffin and froze at the question from someone across from them. Her gaze went to Will's, which was on her and not on the elderly gentleman asking the question.

After a short while, Will turned his gaze to the man's and answered smoothly. "Sometimes it feels like thirty years. Sometimes it feels like two months."

The man laughed and shook his head at Will's answer. Jessica swallowed the muffin bite, but had to chase it with coffee still hot enough to burn her tongue.

"That's honest, don't you think?" Will finally asked Jessica, taking a bite of his breakfast sandwich while he waited to see what she would say.

Just like that—whether they were ready to discuss it or not—their talk last night was hanging out there between them, demanding to be acknowledged, demanding to be put to rest somehow. Only Jessica didn't know how to put it to rest. It had awakened her at 5 a.m., and she had mentally worked two hours on setting it aside just so she wouldn't brood about it today.

Jessica stared at Will as she sipped her coffee, debating on how honestly to reply to what he said. Since she didn't know how to answer in a way Will would understand, she turned and smiled at the man who asked the original question.

"I made the mistake of confessing to Will that he reminded me of my husband who died thirty years ago. I don't know if he's ever going to let me forget it. The truth is Will and I have only known each for a couple of months," Jessica said lightly, breaking off another bite of muffin to stuff in her mouth to stop herself from saying more.

"Two months? You two sure act like a married couple," the man's wife said, joining into the teasing. "You thinking about keeping him, honey?"

Jessica tilted her head at the woman's teasing question, and smiled wickedly around a bite of muffin. Teasing she could handle.

"Well, I have to say that now and again it seems like a good idea. Did you see the size of his bike in the parking lot? That machine is amazing, and Will gives a good ride," she said in her best sexy voice, her amused gaze on Will as he reacted to her words.

"Hot coffee," Will said to the couple, flushing and coughing to clear his throat.

Jessica held his gaze across the table and Will watched her eat bite after bite of muffin, licking the remaining blueberry and butter from her fingers on the last one. He was completely unable to hold back a sigh, but he bore her teasing by planning what he was going to do to her when they got back to her place.

"Jessica and I have a lot of fun together," Will said, smiling at Jessica, knowing his gaze was warning her he would seek retribution. "It only gets interesting when we fight."

"You know, I cannot believe how hungry I suddenly am," Jessica said, leaning over the table to pluck a bit of bacon off his plate, and letting him look down her shirt at the leopard print bra she had worn. Thirty years of dating had taught her many ways to distract men and keep them from delving too deeply into her psyche or asking too many questions.

Will looked down Jessica's shirt as he sipped his coffee, wondering how he was ever going to convince her to devote herself to one man. No matter how much Jessica teased or flirted, Will knew great sex alone was never going to be enough for him. Even if he believed Jessica's flattery about being the best lover she'd ever had, Will now knew his competition for her heart wasn't guys like Steve Lipton or the math teacher.

It was Nathan Daniels that Jessica called out for in her dreams. Will had no idea how any live male could ever compete with a ghost she still loved.

~

After breakfast, they rode over to Versailles and then looped back the way they had first come to enjoy the scenery through the horse farms again. It was a beautiful, crisp day, and the breeze was perfect.

When they got back to the house, Will hung up his jacket and tossed his helmet on the bench. He took Jessica's hand and tugged her into his arms, pulling the shirt from her body and tossing it beside the helmet. He pulled his own over his head and tossed it there as well. When he leaned back with her in his arms, she ran restless hands over him and ended up unsnapping his jeans almost like a reflex action.

"Just so you know," Will said roughly as her hands explored him, "this time is going to be just for me. I'll try to make sure you get there, but no promises."

Jessica unzipped him and slipped a hand inside the front of his jeans. "Okay. Tell me what you want."

"I'm going to make this really simple. I want to take you upstairs and try to break your girlie bed again," Will told her softly. "And I want you to look me in the eye while I do it."

Jessica shook in anticipation and her hand trembled as it cupped Will's growing desire for her. "Let's go," she said hoarsely, reluctantly removing her hand.

They walked upstairs together and in the bedroom shed the rest of their clothes. When they were both completely naked, Will kissed Jessica and pulled her down beside him on the bed. Then he rolled her sideways and pushed her back, moving over her until he could feel her heart beating frantically.

"Excited or scared?" he asked, pressing his lips to the side of her neck.

"Both," Jessica answered honestly. "Will, I think you're always going to scare me a little. I'm just not used to a man who excites me as much as you do. It's like you have a power over my arousal that makes me nervous."

"If you expect me to apologize for that, you're going to have a hell of a long wait," Will said, bracing himself at the entrance to her body. "Let me inside you, Jessica. Invite me in."

"What do you mean?" she asked, feeling just the fingertips of one of Will's hands skimming the inside of her thigh.

She bent her knee and raised her leg to grant him more access.

"You know exactly what I mean, or at least your body seems to know," Will told her. "How ready are you?"

"Why don't you find out for yourself?" she asked, her body flushed as his fingertips explored but never went where she needed them most, where he would have known the answer to his question. Instead, he pressed just the tip of his erection into her.

"Is this for me?" Will asked, pushing into her a fraction and stopping.

"Yes," she said, arching her hips to offer more, moaning in protest when Will didn't deepen the contact.

"Are you sure?" he asked against her mouth. "I only want what's mine."

"If this is a quiz, the answer is yes. Damn it. Yes," Jessica said fiercely. "I want you. Do you always have to talk so much?"

She watched Will's gaze darkened and eyes narrow at her criticism.

"Keep your eyes open or I stop," he told her, sliding in a little more, stopping, and retreating when she closed her eyes in pleasure. "No. Look at me. I want to be sure you see me. Today is my turn, and I want you to want me—only me."

Jessica forced her eyes open to hold Will's gaze as he slid into her inch by agonizing inch. When she felt him go in as far as he could, she watched his face as he pulled almost all the way out, and saw the flash in his eyes as he drove hard into her, slamming his hips to hers in possession. Jessica lifted both knees and braced for the next thrust and really had to work at keeping her gaze on his fierce one. One more thrust with him looking at her that way and she was going to shatter beneath him without finesse.

"Jessica, I want the power you give me over you. I want to be the only one you let inside for the rest of our lives. So factor that into your thinking," Will demanded roughly, caught on the edge of sanity by what he was doing. "I was trying like hell not to say anything so possessive, but damn, lady—I can't seem to ever be with you without thinking of you as completely mine."

"Will," Jessica said, her heart expanding again until she thought for sure it would burst in her chest.

"Oh shut up, you talk too much," he said harshly, laughing at her. "Less talking, more moving. And look at me, damn it."

Jessica held his gaze as he demanded, until the wave hit. Then her head rolled back as her body rose up against his. Jessica heard Will make a sound above her, the sound a guttural groan that came from deep within him, and then he called her name as she instinctively tightened around him. All through her climax, Will's body staked its possession of hers until Jessica finally felt his release sweep over him.

As they lay in the broad daylight sideways across her bed afterward, Jessica wrapped an exhausted Will in her arms and held him as he slipped quietly into sleep on top of her. She didn't move him, nor did she want to disconnect them. Instead, she thought about the conflicting emotions Will brought to her each and every time they were together.

Their discussion last night had given her the gift of some old, sweet memories back. That didn't mean she would ever use Will as a substitute, though she could understand Will might have concerns about it.

Today, Will had selfishly demanded equal time with her. Jessica's heart beat hard as she thought about just how much she had wanted to give Will his own time, how much she had wanted to obey his directions, and how close she had been to agreeing that he could have all he wanted of her forever.

But an unexpected side benefit of last night was an understanding of the source of her recent PTSD symptoms. As crazy as it seemed after thirty years, Jessica realized she wasn't over the death of her husband. It was like the rape had disrupted her grieving for Nathan. Instead of going through it, she had just set it aside until she had starting falling in love with a man who some similar traits.

Last night, she had remembered her marriage, and in remembering had missed Nathan Daniels with her entire being, even though she woke this morning nothing but grateful to see Will's sleeping form beside her in bed. It was confusing, painful, wonderful, and upsetting all at the same time.

Jessica decided she was going to have to move up her yearly maintenance appointment with her therapist. She needed to find out if there was a possibility that she might actually be able to love another man.

CHAPTER 18

When Will came home Sunday evening, Michael was in the courtyard feeding a fire in his gas fire pit with a small black kettle on the grate. Instead of his customary ponytail, Michael's long hair was hanging free to the middle of his back. Will smiled because his son looked like a wizard bent over a cauldron. Whatever he was brewing, the look of concentration on his son's face would be very intimidating to anyone who didn't know it was just how Michael looked when he was absorbed in his work.

Will slid the patio door open and walked out to join him. Michael's head came up, and he nodded, but said nothing in greeting. He walked a little closer and peered into the kettle.

"Is that gold?" Will asked, surprised to see the molten liquid.

"Yes. I'm making wedding rings," Michael said, finally meeting his father's gaze. He sighed, and then just said the words. "I'm getting married, Dad."

Will arched an eyebrow. His oldest son's facial expressions had always said more than his words ever had. What Will saw in Michael's face was a combination of complete shock and absolute determination. "Most people just buy rings these days."

"Not a metal sculptor, and not for this woman," Michael said sincerely. "When I put this ring on her finger, I want to have breathed life into it myself. My every interaction with her from here on out is going to communicate my commitment."

"Something happen this weekend you want to tell me about?" Will asked, running a hand over his face. Seeing Michael in this hell-bent determined state was like winding back the clock thirty years for him.

"I haven't asked her to marry me yet, but I'm going to this week," Michael said quietly. "She's having my baby, and I intend to marry her whether we stay that way or not."

Will stood for few moments saying nothing as he absorbed the full magnitude of what Michael was sharing. He studied the molds standing by waiting. One was smaller and obviously a woman's ring. The other was its mate. His guess was that it would never get any more serious for Michael than crafting the band he would use to bind the woman he wanted to him.

When he finally forced his gaze to Michael's determined face and hard jaw again, for a moment all Will could see was the sensitive, emotional boy he'd been. Now that boy was going to be a father. Will knew full well all the changes that meant, and they were enormous. After the baby came, Michael would never be a boy again. He could only hope his son was up to the challenge.

"Carrie Addison?" Will asked finally, though it hardly needed asking. He knew Michael hadn't been out with anyone else but her in a couple months.

Michael's eyes flashed at the name. "Yes. Carrie Addison. She came to see me last night to tell me I'm going to be a father. I called Dietrich this morning and made him sell me gold today because I wanted to get these done while I'm inspired. I'm making hers a common small size and thicker. It will be easy to heat and stretch it when I get the exact measurement. If I have my way, you and I are going to get a permanent roommate in a week or so. I hope you're okay with that."

"Sure, I'm fine with it. I need to look for my own place anyway. What happens if Carrie doesn't want to live with you?" Will posed, trying to make sure his son realized that he wasn't going to be able to force the woman to do anything, pregnant or not.

"Carrie's sick all the time and can't take care of herself. She needs me to agree to certain things, so I'm making marriage and living here a condition of our—contractual agreement. It's not like she hasn't been married before," Michael said harshly, not wanting to remember that she said she married those other men just to stay away from him.

In fact, all last night he'd thought about how long he'd wanted

Carrie, how many years he'd felt like she should be with him. So he had decided he would just get over husbands one and two, and Carrie Addison was just going to have to get over the bad past with a selfish boy Michael no longer remembered.

Then after he married her, he was going to make the relationship legal in every way. And when he made love to his wife, it was going to be even more meaningful than the night they conceived the baby. If Carrie ended up leaving him eventually, Michael intended to make it as hard as possible for her. He wanted to make staying with him seem like the only option that made any sense.

"Dad, did you ever do anything you regretted with a woman?" Michael asked finally.

Will put his hands in his pockets as he thought about it. "Sure, I think everybody has something in their love life they regret. If you date a lot, it just increases the odds that you're going to mess up. Somehow we all seem to move past our mistakes eventually. Why?"

"Carrie told me we got together in college and that I treated her badly. I don't even remember her, but it's true I treated a lot of women badly for a short period of time. Maybe I'm becoming an even bigger bastard because I'm not going to let the past get in the way of marrying her now that I have the chance." Michael looked at the ground and not at his father.

Will could tell that nothing he said was going to deter Michael from trying to force Carrie to marry him, but what you said to a twenty-year-old and what you said to a man heading to age thirty-five were different things. His son had lived too long to not have made some mistakes, but all a person could ever do was make it up as best they could.

"Well, every man is a bastard at some point," Will said carefully, putting his hands in his pockets again, this time to keep from physically reaching out to comfort his suffering son. "From my perspective, it doesn't seem like you stayed one. Otherwise, why would she have let you spend the night recently? Carrie seems like an intelligent woman. Maybe she just needs time to accept that you've changed."

Michael snorted and shook his head, wanting to cry at how good his father was.

"I can always count on you to see the bright side. God, I want to be just like you when I finally grow up," he said sadly, lifting the kettle and pouring the liquid gold carefully into the tiny molds. "It's truly not just about the baby. The baby is just giving me an excuse. I want Carrie to be my wife. I've wanted her even when she was married to other men. Even Shane can't figure that craziness out."

He set the kettle on a nearby table to cool. Taking a tiny rubber mallet, Michael tapped the molds gently to make sure the air bubbles left the now cooling gold.

"You want to be like me? Son, you already *are* like me," Will said, laughing roughly as they watched the gold pool and solidify. "That's what got you into this mess. Your mother was pregnant with you when we got married. Granted, we married when she was only a couple months along, so no one really knew but us. We didn't even tell our folks anything other than we were tired of waiting."

Michael looked at his father and laughed. "Seriously? You knocked up Mom before you married her?"

Will rolled his eyes at Michael's description and shrugged. "It was just one of those attractions too big to fight. I had no regrets at the time. Neither did your mother. At the time, I wanted both of you badly. She wanted the same things. We couldn't stay away from each other."

He looked deep into Michael's eyes to make sure his son was hearing all his words. "Your mother and I have always agreed we would have ended up together no matter what. That part of our past didn't change even when we divorced. Some relationships in life just seem to be inevitable and happen when they happen. I have never understood people who choose to spend their entire life being in denial about someone they love. I'd rather go through the divorce again than to not have you or Shane."

"I get that—I really do. I want both of them so much it hurts. God, maybe I really am like you," Michael said, his mouth curved into a half smile, half sneer. "I know I ought to feel more guilt about the past. Maybe I will someday. All I can think right now is that she needs to be with me so I can take care of her and the baby. Anything else seems too wrong to contemplate. I don't know how in the hell I'm going to convince her to marry me though."

"Then we're both in the same club," Will said quietly. "Since I can't get Jessica pregnant, I'm going to need to convince her to make the choice willingly. That's going to be tough since she's still in love with her dead husband. I know that for sure now. Those guys she dated were never in the running. I am, but she has a thirty-year list of reservations."

"Maybe she still loves a dead man, but Jessica is also crazy about you. Carrie all but hates me. Emotional blackmail may be all I have," Michael said, grinning now. "But before I go that route, I'm going to see what my clever brother thinks I should do to win her over. I'm not going to be able to hide this from him, so I might as well use his skills. I hope he's not too disappointed in me to help."

"Well, I don't have a doctorate in psychology, but I suggest saving blackmail as a last resort," Will said. "What could you possibly have on Carrie Addison to blackmail her about?"

"She wants something huge from me," Michael said easily. "I'm willing to do a prenuptial agreement about it so long as she marries me."

"She wants money?" Will asked, surprised and having trouble believing Carrie was mercenary.

"No," Michael said, laughing. "Carrie doesn't want my money. The problem is she wants nothing at all, including the baby or me. I'll have to promise to give her freedom after the baby is born. That means I only have seven and half months to change her mind."

"That's a pretty big gamble if she's not interested in a relationship with you," Will said slowly. "I'm sorry she doesn't want the baby, Michael."

"She has good reasons," Michael said quietly, "but I hope to change her mind."

Michael saw the gold had hardened, formed the rings. He picked up the hammer and smashed the molds around them to free the gold.

"I'm only planning to do this marriage gig once," Michael said, ruthlessly crushing the plaster casting, "and I will do my best to shape our relationship to be what we both need. I hope one day I can thank my child for helping me find a way into its mother's heart. If that doesn't happen, I will at least know I did my best. I'll just have to love it enough for two parents."

Will let the worry wash over him, but he said nothing. He'd seen Michael the morning he'd come home from Carrie's devastated about her sending him away. It was easy to understand Michael's determination to have the woman in his life. Will felt both admiration and concern, feelings that he experienced frequently with both his sons. Michael was a lot like him when it came to love and fidelity.

Hopefully, Carrie would recognize and appreciate that trait over time.

He watched Michael inspect the gold bands and then smile as the rings clinked together in his hand. Judging from the glint of satisfaction in his son's eyes, it seemed Michael had indeed infused the rings with his emotions. He only hoped Carrie Addison's nature turned out to be as malleable as the gold.

Will left Michael smoothing the edges from the bands. As he headed to his room and bed, he promised himself that he was going to stop worrying about Michael and Carrie getting married and think positively about the situation.

He decided to let himself dream for a while about what being a grandfather was going to be like.

CHAPTER 19

"Retirement already? Wow. Your replacement certainly didn't last long. You're obviously tougher than I gave you credit for, Dad," Shane conceded, picking through the bowl of bright red apples on the kitchen table until he found one he liked.

He came back to lean on the cabinet nearest the sink where his father was loading the dishwasher. Shane preferred to look at a person's face as they talked.

"Ray only took the job as principal because I talked him into it. He was ready to stop teaching when I left. It wouldn't be right if I didn't at least make an appearance at his retirement dinner," Will said, thinking out loud more than addressing the comment to his son. "But I am not looking forward to showing up with my bald head shining."

"If you're self-conscious about your shaved head, wear a cool hat," Shane said, taking a huge bite out of the apple he snagged. "I bet Michael has some hats. All artists wear crazy hats. Remember when Michael used to pretend to be French. Man, I wish we had some of that on video."

"I'm not self-conscious about my head," Will denied easily, ignoring Shane's comment about Michael. "I just don't want to be the total topic of conversation all night with everyone who used to know me dragging everyone else over who doesn't just to see my completely bald head. Then on top of that, some of them are still trying to hook me up with women to date."

"Dad, you look great," Shane said laughing. "It's been almost two school years. People will expect you to have changed some in that time."

"They will not expect their former principal to have a shaved head and be wearing a earring. Trust me," Will said emphatically, gaining a laugh from Shane.

Shane grinned, undaunted by his father's complaining. "But I was right, wasn't I? Jessica really liked the earring, didn't she?" he demanded, pointing the half-eaten apple at his father. "I'm rarely ever wrong when it comes to women. It's a gift."

Will shook his head. His youngest attracted more women than any other adult male he'd ever met. Shane oozed "good time" doing nothing more than just leaning against the counter and grinning.

"Yes. Jessica liked it," Will admitted, placing the last of the dishes into the dishwasher. "It was one of the first things she noticed."

"There's the answer then to both your problems. Take Jessica along as your date," Shane said, smiling and shrugging. "Her presence would explain everything, stop people from fixing you up, and you wouldn't have to deal with the teasing about your head because she'd intimidate them with her presence."

Will sighed. "I like your thinking, but I can't ask her."

"Why?" Shane asked incredulously, managing to swallow a mouthful of apple as he watched his father's guilty expression get even more so. "It's a retirement dinner. She's a teacher too. Isn't she the perfect date?"

"She's perfect in a lot of ways," Will said sincerely. "But Jessica thinks I'm only an artist. I never told her anything else."

"So tell her," Shane said, wrinkling his face and shrugging "What's the big deal? It's not like you're ashamed of what you did for a living. I mean, you aren't—are you?"

"No, but I'm ashamed that I waited so long to tell Jessica about something that was a big part of who I've been most my life," Will said. "I'm ashamed I kept something so simple from her. I kept meaning to tell her, especially as we kept getting closer. It just never seemed to come up at the right time. I guess I've been waiting to work it into the conversation, but we've had bigger things to deal with that side-tracked me from confessing."

Will stared out the window over the sink. This wasn't a big deal.

"No, I'm going to Ray's dinner alone, and then I'll tell her after. Jessica can go with me to the next one."

"Mom's going," Shane said, tossing the apple core in trash. "I think she's going by herself too. When Luke called last night, she mentioned it to him, but I think he said no. She cried for an hour after she hung up. It's not working out so good for them."

"Yeah. Your mother makes sure I'm fully aware that it isn't working out for them," Will said bitterly. "You're not thinking she and I will get back together are you?"

"God, no," Shane said earnestly. "Mom and Luke genuinely seem like they belong together. They both enjoy the same pretentions—I mean, activities. I'm just feeling sorry for Mom. She seems hurt and confused about what Luke expects from her. I also don't think she's very happy with her life in general."

Will knew Shane always had a soft spot for Ellen and her melodrama. His son had even once seriously dated a woman that could have been Ellen's clone in everything except hair color, complete with a negative attitude toward his art.

Will sighed again, this time with resignation. "You want me to talk to her, don't you, son?"

"I just think that you and Mom need to continue to work on being friends," Shane said. He punched his father lightly in the arm, still knocking him sideways from the sink, making both of them laugh. Shane was famous in the family for breaking things because of his strength.

"I read that it's good for the children of divorced parents to know their mother and father have a solid relationship, despite their differences," he told his father.

"Really? Are you going to expect Jessica to follow your sage advice if she becomes your stepmother, Dr. Larson? I can tell you your biological mother has already burned the friendship bridge with Jessica a couple of times," Will said, flicking Shane sharply with the end of the dish towel and making him yelp. "If you want to help someone, talk to your mother about your theories of friendship. She's in great need of some counseling about honoring people's personal boundaries."

Shane snickered. "You don't have to use my lingo to try and soften the truth, Dad. Michael already told me Mom made a pass at you," he said, laughing openly. "My brother is bribing me for a share of the profits from my book."

Will snorted about the book. "Michael talks too much. He needs to worry about his own life more," he said, staring out in the courtyard.

Shane studied the worry in his father's gaze. He had tried really hard not to be the cause over the last couple of years. That's why he had paid for the rest of his education himself when he saw his parents were having problems getting along. He didn't want to be an additional burden.

"Well, I just want you to know that I use a condom every time with no exceptions just like you made me promise to do when I was a teenager," Shane said sincerely. "You do not have to worry about me getting anyone pregnant. It's not going to happen."

"Michael said he and Carrie used one every time as well," Will said quietly. "Sometimes the unexpected just happens, Shane. That's why it's good to be selective and only get to that level of intimacy with women you genuinely like. If it does happen, you really want it to be with a woman you care about or love, not just some random stranger you picked up in a bar."

"I stopped picking up women too," Shane blurted. "I mean—you don't have to worry about me getting some random woman pregnant. I'm not doing the bar thing anymore. I haven't been with a woman at all in almost five months now. I just wasn't broadcasting the fact."

Will turned and stared at his son in open-mouthed shock. "Seriously?"

Shane nodded and held his father's gaze. "If I hadn't already stopped, I would have when Michael told me what happened to him. I honestly don't want that to happen to me."

"I know waiting gets a little lonely, but being selective doesn't mean the right one won't come along sooner than you think," Will assured his son. "Trust me. I just stopped by the café for coffee, and the next thing I knew I was zipping to Berea with a sexy redhead wrapped around me on the bike."

"God, that sounds good," Shane said, sighing. "I'd like to just have a girlfriend to do things with when I wasn't working. That's actually what I want."

"Well, having a girlfriend is good," Will said, nodding. "Having a wife is even better, but that may take a while to happen. The best relationships always seem to need the most work."

"Well, my money is on you marrying Jessica," Shane said, smiling. "Michael though is going to need some divine intervention because he doesn't stand a chance in hell of making up for what he did to Carrie in college. He doesn't even get why it still hurts her, but that kind of betrayal causes some major damage. Trust issues are probably going to come up time and again in their relationship, even if by some miracle she ends up staying married to him. Their odds are not good. I told him that he needs to start planning on being a single father."

"Maybe, but sometimes you just have to believe in what you feel and go for it," Will told his youngest. "Screw the odds."

"*Screw the odds*," Shane repeated. "Now that sounds like a good chapter title for my book. I think it belongs on the one about the father who remarries a tall sexy redhead after his traumatic divorce from the cool sexy blonde who threw him over for a younger man."

Will flicked him sharply with the dish towel again, sending Shane dashing for the kitchen door while he laughed.

~

"JESSICA! IT'S SO GOOD TO SEE YOU. I'M SORRY TO GET YOU IN SO LATE IN the day, but I asked the office to schedule you as soon as possible. I can't stay over, but hopefully we can still get to some of what you need to talk about. My notes said you had a new issue to discuss."

Jessica smiled at the woman who was a decade older than her, but looked a decade younger with her trim pink suit and a fashionable haircut that a runway model would envy.

"Dr. Whitmore, are you hiding the fountain of youth somewhere and not sharing? I swear you look younger every year," Jessica told her. "You could practically pass for my daughter."

"Look who's talking," the woman replied with broad smile. "Your body still looks like it did when I met you, or at least like it did after Brooke was born. Super models would kill for your trim figure."

"My figure is an optical illusion created by quality spandex and expensive lace support bras," Jessica teased. "My breasts have succumbed to gravity at last. It makes me sad even though the guy I'm with right now doesn't seem to mind that they sway in the breeze. He seems to think it's sexy. I really appreciate that about him."

"Is that what you need to talk about today?" Dr. Whitmore asked, leaning excitedly on the desk. "I'd love to hear about a new guy. Is he as yummy as all your others?"

Jessica sighed at the old term they'd shared for all the years she'd been seeing the same therapist.

"Yes. Will is very yummy. The problem is that he reminds me of Nathan. I've been having dreams. Some of the memories of my time with Nathan are starting to return."

"Really? After all this time, that's pretty amazing. Does this seem like a good thing to you?" Dr. Whitmore asked carefully.

"I don't know," Jessica said honestly. "He—Will reminds me of Nathan in many ways and encourages me to remember him. I don't get them confused, but I also don't know how I feel about either man sometimes. Do you think I could still be grieving for Nathan after all this time? Every time I think about how I feel about Will, I start to feel guilty and think of Nathan. Is that normal?"

Dr. Whitmore laughed. "Anything can be normal. The question is does it *feel* normal to you? If it does, then it's normal."

"I've never cared about any other man enough to walk through your office door and talk about marrying again, so no—what I feel about Will doesn't feel normal to me," Jessica said, closing her eyes. "But the idea of never being with him again feels worse."

"Are you falling in love at last?" Dr. Whitmore asked, trying not to sound as surprised as she felt. "What was his name again—Will?"

Jessica nodded. "Yes. Will—Everett Williams. I like him. I care about him. I don't want to date other men. Do you think I'm falling in love with him? I never loved the other guys."

"You've forgotten how this works," Dr. Whitmore teased. "I'm the therapist and I get to ask the questions. You have to answer them. So what do you like about this man?"

"Will is a stone sculptor. He does nudes," Jessica confirmed. "They're incredible. That's all he does as far as I can tell, but he seems to make a good living from it."

"Why would you care if the man is financially successful?" Dr. Whitmore asked. "Is his success important to you?"

Jessica suddenly had trouble swallowing past the lump in her throat. "It's important to me for Will to be happy."

Dr. Whitmore leaned over her desk and smiled at Jessica. "Do you know what would make Will happy?"

Jessica squirmed in her chair. "Being with me—being married to me. That's what Will says he wants."

"How about you? What do you want?" Dr. Whitmore asked, trying to settle her heartbeat as she studied the flushed face of a woman who had struggled her way out of the darkness of her past. If anyone ever deserved a happy ending and a husband who loved her madly, Jessica Daniels did.

"I don't know what I want—other than to not be confused," Jessica said softly.

"Do you want Will?" Dr. Whitmore asked.

"Yes," Jessica said, breathing a sigh of relief to be able to say at least one thing with confidence.

"Do you want to keep Will in your life?" Dr. Whitmore demanded softly.

Jessica searched for that answer and found it waiting in the same place as the other one. "Yes. I want to keep him in my life. It's been a long time since I've wanted to extend a relationship."

"So start there," Dr. Whitmore said. "Make keeping Will in your life okay for yourself and just see how it goes. Come back in about a month and we'll talk about whether you are falling in love again."

"What about the memories of Nathan?" Jessica asked.

Dr. Whitmore stood and walked to her bookshelf. She pulled a book and brought it over to Jessica. "Take this and read it. This book offers some practical ways to deal with your grieving. I believe you'll find it helpful. Most grieving is just a process of letting go. You're a master at that, Jessica. So use those skills to help yourself let go of Nathan. I believe it's time."

"Is there any way around remembering or going through all the crying stuff?" Jessica asked.

"No. Not really. If you have a bunch of grieving stored up, you have to let it out. But the big grief eventually passes, and then if you're lucky, sweet memories linger. There's no one process that works for everyone," Dr. Whitmore said kindly. "In the meantime though, I would suggest you limit talking in bed so you won't accidentally call Will by Nathan's name. I've known that to cause problems."

Jessica flushed remembering all the times she fussed at Will for talking too much.

"I don't like to talk anyway," she said, half laughing. "It messes with my concentration. I don't like my lovers to talk either."

Tucking the book under one arm, she stood to leave, and so did Dr. Whitmore.

"Do come back in a month," Dr. Whitmore entreated. "Let's move you past this quickly."

"Sure," Jessica said, not really intending to visit again. "Sure. I can do that."

~

AGAINST HIS BETTER JUDGMENT, WILL DROVE BY SHANE'S AND PICKED UP Ellen on the way to the retirement dinner. He really wanted to reach some sort of platonic level of friendship with his ex-wife, but didn't hold much hope Ellen would meet him on that playing field. He would try for Michael and Shane's sake, but they were his only reasons.

"I really didn't feel like driving. Thanks for giving me a lift," Ellen said quietly. "I also didn't want to spend another evening alone with Shane. The only time that boy ever sits is when he's drawing. Then a bomb could go off and he wouldn't notice."

Will laughed and nodded. "At least he's learned to focus all that energy on one or two things. I still don't know how he got through school and did so well. Remember the tutors through middle school who said he'd never be able to concentrate long enough to learn anything?"

"Remember the high school counselor telling us we would be wasting money if we sent him to college?" Ellen asked, smiling at Will.

"Oh yes. We always knew the counselor was wrong. Michael said Shane's going to submit his dissertation for review this year," Will said proudly.

Ellen's eyes were huge. "Well, why hasn't Shane said anything to us about it?"

"I don't think he wants us to know until it's done. So don't say anything," Will said, grinning. "I'm sure he'll tell us eventually. Actually, I think Michael dared him into finishing his degree. They have a thousand dollar bet riding on it."

Ellen laughed, leaned her head back, and closed her eyes. "Reckless heathens. Your sons are heathens, but brilliant, handsome ones. Thank you for being a good father, William. I truly am grateful for that and how you stay so involved in their lives. Luke's daughter barely even talks to him."

"Well, you always wanted a girl. Maybe you can win her back to the family," Will said easily. "It can be another chapter in Shane's book. We'll be that weird blended family everyone talks about, and we'll sue Shane for a share of the money he makes during the TV interviews about us."

Ellen was openly laughing now. "Shane and his damn book. Are we really that awful?"

Will stopped laughing and glanced over at the woman he'd spent most of his life with, but no longer wanted in the same way. "We're not awful at all. We're just changing and trying to do it with as much grace as possible."

"Forcing us to change was my fault," Ellen said morosely. "I became terribly unhappy with both of us and just couldn't figure out what to do about it. When I met Luke, he made me happy again for the first time in years. My leaving was never about you, Will. It was just about some restlessness in me. I hope you can believe that."

"I'd like to believe it. So why the press to get me back? I know you still love your husband," Will told her sharply.

Ellen looked at her hands. "Yes. I still love Luke and I want him, but he's not making me happy anymore, either. I feel like his social director more than his wife. Frankly, I was less miserable with you than I am with him now. Luke says he can't stand seeing me unhappy, but I don't know how to fix myself. I'm in the same place I was right before we divorced."

"So let me get this straight—you just wanted me back because I was the lesser of two evils and more tolerant of your miserable personality," Will summed up, grinning.

Ellen sighed and shook her head. "It's not as bad as you're making it sound."

"It's not good either," Will declared, laughing. "I don't want to be your back-up plan, Ellen. Have you told Luke how you feel? Maybe he might have some ideas about how to make you happy."

Ellen nodded. "He's logical, but not in the same way I am. He didn't even get mad at me when I told him I was unhappy in our marriage. He just withdrew, and now we're hardly talking. He wouldn't come with me tonight. I'm guessing I'll be getting divorce papers from him shortly. Legal speed is a side benefit of marrying a lawyer."

Will sighed in sympathy but firmed his tone to make sure Ellen knew he was serious. "Well, I'm sorry about the problems between you and Luke, but you need to get your shit straight about men."

She shrugged. "I know. I brought this on myself. Maybe I'll move in with Michael and his new bride after the baby comes. I can be a live-in grandmother. That will give me something to do."

Will roared with laughter. "You're going to want to steer clear of that couple unless they beg for help. I'm getting my own place in a couple of weeks because Michael's house is going to be an emotional war zone for a while. They have a lot to work through."

Ellen laughed. "I know you're right. Michael and his stubbornness are not easy to live with anyway. So what do you think I should do then? Retirement is boring. Luke's career gave me a hobby at least. Without him, I have nothing to do."

"You have your master's degree. Go back to teaching. Teach at the college level this time. It will be a whole new group of friends too," Will suggested.

"I guess that would be better than doing nothing," Ellen said, sighing. "I can't believe you're happier now."

"I took my time and waited for the right person to come along. That's part of it," Will told her. "The other thing is, I have always had my art. I know you don't get it, but it's the most important thing I do with my time. When I see a finished piece, it satisfies me in a way nothing else can."

"I don't remember you being so difficult to satisfy when we were married. I know I'm better in bed than she is," Ellen said, trying a bit of flirting.

"There's a lot I'm not going to say to you, but just know I've gone to a whole new level with my expectations," Will warned. "Jessica exceeds everything I thought I wanted after I got over you."

Ellen reached over and patted his hand. "Don't worry. I won't put any more moves on you, but I will tell you that if I get divorced, you can come back to me anytime you want."

"Better put all your energy into saving your marriage with Luke. You'll have a better chance of being happy," Will advised, pulling into the parking lot of Art's Place downtown. "I'm planning on marrying Jessica Daniels as soon as she agrees."

"Well good luck with that one," Ellen said, climbing from the car. "I think she only ever married the first guy."

"That's a truth, but I intend to be the last man in her life whether she marries me or not," Will said, holding the door open while Ellen walked inside.

~

"SO WHERE IS THIS GUY YOU WANTED ME TO CHECK OUT," JESSICA ASKED her teacher friend, Susan Rafferty. "I need to look quickly and go. The guy I'm dating is not going to like me scoping out future men to date when he's not around. I'm feeling guilty already."

"*Guilty?* You—the queen of no regrets? Well relax, this is not a bar and you're not picking anyone up," Susan told her laughing. "I won't even introduce you unless you want me to. I just wanted you to *see* him."

Jessica sipped her coke and studied her knee length black dress and sedate pumps, both leftovers from her Jack the Jerk days. Dating him was probably the last time she bought formal clothes. Wearing the bland formal clothing always depressed her, but it was such high quality that she saved them for school events. She couldn't wait to get home and back into her jeans.

"Oh damn," Susan said in a whisper. "He looks great, but he came in with his ex-wife. Now I'm sorry I even talked you into coming."

Jessica turned and her gaze went immediately to the door, where she saw Will ushering Ellen inside. At first, all she could think was how silly Will looked in a hat. Then the truth of what she was seeing hit her with the impact of a semi-truck colliding with a compact car.

"Who—which guy are you talking about?" Jessica said, fighting to keep the tremble from her voice.

Susan sighed. "The guy in the silly hat is the one I wanted you to see. His name is William Larson. He's an absolute doll, one of the nicest men that ever walked the earth. He was the principal at my school for years. His wife left him for a younger man, but I hadn't heard they had gotten back together. The woman was always a pill. I hope you believe I'm truly surprised."

Jessica swallowed hard. "Sure, even people you think you know well can surprise you sometimes," she said, anger at the situation finally kicking in and overwhelming the hurt. "Why don't you introduce me anyway? Let's liven up the evening and give Larson's ex-wife something to think about."

"Are you serious?" Susan asked, her eyes widening. "Does Larson look that interesting to you?"

"Yes. He does. In fact, I've never been more interested in a man in my life," Jessica said, the irony of her words making her tone far more enthusiastic than she was feeling.

"Well, let's do it then," Susan said on a laugh. "I was trying to pay you back for introducing me to Steve by finding you an equally great guy. Little Miss Ex-Wife better look out if Jessica Daniels is interested in her man."

"You and Steve are both sweeties, and I couldn't be happier," Jessica said sincerely, putting her plans for murder and mayhem on the back burner for a moment. "Some of us have a lot harder time finding a good man."

"You had Steve once," Susan reminded her, though she knew that was over long before Steve landed in her life and took over her heart.

Jessica sipped her coke. "No. I never really *had* Steve. I dated Steve, but we never connected on the super important levels. What you two have is the way it's supposed to work."

"So you think you're going to connect with William Larson?" Susan asked, looking across the room at the giant man who didn't seem very interested in anyone this evening.

"I can guarantee it," Jessica stated emphatically.

Susan laughed and thought for the millionth time since she'd known her that Jessica was the bravest, boldest woman she had ever met in her life.

"Well, let's do this then," she said brightly, taking Jessica's arm and leading her across the room.

~

LUKE CANNON HAD BEEN WALKING AROUND THE CROWD LOOKING FOR HIS wife when he spotted her coming through the door with her ex-husband's hand at her back. He had missed his wife and had wrongly assumed she would miss him too much to stay away this long.

Maybe he should have just agreed to come with her tonight, he decided, but it never occurred to him she'd hook up with Will if he didn't. Coming here with Will was probably just to spite him, but still it stung his pride. His wife's lingering admiration for her ex was one of many sore points in their marriage that still needed to be worked out, even though Luke had never doubted Ellen's love for him.

Seeing them getting along bothered the hell out of him, but it was just jealousy. Or at least Luke hoped it was.

Ellen and her ex couldn't be getting back together. He refused to believe it. Larson lost her, Luke thought bitterly, and the man needed to accept the fact.

Once he and Ellen were back together, Luke was going to make damn sure she never spent another night away from him—starting with tonight.

~

WILL WAS TALKING TO A GROUP OF PEOPLE HE HADN'T SEEN IN YEARS AND so absorbed in the conversation that he didn't see the additional two women step up to his side. From the corner of his eye, Will did finally recognize Susan Rafferty, a teacher from his school, when she placed a soft hand on his sleeve.

"Will? I'd like you to meet a friend of mine. Jessica, this is William Larson. Will, this is my friend Jessica Daniels. She teaches art at Henry Clay High School," Susan finished and drew Jessica forward.

Will froze in shock as he met Jessica's accusing, furious glare.

"Mr. Larson. How very interesting to meet you. You look remarkably like the man I've been dating for two months. You wouldn't have an evil twin would you?" Jessica said, her tone daring him to lie to her in front of witnesses.

Will was trying to think of what to say when Ellen slipped an arm around his waist from the back and stepped to the other side of him.

Ellen started to tell Will someone was looking for him when her eyes raised to the tall redhead dressed in formal black who was currently glaring down at her like she was a bug that needed squashing.

"Either take your hands off Will or get your ass kicked in public," Jessica told Ellen, smiling as the woman took two steps away.

Everyone who had been talking to Will bit their lips to keep from laughing, but they still slipped away discreetly. Probably to get a better view of the whole drama from a safe distance, Jessica thought meanly, wishing she could bite out her tongue for what she had said to Ellen and how totally possessive it had sounded.

Then Jessica felt a firm hand on her arm and turned to see a well-dressed, handsome man looking kindly into her eyes. He rubbed her arm in a friendly manner and walked around her.

"If you kick Ellen's ass that would be assault, and I'm afraid I would have to sue. She's not always the nicest person, but I can't really let you physically harm my wife," Luke said, walking to his wife's side.

Ellen stared up at her husband in shock and looked at Will, who still hadn't said a word. She looked at Jessica, and then back to Luke.

"This is not what you're thinking, either of you. Will and I are not here together. I swear, he just gave me a ride," Ellen said.

"Oh, I have no trouble at all believing Will gave you a ride," Jessica said, snorting.

"Now look," Will said, finally finding his voice and glaring back at Jessica for the insinuation. "You know damn well that's not what Ellen meant. She's not my date. We just drove here together. Trust me."

"Trust you? You mean—I should just believe you because you're such an honest guy, *Mr. William Larson*? Do you have any other aliases you're hiding from me?" Jessica asked sardonically, crossing her arms.

"I didn't mean to not tell you about being a principal. It just was one of those weird things," Will said. "It seemed so much less important than everything else that was going on."

"Sure it did. I mean I've been keeping all kinds of things from my life secret from you. By the way, my friend Susan is Steve Lipton's fiancée. She brought me here specifically to meet you. If she had said your damn name before I got here, I'd already be shopping for the next guy I intend to date."

"Wait. You mean you already know Will?" Susan asked, confused—and alarmed at the fury and pain showing in her friend's face.

Ignoring everyone else around them, Jessica contemplated Will with a combination of disgust and disappointment. "No. I don't know Will. I know a man named Everett Williams. Or at least I thought I did, but sleeping with someone really doesn't give you any insights into who they really are. Two months and this man never even told me his real name. Of course, you'd think I'd have figured it out when I met his son, *Michael William Larson*. I just never thought to ask the obvious question because I was told over and over and over how much Will hates lying. I just figured the children had taken their mother's name or some other strange thing."

"Look, maybe we could just go somewhere more private so I can explain. I swear I never meant to not tell you," Will pleaded. "This is not a big deal. I just wanted you to know about my art first."

"Right, and that worked out so well for us. Remember the fight in Berea, Will? Using that same reasoning, I guess from your standpoint, me seeing you walk into a place I didn't know you would be with your hand on your ex-wife's back is also no big deal, right?" Jessica asked.

"I admit it looks strange," Will said quietly. "But it's not what you're thinking."

"You never even mentioned your plans to me tonight or that you intended to bring your ex as your date. I told you I had a school function," Jessica said, uncrossing her arms and sighing. "You told me nothing."

"I didn't want to get into it until I could explain why I never told you," Will said, but his defense sounded weak even to his own ears. "And I didn't bring Ellen as my date. I just gave her a ride." At her furious glare, Will blushed. "Damn it Jessica, you know what I mean."

Tired of looking at Will's guilty expression, Jessica looked over at Luke Cannon, and then at Ellen who stared blankly at all of them, still showing no signs of remorse. The need to even the score with the woman was suddenly just too much to fight. No one would ever have accused Jessica of being noble, because she wasn't. Twice now the woman had made a fool of her with Will, but there was not going to be a third.

"Maybe next time you make a move on Will, you'll get the response you wanted from him last weekend. You win, Ellen. I give up. You can have Will back now. I'm done with him."

Ellen's shocked gaze swung to her husband, whose injured look moved between her and Will in disbelief that all too rapidly changed to acceptance.

"Okay. Well, I guess there's no use wasting my time chasing after you," Luke said, turning on his heel and walking to the door.

Ellen looked at Jessica, still having trouble believing the woman had said all she had, and then chased out the door after her husband. "Luke," she called, trying to get him to stop and listen. She still couldn't believe he'd come looking for her.

"That was a pretty mean thing to do," Will said, frowning. He never would have guessed Jessica could be so vindictive, not that Ellen didn't deserve a little of that heat.

"Yes, it was completely mean, but it was also brutally honest. Now if they work things out, her husband will know what kind of woman his wife really is," Jessica said without remorse. "And here's a piece of brutal honesty for you—we are over."

"No, we're not," Will denied, pulling the hat from his head, his temper starting to flare as his own frustration grew. "You're just mad at me. I can see why, but I swear tonight is nothing—absolutely nothing like you think it is. Ellen was never my date."

"Right. I'd stick with that story myself. It sounds great. By the way, keep your sons away from me too. I will not be nice to them next time either. I never want to see any of your family ever again," Jessica said.

She turned to look at the woman she'd used to blast Will. It was her single regret of the evening. "Susan, I'm sorry if I embarrassed you. I was shocked and—well, I'm sorry. I just couldn't believe Will had kept something so simple from me, but I should have told you I knew him when you first pointed him out. It was a shock to see him with his ex-wife and I overreacted."

"Are you going to be all right?" Susan asked, ignoring everything except the shattered expression on her friend's face.

"I'm a survivor," Jessica said enigmatically. "Tell Steve I said hi. I'll see you guys at the wedding."

Jessica walked to the door, down the steps, and out to the parking lot on the side of the building where a crying Ellen was sobbing as her husband stood with his arms crossed glaring down at her. She wanted to walk past them, climb in her car, and get the hell away from anyone connected to the Larson family. Instead, she walked over to the fighting couple because she wasn't quite as hard-hearted as she wanted to be.

"Please tell Luke I never cheated on him. I didn't. I wouldn't," Ellen implored. "Neither did Will. He hasn't touched me since the divorce. I swear."

Jessica looked at the good-looking man with pain in his gaze and a clenched jaw that was uncompromising at that moment. Ellen was going to have to do a lot to get back into his good graces, but Jessica knew it went both ways. Being eye-to-eye with the man helped make sure the man held her gaze as she spoke.

"Mr. Cannon, what I said was the truth, but I don't think anything happened. Don't get me wrong, I'm still plenty pissed about Ellen flirting when she knew Will and I were lovers. I didn't bother kicking her ass that day because Will did a good job convincing me he wasn't interested in her any longer. I don't pretend to know how these people think, but I have been in therapy for thirty years. If you love your wife, it's your job to help her work out her problems," Jessica said. Then she turned and looked at Ellen. "I believe Will didn't touch you, but it wasn't because you didn't try. You're not the injured innocent here, and you need to admit that to yourself."

"Ms. Daniels—Jessica," Ellen called. "Will does love you. That's mostly what we talked about on the trip over here. I don't know why he didn't tell you about his teaching work, but it's nothing compared to how much he cares about you. You need to forgive him."

"Really? Would I be forgiving Everett Williams the stone sculptor or William Larson the retired principal? Will just yanked my trust foundation out from under me and I don't know what to believe anymore. You'd be upset too if you were in my shoes," Jessica said.

Ellen just blinked at her as Jessica shook her head and walked on.

CHAPTER 20

Tucking the papers he carried under his arm, and gripping a jeweler's box in his hand to discreetly hide it, Michael walked into the offices of The Main Event Marketing and Promotion Company. He smiled at the receptionist, suddenly glad he had never dated the beautiful blonde who smiled at him in welcome each time she saw him.

"Hey, Belinda. Is Carrie in?" Michael asked.

"She is, but I'm not sure she's seeing clients today, Michael. Carrie's not been feeling well," she said sweetly. "Can I give her a message?"

"This is not a business visit. It's personal, and Carrie's expecting me. You can tell her I'm here if you want," he offered.

Belinda blinked and raised her eyebrows at his tone. "She didn't mention you were coming by, but if she's expecting you, then I guess you can go on back."

"Thanks. I just need to drop something off with her, and then I'll be on my way," Michael said, rapping the knuckles of his free hand on her counter as he walked by.

Carrie's door was mostly closed, but not completely. He could see through the crack that she had her head down on the desk and a trashcan at her feet. There had to be something she could take for the sickness, Michael thought, his own stomach contracting in empathy.

He knocked lightly and pushed open the door. She raised her head and tried to sit up straight when she saw him. Michael closed the door behind him and walked over to sit in the chair across from her.

"Are you this sick all the time?" he asked softly, keeping his voice quiet.

"It comes and goes," Carrie said weakly. "I hear I only have two more months of this before it gets better."

"Well, that's depressing as hell," Michael said seriously, getting a little laugh out of her when he wasn't even trying. "There has to be something you can take to help with the sickness."

"I'm going to ask tomorrow at my appointment," Carrie said. "I should have just stayed home today, but I haven't been at work in over a week.

"I'd like to go with you to the doctor tomorrow," Michael told her. "What time is your appointment and where?"

"You don't have to do that," Carrie said, looking away from him.

"I want to," Michael said firmly. "I have a lot of catching up to do and a lot to learn about having a baby. I bought some books, but I learn best by talking to people."

"Michael, you don't have to worry. I'll do what I have to in order to take care of the child and me." She pushed her hair behind her ears and again tried to sit straight in her chair. "Why don't you tell me why you're here? I'm guessing you haven't changed your mind."

"No, I haven't changed my mind. In fact, I came to ask you to marry me," Michael told her, watching her face to see her reaction. The shock was swift and drained the remaining color from her face. Well, at least she wasn't yelling at him. He knew she could because he'd heard her yelling at her crew on many occasions.

"No," Carrie said firmly, absolutely certain of her answer. She was not marrying Michael Larson, did not want to bind herself to a man she didn't really like.

"I thought you might say no, but I figured it was worth a shot to just ask in the traditional way first," Michael told her, slipping the papers from under his arm and pushing them across her polished desk to her. "Here are the reasons it's a good idea. They are all in a contract I had my lawyer draw up. It's a prenuptial agreement that requires we marry and stay married until baby is born, which will give me unquestionable legal rights to our child after we divorce. It also requires that we live together so that our marriage will seem legitimate to the world and which will also make it easier for me to establish parental rights."

"What happens if I don't marry you?" Carrie asked, her throat dry and her heart banging against the walls of her chest. What Michael was saying made her suddenly realize that there were many things she had not taken into consideration when she'd offered him the chance to raise their child.

"I have to go through the motions of dragging you and the baby through court to prove I'm the father, which means DNA testing and God knows what else. Then there would be custody agreements and having to explain why the birth mother doesn't want any rights to the child. Every other alternative but marriage is ugly, very public in the legal records, and not good for any of us. If you marry me, I can have the child when we divorce and no one will question it," Michael said, working to keep his tone neutral and his words logical, but it was a battle he was losing. "If you keep looking at me like I'm the worst man in the world, I'm coming around the desk to prove I'm not."

"No, stay where you are," Carrie said, holding up a hand and closing her eyes. "I just—I just hadn't thought about it from the legal standpoint. It's hard to think of rational next steps when you're throwing up all the time."

"I can't even imagine how you're managing to get through the day. So will you marry me? You've been married and divorced twice already. I can be just as civilized as the first two guys," he said carefully. "Marry me, Carrie Addison. Make me the legal father of our child. The prenuptial agreement guarantees you a divorce after the baby is born and is three months old. You don't have to live with me after you deliver the child. I understand that would hard."

Carrie flipped a couple pages of the prenuptial agreement, skimming the contract terms. Everything seemed to say exactly what Michael had told her, but it didn't seem real for her to be even considering marrying the man who had caused her so much pain.

"I need some time to look over this agreement, and I may want changes. However, I do see that marriage would legally simplify our —arrangement," she admitted quietly.

"Is that a yes?" Michael asked, wondering if it was really going to be this simple.

Carrie searched Michael Larson's gaze, looking to see how genuine the man was being with her. She couldn't tell much, but then her head was in a fog of nausea anyway.

"I guess marrying you makes some kind of sense," Carrie said sarcastically. "It's not like it's forever. What's one more divorce in my personal resume anyway? I don't want to have to do some bogus court battle over your rights to your child either."

"Thank you for agreeing with me, but is that a yes to my proposal?" Michael asked.

"I guess it's a yes," she said wearily.

"Good. Here's a ring," Michael pushed the ring box across the desk. "It comes back to me after the divorce, but it will help us build a story that will protect your reputation here. There's no reason for you to let this affect the career you've spent years growing."

Carrie looked at the ring container like it contained poison, but she reached out a hand and pulled it to her. She was so weak she couldn't pry open the tight box.

Michael did jump up then and stalk around the desk. He couldn't stand not helping her any longer. He put a hip on the desk to keep as much distance between them as possible. It was hard as hell not to touch her.

"Here," he said briskly, pulling the box open and taking the ring from inside.

Michael picked up Carrie's left hand and slid the diamond solitaire on her finger. It was just about a perfect fit and he couldn't believe he'd guessed it right when he'd had it sized.

"It probably needs to be a little bigger so you can still wear it as you gain weight with the baby."

Michael let her hand drop gently back onto the desk. Then he moved back around to the chair so he wouldn't give in to the temptation to pull her into his arms and hold her.

"The prenuptial agreement also stipulates that I go to all doctor's visits and check-ups as well as be allowed into the delivery room. If you just rebel at the delivery room idea, I'll try to understand, but I want to be involved in the birth. If I have to do this alone later—well, I just want to know all I can," he said.

And I want to be there to take care of you, Michael thought, not liking the fact that the strong woman he was used to seeing looked like she was going to fall into a dead faint any moment.

Carrie shook her head and shrugged, barely hearing what Michael said. She was still staring at the ring, which was amazing. "It's a beautiful ring."

"It was my grandmother's, but I had it reinforced with more gold." Michael wanted to smile because she liked the ring. Well, he wanted to scoop her up, hold her, and study how the ring looked on her hand, but he knew that couldn't happen—not yet anyway.

"I'll be careful with the ring," Carrie said quietly. "I gave back rings to both my exes. I'm used to the procedure."

"You also need to know that I told my family the truth about our situation, even my mother knows some of it. They know we're marrying for the sake of the baby. They will help us, and I need their help, so I didn't want to have to lie to them," Michael told her. "They won't judge you. They're just glad we're choosing to have the baby. My mother and father are thrilled to be getting a grandchild."

Carrie nodded, opened a desk drawer, and grabbed a tissue. Crying had become another daily activity just as much as being sick was.

"Sounds like you have a great family. I haven't told mine yet. They're still upset I got divorced the first time, much less the second. I'm dreading what they're going to say when I tell them I'm pregnant. I don't think they will understand any of it."

"So don't tell them the truth. It's not worth stressing over it. Tell them the same story you tell the office," Michael said.

"What story is that?" Carrie asked sarcastically, sniffing.

Michael leaned forward, meeting and holding her gaze. "Tell them as much of the truth as you can manage with a clear conscience, starting with the fact that I've loved you for years and that you got pregnant in a moment of unplanned passion. When they see us together, no one is going to think we married for any reason other than love, because that's how I feel about you and it's going to show. Only you and I will know there is a time limit and that you are likely never going to love me back. The details are our business."

"Then I become as bad as I'm accusing you of being. I'm just using you to save myself," Carrie said, tearing up as she thought about all the wrongs that would not be made right by what they were doing.

"It's okay. I can handle the heat, and I owe you," Michael said, clenching his jaw in determination.

He leaned back in the seat, noticing the color was finally coming back into her face. Telling her family must really be worrying her.

God, was he ever grateful for his family, even as messed up as they currently were. They gave him shit over what happened when he told them, but he knew they also would support him. They would support Carrie too.

"So I thought we'd give people a little time to absorb the engagement, and then get married in three weeks before you start showing," Michael said. "In the meantime, I want you to move into the house with me and my father. I'm in the process of moving into a guestroom so you can use the master. It has a private bath. You can have your own space that way."

"Why do you want me in your house?" Carrie asked.

"You need someone to help you until the sickness passes. Then after that, you're going to need support as well, even if it is just to fix you dinner at the end of a long day. I've had both my divorced parents under my roof lately. You can't be any more trouble than them," Michael said lightly. "I do draw the line at the UK ballgames. The TV is solely mine on game days."

"That figures," Carrie snorted, trying to join in the weak joke.

"There's a small television in your bedroom. I'm not completely selfish," Michael said, grinning.

Was she actually agreeing to this madness? She thought of her bathroom at home and how she had been too sick to clean up after herself. That was probably reason enough to let him help her. This was his child after all. Her condition was his fault as well as hers.

"I'm too sick to turn down the offer," she told him finally. "But I'm keeping my own place regardless of how it looks. I want contingency clauses in the prenuptial agreement if it doesn't work out."

Michael nodded his head. "Send your stipulations to the attorney listed on the agreement. He'll let me know. I'll get back to you on anything I disagree with."

"Don't read too much into my capitulation, Michael," Carrie said tiredly. "The situation isn't giving me much choice."

Michael stood and walked to the door. "Come spend a couple days as a trial, and then we'll move your things this weekend. By then you'll have settled into the space."

"If you want to meet me here tomorrow at one, you can drive me to the doctor's appointment," she said weary of the whole situation. "When I get to feeling better, I'm probably going to regret letting you talk me into this."

"We'll deal with that when the time comes," Michael told her. "You want me to take you home?"

Carrie shook her head. "The wave has passed for the moment. I need to get as much done as I can before the next one hits."

"See you tomorrow then," Michael said, keeping his back to her. "I'm glad you like the ring. It suits you."

CHAPTER 21

"Well, at least Jessica's not still mad at you," Will said, sipping his cold coffee just for something to do. "I would have told her it was my fault that you didn't tell, but she's not talking to me."

Melanie topped off Will's coffee to warm it up. The man was barely functional.

"Any other time she would have laughed about finding out about your past. It's a silly thing to be so mad about, and I'm not buying that's the problem," Melanie said, for once taking Will's side over Jessica's. "Something else is going on with Jessica. She's back in therapy. I only know this because she left here to go there and accidentally mentioned it. Then she looked like she wished she hadn't."

Will closed his eyes, feeling the hurt to the depths of him. It was Nathan, he thought. Jessica had gone back to therapy because she was remembering Nathan. Also his fault, he decided, even as he wondered for the millionth time how he managed to do so much unintentional damage to the woman he loved.

"Jessica has survived a lot worse in her life than our relationship," Will said softly. "I'm sure what we had will seem like nothing more than a minor speed bump along the road of her life one day soon."

"I'm not worried about her getting over you. I'm worried because she's stopped flirting," Melanie said briskly. "I've known Jessica Daniels for over a decade. Men come and go, but this is the first time she has gotten to a point where she doesn't flirt, laugh, or tease no matter what a man says to her. Poor old Mr. Beaumont was devastated when she didn't kiss him on the cheek when she left the other day."

"Great. It's barely been a week and she's kissing other men already," Will said morosely.

"No, it's not great. Mr. Beaumont is ninety-two. Jessica always flirts with him and kisses him goodbye." Melanie wiped the counter furiously. "She's not happy anymore, Will. That's what always set her apart from other women. Jessica Daniels was always happy with herself. She was my role model."

Will wanted the ground to just open up and swallow him. His guilt over ruining Jessica Daniels' happy life was so heavy it was breaking his back to stand up straight.

"I can't fix this if she won't talk to me," Will said sadly, rubbing his face as he slid off the bar stool. He tucked bills beside his coffee cup and picked up his helmet. "If you have any suggestions, let me know."

Melanie nodded and watched Will walk out the door. She could think of nothing this time to help either of them. The best she could hope for was for Jessica to come around.

~

"I KNOW IT'S BEEN A WHILE SINCE I CAME BY FOR A VISIT, BUT I MET THIS man I really needed to talk to you about. The funny thing is he's a lot like you."

Jessica dropped to the grass besides Nathan Daniels' grave and sat. The Lexington Cemetery was as beautiful as any park, and you forgot that if you didn't visit much.

"I'm thinking about marrying him, Nathan. What I feel for him has made it pretty obvious to me that I need to let go of you completely before I do.

She plucked at the grass and ran a hand over the ground.

"You were a good husband for the short time we were together. I know you couldn't be there after the rape, but I always thought you somehow sent the good men my way to help me. I just never could get serious about any of them though."

Jessica reached out and arranged the flowers she'd brought with her in the little vase she had buried in the ground by his headstone years ago.

"Okay. So the man's name is William Larson. He's both a retired principal and a stone sculptor. I'm mad at him right now because he—well, it's complicated. And stupid, I guess, if I believe everybody else. I think I have right to be upset, but Dr. Whitmore says I'm just looking for an excuse to push Will away like I did with all the other men since you. Do you think that's true?" Jessica asked sadly, her voice starting to quiver as her eyes filled with tears.

"You know, I told myself after I lost you that I was never going to love any man that much again, and I haven't until now. Dr. Whitmore keeps telling me I need to go tell Will I love him and talk things out." Jessica sniffed. "I miss him, Nathan. I don't know if that means I love him or not, but I miss him more than I even missed you when you died. I hope you think this is okay because I don't think all the therapy in the world is going to change how I feel about him."

She stood and looked down at the grave, sniffling and fighting tears while she tried to finish. "This is probably going to be my last grave visit for a very long time. I would appreciate it if you would stay out of my dreams because I really don't want any more confusion. I'm going to have to go take on an ex-wife who wants Will back, and two of the sweetest, but most interfering adult children on earth. Brooke is going to love them, but the Larson family is not restful or easy. I need a clear mind to deal with them."

Jessica pulled up the bottom of her tee shirt and used it to wipe her eyes and nose.

"You know that I'm usually not such an emotional mess. Will just does this to me. It's one of the many reasons I tried not to get involved with him for so long. But I don't think you can choose who you love.

She looked around the other graves. It wasn't her time yet. And she didn't want to go before she had lived and loved with everything in her. "You know I really loved you, Nathan. Will is the first man I've loved since you, and I just needed to let you know about him before I try to make it work."

"I hope wherever you are that you are happy," Jessica added. "Wish me luck, okay?"

She rubbed her runny nose on her sleeve again as she walked back to her car.

MICHAEL CARRIED CARRIE'S OVERNIGHT CASE INTO HIS BEDROOM AND SET it on the bed.

"So this is your room. I haven't completely emptied the bathroom yet, but I'll get that done before you move in," he said, searching her fearful gaze for signs that she was going to break and run. "Please stop looking like this is a prison cell. Can't you spin it a little bit positively in that business brain of yours?"

Carrie shook her head to clear the overwhelming confusion she felt. "Sorry. You've been great. You were great today and I—I don't mean to be ungrateful for your help."

"Okay, that's more contrition than I can handle," Michael said, walking to her and putting his arms around her to hug gently. She froze in his arms, but he ran comforting light hands over her back until she relaxed against him for a moment. "We've been lovers. You're carrying my child. You have to let me try to be your friend for a few months while we deal with this situation. I'm too emotional a person to walk around here being stoic while you hurt."

"Give me a few days," she said, pulling out of his arms and walking a few steps away. "I'll try to find some way to think about all this that won't be obnoxious."

"You're not being obnoxious," Michael declared, shoving hands in his pockets to stop from reaching for her again. "I just—look, settle in and then come find me. I'm working on a new piece out in the courtyard. Dad's out there finishing a marble bust that I think you'd enjoy seeing. My mother is picking up food on the way over. I hope the medicine will let you eat."

"Okay," Carrie said, because it seemed the only polite answer to give. "Thanks, Michael."

When Michael walked out of the room and closed the door softly behind him, Carrie collapsed on the bed and thought about how much the room smelled like him. It was the only scent that didn't seem to send her immediately running to be sick.

She stretched out with her shoes still on and closed her eyes, thinking she'd just give herself a few moments to rest. A couple minutes later she was fast asleep.

"CARRIE'S IN THE BEDROOM SETTLING IN," MICHAEL TOLD HIS FATHER AS he watched him remove the dust from the bust's breasts with a soft brush. "That's absolutely some of your best work."

Will turned and looked at his son. "I know, and thanks."

"Why a bust?" Michael asked. "Why not a full statue? A Venus de Milo with Jessica's body and face would be an amazing piece of work. Your girlfriend's hot."

"Overlooking the *hot* comment from the newly engaged man, I'm just going to tell you I chose a bust because the look on Jessica's face is what I miss the most when we're not together," Will said quietly. "The first time I picked her up to go out, she had the most eager, open expression I've ever seen on any woman over seventeen. There are very few circumstances that put that level of happiness on her face. I hope she finds someone to do that for her again. I carved what I wanted for her—for both of us."

"Jessica's coming back to you, Dad. She just needs some time to get over the fact she overreacted. I think I understand her. She and I are a lot alike," Michael said. "Damn if Shane's touchy-feely lingo isn't rubbing off on me."

"Did I hear my name being used in vain?" Shane said, walking up to his brother and father. "Where's the woman we're supposed to meet? Gee Dad, nice bust of Jessica."

"Thanks," Will said, smiling at Shane's unabashed appraisal.

Shane walked over and ran a hand over the statue's face and his fingertips over her breasts. When he looked at his father, he simply couldn't stifle the laugh at his dad's angry expression.

"What? You created it. Better get used to it being touched. It's damn near irresistible. All your statues are, Dad," Shane said, grinning.

Will sighed and frowned at him. "Put my reaction in your damn book and you will die a slow, tortuous death. Fathers have sacrificed their children throughout history. I'm still young enough to make another child to replace you."

Shane exchanged a wicked look with Michael, who was grinning but saying nothing. "Tell me you haven't wanted to touch it."

"Don't look at me, bro. I have enough problems," Michael said. "I don't need Dad upset with me."

"Your mother move completely out yet?" Will asked Shane, trying to get the conversation onto something other than the bust of Jessica and how appealing it was.

"I have the rest of her stuff in my car. She and Luke are coming to dinner, right?" Shane said.

Michael nodded. "Yes. I thought we would do one dinner meet and greet with Carrie to get it over with quickly. She's still pretty sick, so she may end up heading to her room for most of the evening. Mom is picking up the catered food I ordered. I didn't want to fill the house with cooking smells until Carrie's medicine starts to take better effect. The doctor said it would be two or three days."

Will patted Michael on the shoulder. "That was very thoughtful. Your mother was sick both times she was pregnant. It's really awful watching someone go through it. I can't imagine how it is to be the one sick for months and months."

"If there's anything I can do to help, just let me know," Shane said, keeping his voice quiet.

Michael nodded. "Just try not to scare her with your ugly mug. Are you ever going to get a haircut again or shave on a regular basis?"

Shane raked a hand through his shoulder length blond locks and tucked them back behind his ears. "There. Is that more respectable?"

"No. It's still on your head," Michael said on a laugh. "But I guess it will have to do."

A rap on the patio door had them all looking at the cool blonde smiling and waving at them.

"Mom looks so much happier. I don't know what happened, but it was good," Shane said, smiling.

Will looked at Ellen and watched her setting the food out on Michael's kitchen table. He walked back to the bust of Jessica.

"I guess Luke forgave her," Will said softly, taking a cloth and wiping the rest of the dust away.

"Yeah—thanks to Jessica," Shane said sharply. "Mom said she stopped in the parking lot and told Luke it was his job as her husband to help her be happy. Evidently, he took her advice."

Will stopped wiping to look at Shane. "I think it was a toss-up who Jessica was more angry with—me or your mother. I guess it must have been me since she actually talked to Ellen and Luke. Hell, I was just the guy sleeping with her. Why should've Jessica talked to me and given me a chance to explain?"

Shane looked at his brother. "Now I know where you got all that emotional stuff from. Dad whines just like you when he gets upset."

"*Whines?*" Michael exclaimed. "I do not whine. I express myself in a healthy way, and I'm about to sit on you while Dad takes his turn expressing himself."

Shane burst out laughing. "Well I guess before you guys gang up on me, I'll just go help Mom in the kitchen."

"Running away would be a wise choice," Will said, fixing his youngest son with a narrowed gaze. "I'm pretty physically frustrated right now. Kicking your ass appeals to me as a healthy outlet for my emotions, Dr. Larson."

Shane walked off laughing, satisfied that the only emotion the men in his family would be expressing this evening was some bullshit anger.

Michael stood there for a moment frowning at the patio door after Shane had gone inside.

"I do not whine," he said firmly, his head turning sharply at his father's belly laugh. "What's so funny?"

"If my parents were still alive, I would tell them how grateful I am to be an only child. Shane yanks your chain, and you strain on the end of it every time," Will said. "One day you're going to learn not to let him see that he's getting to you."

"He insulted you too," Michael reminded him, grinning.

"Yes," Will agreed, laughing again. "But I don't care as much about what he thinks as you do. He may be a boy genius in his field, but to me he will always primarily remain my smart-ass son."

"One day I'm going to get even," Michael said, crossing his arms.

Will snorted. "Right. That's very mature for a man about to get married and become a father."

"Beats whining," Michael said, enjoying his father's rolling laughter. He hadn't heard it much lately. "I'm going to check on Carrie. How near done are you?"

"I can stop anytime. Just let me know when you want me inside. I'm not keen on making casual conversation with your mother and Luke until I have to."

CHAPTER 22

Ellen knew Shane and Luke were in the living room watching the sports highlights for the week. She had seen Michael creeping down the hall and quietly into the master bedroom. The kitchen table was laden with food, and it wasn't time to make final preparations.

There was nothing else to do now except the one thing Ellen Cannon didn't want to do, but needed to. She needed to go out to the courtyard and apologize to her ex-husband. So sliding the patio door behind her, she walked carefully through the courtyard to where Will was cleaning his tools and putting them away.

"Will?" she called, then stopped as her eyes landed on the bust. "Oh. That's so beautiful. Look at her face. She looks radiant."

"Is that actually a compliment on my art?" Will asked sarcastically, but smiling to soften the question.

"Yes. It's a compliment," Ellen said quickly. "And I can't believe how amazing Jessica Daniels looks in marble."

Will shrugged. "Thanks."

"I'm sorry Will. I'm sorry I caused you grief in your new relationship and sorry I thought only of myself for a long time. I never meant to hurt you. I just couldn't seem to avoid it," Ellen said, her eyes tearing up. "I'm sure Jessica will get over this. She's a passionate, hotheaded woman, but I don't think she's totally unreasonable. In fact, she seems like the perfect match for you."

"Yeah, well—you can tell her that next time you talk to her. She's still not talking to me. I tried calling and going by the house. She's ignoring me pretty well," Will said.

"If you want me to go talk to her, I will. I owe both of you that much. Luke has been a different man since she talked to us in the parking lot. I don't want to repeat that awful night, but it may end up being the best thing that ever happened to my marriage. I'm happy, Will. I want you to be happy, too." Ellen looked at the bust. "I want you to be happy with Jessica Daniels."

"Keep saying it. I'm starting to believe you," Will said, closing the box and walking to where Ellen stood. "I would like us to be friends—real friends. We're going to be grandparents. Michael's situation is not good, and we're going to need to help him. I don't want the kids worrying about us, too."

"No. I agree with that," Ellen said, meaning it. She looked at the bust again. "In all the years we were married, you never carved me, Will. A relationship that inspires your art this much is worth fighting for, don't you think?"

"How can I fix it if the woman won't talk to me?" Will asked sadly, letting his true frustration show to a person that had known him through many hard times.

Ellen grabbed his arms and shook him while she laughed. "William Everett Larson, use that incredible stubbornness of yours to go after her. Stop feeling sorry for yourself."

Will laughed in return, feeling more hopeful than he had in days. It was the most natural thing in the world to put his arms around Ellen for a comforting hug.

~

NOT HAVING THE HEART TO WAKE HER YET WHEN SHE WAS STILL SO PALE, Michael had left Carrie still sleeping on the bed. They could wait another half hour, he thought.

He started to veer into the living room to hang with Shane and Luke when the doorbell rang. Bypassing the living room, he glanced in the kitchen and saw his mother was not around. So he headed to the door wondering if she'd locked herself outside. The last person he'd expected to see was Jessica standing on his front step.

"Jessica. Come in. You're just in time to meet my fiancée," Michael said.

"*Fiancée?* When did this happen? I thought she was marrying someone else," Jessica said, her forehead wrinkling in confusion.

"Dad didn't tell you?" Michael said, shock on his features. "Well, a lot has happened to me lately. Getting her pregnant moved me up in line on the next-guy-to-marry list."

"Decided to throw everything you had into the relationship, did you?" Jessica said, a twinkle in her eye.

"Well, I always did like cranking up the heat under a burning flame," Michael said, as he laughed and slipped an arm around her waist. "I'm really happy about this, and I'm sorry you were the last to know."

"I've been ignoring your father. Now I've decided to come fight again. Can I talk to him?" she asked.

Jessica wiped sweaty palms on her jeans as Michael let her go.

"Sure—but you should know Mom and Luke are here. So is Shane. We're just sort of hanging out until Carrie wakes up. Dad's in the courtyard working if you want to go on out. There's a new piece of art you should see anyway. He's been working on it non-stop for a couple of weeks now," Michael said.

Jessica took a deep breath. "I guess it doesn't matter who's here. I owe your mother and Luke an apology, too. What's one more humbling circumstance?"

Then she looked out the patio door and saw Will hugging Ellen and laughing. "On the other hand, I may just kill both of them and bury their bodies in my backyard after all."

"What do you mean?" Michael asked. Then he saw what Jessica saw.

"That's not what it looks like," Michael assured her. "I don't know what it is, but it's not what you think."

"Did you get that denial thing from your father, or did he get it from you?" Jessica asked snidely. "I'm getting really tired of hearing how there's nothing going on, but yet this is what I see." She pointed to the courtyard.

Michael laughed because the situation was funny even if the look on Jessica's face was not. "I'm sure there's a perfectly reasonable explanation," he said, trying to keep a straight face.

"The hell there is. Get out of my way, Michael. Your mother's ass is mine," she said firmly, sliding the patio door open and walking out.

"Shane! Luke! Get in here. Jessica caught Mom hugging Dad

again," Michael yelled, sliding the patio door open and walking outside after her.

~

"So are you two getting back together or what? Just tell me so I can stay the hell away from you both," Jessica demanded, striding towards the couple that sprung apart like guilty kids caught necking.

"No, of course not," Ellen replied, stepping toward the angry woman. "Look—Jessica, this is not what it seems."

"Better stay where you are, Ellen. I wouldn't suggest being within reaching distance of me while you answer my questions. I have six inches on you and probably out-weigh you by thirty or forty pounds. Even my therapist couldn't talk me down from kicking your ass right now," Jessica warned.

"Jessica—wait," Michael called.

She swung around, pointed her finger at him, and stepped back towards him. "Stay out of this, Michael," she ordered. "I know the woman is your mother, but she's also a grown woman who needs to be held accountable for her actions. I'm not going to kill her, but I am going to have my say. If you're going to stand out here, then shut up and let us get on with this."

Michael held up his hands and took a few steps back to show Jessica he was complying. Shane and Luke came out of the door together just in time to see Michael with his hands raised in the air.

"What's up?" Shane asked. "Besides your hands, that is."

"Jessica is planning to kick Mom's ass," Michael said, torn between distress and laughter.

"Cool," Shane said. "Why?"

"She was hugging Dad again," Michael said, looking at Luke.

He was surprised when Luke snorted and laughed. "Something funny about your wife hugging another man?" Michael asked.

"Yes," Luke said, his body still worn out from last night's most recent marathon with Ellen. He was completely convinced that his wife didn't want her ex-husband sexually anymore, but if she was dumb enough to get caught hugging him again, then he was just going to enjoy watching her learn her lesson. "I haven't seen a good cat fight since high school. You didn't say there would be entertainment tonight, Michael."

"My last cat fight was my sophomore year in college. I was dating several girls in the same sorority. Well, as you can imagine that didn't work out so well," Shane said, sighing. "But the fight was a lot of fun to watch."

"So am I the only one appalled at this?" Michael asked, pointing at the yelling, swearing women down the yard. His father looked like a referee trying to separate two wrestlers.

Shane and Luke looked at each other, then at Michael and shrugged.

"Unbelievable," Michael said, laughing at the men who were contentedly watching the show.

About that time Carrie slid open the patio door. "Michael? I thought I heard yelling. What's going on?"

Shane looked down at the pale brunette with incredibly beautiful turquoise eyes. He smiled in welcome. She didn't even blink at his appearance.

"Hi. I'm Michael's brother, Shane. This is his stepfather, Luke. The tall screaming redhead down the courtyard is my father's girlfriend. Our father would be the sputtering bald guy caught between the two women. The pretty blonde woman trying to hide behind him and use him for a human shield—well, that's our mother. It's nice to meet you, Carrie," Shane said, sticking out a hand and laughing as she took it. "Welcome to the family. What chapter in my book do you want?"

Carrie could tell Michael's brother was trying to get her to have a huge reaction, so she denied him the pleasure and looked at Michael instead.

"Seriously? This is your family?" she asked. "And this is your idea of a quiet dinner?"

"No. Actually, this is my idea of hell. The quiet dinner to meet the family was a dream I once had," Michael said. "That dream is gone now. Lately, this is as good as it gets. See why I told you that you wouldn't add anything to my drama? My parents have lost their damn minds lately."

They all turned their attention to the courtyard as Jessica screamed and Ellen yelled pulling backward on Will's shirt to keep him in front of her.

"How old are those people? Aren't they all over 50?" Carrie asked, shaking her head in disbelief. "This is not high school."

"Well, they were once all teachers. No—wait, Will was a

principal for a long time," Luke said, laughing at Ellen cowering behind Will and trying to reason with the hot-tempered redhead. This was even more entertaining than he'd imagined, Luke thought. It was even better to learn how passionate his wife truly was under all that reserve. He was more in love with her now than when he met her.

"Teachers? They're teachers? You're kidding, right?" Carrie asked.

"Well, teachers are just as human as the rest of us. They just have better self-control—usually," Shane said, laughing. "Love always makes a mess of everyone."

Carrie blinked in shock again, realizing they were going to do nothing to stop what was happening. She looked at all three of the men.

Luke smiled, Shane smiled, and Michael closed his eyes and shook his head from side to side. Unbelievably, Carrie felt sorry for Michael Larson. He seemed to be the least crazy person in his messed up family.

She sighed and put a hand to her stomach. "Well, I guess I need to go meet everyone else before I do anything more serious to stop this craziness."

She started forward toward the group of fighting, yelling people.

"Carrie, no. You might get hurt," Michael said, rushing after her.

Shane burst out laughing. "Welcome to the family, Carrie," he called out.

Michael turned around and gave his brother the bird.

Shane looked at Luke, who was still smiling. "Does your older brother treat you that way?"

"All the time," Luke asked. "He kept flirting with your mother when we were dating, so I had to pound on him to keep him away from her."

"Wow. My fifty-two-year-old mother had two young men fighting over her," Shane said. "I'm going to be a rich man after I finish my book."

"You're going to want an attorney to read the contracts," Luke advised. "Good thing you have one in the family."

Shane laughed and turned his attention back just as Carrie let out a loud yell and clapped her hands really loudly. Now he and Luke were riveted.

On her way, Carrie had spied the marble bust sitting a table. It was the most marvelous thing she'd ever seen. It was also obvious who had been the model.

"Hi. I'm Carrie. Do you want to meet me now or after the police are called to break up this domestic disturbance?" she asked, trying to be as imposing as she could be.

Jessica turned her furious gaze on the pale, weaving woman who looked like a hard wind would knock her down. "Honey, you look like you're going to faint any second."

"That would better than listening to you all fight all night," Carrie said in reply.

Jessica laughed and walked to the woman. "Jessica Daniels. I can already see why Michael likes you," she said, sticking out her hand to shake.

"You're the bust woman," Carrie said, looking up and studying Jessica's face as she shook hands.

"I'm the what?" Jessica asked, laughing.

Carrie pointed off to the side. "That's you, isn't it?"

Jessica looked in the direction she pointed and her jaw dropped. Like a woman in a trance, she walked over to the bust to reach a hand out.

"That's what I kept trying to tell you," Ellen said to Jessica, exasperation and more in her tone. "You're every bit as stubborn as Will. God help you both because you're going to need it."

Ellen walked to the pale brunette who was the same height she was. "Hi. I'm Michael's mother. I hardly ever fight, but it's been a really interesting month for me. It's so nice to meet you. I'm going in to finish getting dinner ready now." She turned back to Jessica. "I was just hugging Will to wish him luck on getting you back, you hellish-fire-breathing-dragon witch."

"Name calling? Oh, that's very mature, Ellen," Jessica said, but then she started laughing as she finally heard the type of angry exchange the others must have been hearing all along.

"Yes. Well, you seem to inspire everyone in this family one way or another. I was going to thank you for saving my marriage, but go to hell first," Ellen said, laughing herself. "I'll thank you later."

"Fine. I'm glad it worked out for you," Jessica said, tears of embarrassment finally starting to flow. "I hate being an idiot."

"Well, don't cry about it," Ellen said briskly. Then she looked at Will and pointed her finger. "Well, don't just stand there with your mouth open like a gaping fish. Make up with her William, and then make her stay for dinner. How else are we going to work on being friends?"

Michael stepped up and hooked an arm around Carrie. "Easy there, General Addison. You're as white as a sheet. Let's go find you a chair." He scooped her up into his arms. "Good job though. You actually did break up the fight. We might get that quiet dinner after all."

"The medicine makes me sleepy, but I think I'm hungry," Carrie said, smiling weakly into Michael's face. "You have a crazy family. I thought mine was bad."

"Sorry. You can add limited exposure to them in the agreement if you want. They will all be leaving later. I promise," he said, walking away with her. Then he stopped and turned around. "Dad, are you going to be okay?"

Will was watching Jessica cry and touch her own face in marble. "Yes. I—give us a few minutes and we'll be inside."

"Take your time," Michael said. "Carrie has to eat though. We don't want the medicine to wear off before she does."

"You don't have to worry so much about me, Michael," Carrie scolded. "I'm fine."

"Absolutely," he said, carrying her through the door Shane was holding open as wide as possible. "You're absolutely the finest woman I know."

~

WHEN THE COURTYARD HAD EMPTIED EXCEPT FOR THE TWO OF THEM, WILL walked over to stand next to Jessica.

"I can't believe I was ready to fight the woman over her hugging you," she said, sniffling. "You must be embarrassed to death."

Will ran a hand over his head, smiled, and decided complete honesty was the only choice.

"I liked the screaming and yelling a lot better than your logical reaction to her waiting for me in the bedroom a few weeks ago. Being a man, and still stupid even at my age, I have to admit it was kind of hot to know my girlfriend would fight my ex-wife over me," he said, rubbing his face. "Even if there was *absolutely no reason*. Ever. Not even if we don't work out, which we will, because you are all I can think about."

Jessica sniffed. "So you say."

Will reached out and touched the face of the bust he'd made of her. "My one predominant thought is how to get you to look like this for me again. I can't bear the idea that being with me has changed you to the point you can't be yourself or be happy. When you stop kissing ninety-year-old men, something's not right in Jessica Daniels' world."

"Does Melanie tell you everything?" Jessica asked, laughing.

"Well, I tip her with money instead of condoms. That helps. But I think I also remind her of her dad. She feels sorry for me a lot," Will said. "Can I hug you now, or you still in the mood to kick someone's ass?"

Jessica turned and lifted her arms so Will could walk into them. He scooped her up so hard that she almost couldn't breathe.

"I missed you so much," he told her.

"I missed you too," Jessica told him. "But I had to get over being mad and say goodbye to the other guy."

"What other guy?" Will asked carefully, drawing back and looking at her. "Are you dating again?"

"No. I had to say goodbye to Nathan," Jessica said softly. "I told him I loved you and wanted to marry you. He seemed to understand."

"Well, I'm glad Nathan took it so well," Will said, not sure his legs were going to hold him up. She loved him. He squeezed her tightly. She was going to marry him. "How about Mr. Beaumont?"

"William," Jessica said, using her best teacher voice, "there are just some men that a woman can't give up. You're going to have to learn to share me more or our marriage is never going to work out."

Will pretended to give that some consideration as he ran a hand up her spine until it tangled in her hair. He touched his forehead to hers.

"I guess I can be content with being the favorite," Will said, "but if the math teacher comes back around again, I'm seriously going to kick his ass. You lifted the bar on that this afternoon when you chased Ellen around me. Did I tell you that was totally hot?"

Jessica lifted a hand and smacked Will lightly in the back of his head, making him laugh even when he called out in pain.

"Don't even get me started on math teachers. You married one yourself—yet another thing you never told me even though I heard about Adam a hundred times," Jessica complained.

"I wanted you to like me for my art, for being an artist. I wanted to be with someone who loved me more than a math teacher ever could. I never meant to not tell you. I just never thought about the past when I was with you," Will explained. He kissed the corner of her eye, the edge of her mouth, and down her neck until her heart beat strongly under her lips. "You're not like anyone I've ever known. I've not been sure of anything since I met you."

"You can be sure of what I feel about you. I've belonged to you since the first time you put your hands on me," Jessica said hoarsely. "Marry me, Will. Drive me crazy for the rest of my life. You're the last man I'm ever going to make that offer to."

Will thought being happy felt a lot like being drunk. "Well, since you asked so nicely—yes, I'll marry you," he said, meaning every word. "I'm ready for a new name anyway. William Daniels. I like the sound of it."

"It will never work. You'll just be a crazy Larson underneath, so we might as well use your name," Jessica said, smiling at his grin. "I was tired of being a Daniels anyway. Thirty years is long enough."

"Well, if you're sure," Will said seriously, thrilled to know she was truly ready to let Nathan Daniels go. "Jessica Larson. Sounds like a good name for a vagina artist."

"No, no more vaginas. Your lovemaking has inspired me to try something new. I'm making breast art now. I'm planning to sell it to women's hospitals and birthing centers," Jessica said, laughing again at the pride and understanding she saw in Will's gaze.

"I can't wait to check out the source of your inspiration. Have the *girls* missed me as much as I have them?" Will asked, laughing.

"Yes," Jessica said emphatically. "We've all missed you. They think we should buy a house together so we never have to be apart again. It needs to have a place for you to carve and another where I can work in clay."

Will lifted and spun her as they kissed to seal their agreement. When they stopped spinning, it was to see the crowd assembled at the patio door laughing and clapping.

— THE END —

NOTE FROM THE AUTHOR

Thank you for reading *Carved In Stone*!

If you enjoyed reading this book, please consider leaving a positive review or rating on the site where you purchased it. Reader reviews help my books continue to be valued by distributors/resellers and help new readers make decisions about reading them.

You are the reason I write these stories and I sincerely appreciate you!

Many thanks for your support,
~ Donna McDonald

www.donnamcdonaldauthor.com

Join my mailing list to hear about new releases.

CREATED IN FIRE

BOOK 2 OF THE ART OF LOVE SERIES

CHAPTER 1

It wasn't the first time Michael Larson had awakened in a strange bed early on a Saturday morning, but it was the first time the strange bed was one in his own house.

He listened for a moment to a silence that was broken periodically by the sound of the master bath toilet being flushed. It took only a few seconds of total consciousness to know the sounds meant that Carrie Addison, the mother of his future child, was sick again.

Jumping from the bed, Michael tugged sweat pants on to cover most of his nudity before bolting to check on her. Tapping lightly, he opened the bedroom door a crack and saw no one in the bed.

"Carrie?" he called softly. Hearing no answer, Michael walked quietly inside and across the length of the room to tap lightly on the partially closed bathroom door. What he heard on the other side of it made his own stomach clench in sympathy.

Michael opened the door gently, calling her name again just as she was flushing the toilet yet another time.

"I'm okay," Carrie told him sadly, not the least surprised to see Michael with all the noise she was making. "I think the worst is over now."

Glancing up at his face and seeing pity there brought stinging hot tears of regret to her eyes. She rolled off a handful of toilet tissue and used it to wipe them away. "Being sick is not nearly as bad as feeling sorry for myself. I'm never this wimpy. I hate the constant crying as much as throwing up. I hope the crying stuff doesn't last the whole pregnancy."

Michael walked around where Carrie sat on the floor to get to the sink. Reaching over to a shelf to snag a washcloth, he quickly ran cold water until it was as frigid as possible before wetting the cloth and folding it. Bending over to Carrie, he wrapped it around the back of her neck.

"Hold this in place. It will calm the gag reflex," he ordered softly.

Then Michael returned to the sink and wet another cold cloth, all the while thinking that for the last month now Carrie had been alone every time this happened. It made him really glad she had agreed to move in with him for the duration of the pregnancy, no matter the conditions.

Carrie snorted in disbelief, but pulled the cold cloth tighter around her neck. "Thank you, Dr. Larson," she said sarcastically.

"No, the closest to a doctor in our family would be Shane, who I wouldn't let put so much as a bandage on me or anyone I care about. Actually, Mom used to do this cold cloth trick for us when we were sick. It worked every time," Michael told her.

He dropped to the floor to sit beside Carrie, wrapping his body around hers, which was currently hugging the toilet. Reaching around the front of her body, Michael patted her forehead and flushed cheeks with the second cloth.

He was surprised when Carrie started crying long streams of really hot tears. "Hey now," he said, his arms going around to hug her before he could censor the action.

"I'm sorry. I just hate this," Carrie said, choking on the apology through the tears. "I can't seem to stop crying. There's nothing really wrong. "

"Good to know. A little human kindness is no reason to dissolve into tears," Michael joked, trying not to frown at how vulnerable she seemed.

It was so unlike Carrie's usual take-no-prisoners' approach to her life. Watching her cry this morning was like an instant replay of the night she'd come to tell him about the baby. Trying not to think about all she'd shared that night, he used the cloth to wipe the tears even though nothing he did seemed to be slowing them. Her body was tense, and through the tears Michael saw her frustration.

It was amazing how much he truly wanted to soothe her. All he wanted was to hold her and make sure she knew he was there for her.

Scooting closer, Michael wrapped his body more tightly around hers, creating as much contact as possible.

"You're the strongest woman I know, and every time you cry it kills me. I'm truly sorry you're so sick. No one should have to go through this without choosing to," Michael said gently.

"I think we both know what I chose that got me into this situation," Carrie said tearfully, tone full of honesty and self-pity.

Michael's very impressive, very hard erection was even now pressed against her hip as he held her. Her tears of self-pity dried up only to be replaced by mortification as she felt herself becoming aroused.

"You mean, this old thing," Michael teased, grinning and pressing himself even closer. It was heaven to even imagine the possibility of being with her again, but he'd settle for making her laugh this morning. "No worries about that being a problem, honey. That's just a morning thing for most guys."

Carrie snorted and laid her head on the seat rim of the toilet. She could laugh only because she knew that not even the worst man would seduce a woman who was retching every couple of minutes. Michael was lecherous by her standards, but he wasn't that horrible.

"I was married twice. I know what men are like. It was just the irony of throwing up while thinking about. . .never mind. I think the sickness is passing now. You can let me go," Carrie told him, taking the washcloth from Michael's hand and wiping her entire face. "It would help if you got me a glass of ice water so I can take the nausea medicine."

Michael ran a hand down the back of her short cap of brown hair and flipped the cloth on her neck over to a cooler side. "Sure. I don't mind taking care of you. I want you to ask me to help when you need help."

"So you keep saying," Carrie retorted, sighing and nodding, keeping her face and expression hidden in the washcloth. "I'm going to start crying again if you don't leave right now. Niceness seems to activate the water works."

Michael slid away from her and used the sink to pull himself up. "Stay down there until I get back."

Rolling her eyes, Carrie pulled the washcloth away from her face and watched Michael Larson's very attractive back and rear disappear quickly through the now open bathroom door. His dark hair was loose from sleep, and she marveled again that it hung longer than most women's. What would have been effeminate on many men only enhanced the masculinity he seemed to exude without even trying. Memories of her hands in his hair had arousal tugging at her even through the waves of nausea.

"And that feeling, you stupid, hormonal woman, is exactly how and why you got yourself knocked up again by the man. You never learn, Carlene," she lectured herself. Her words echoed softly in the empty bathroom as she sniffed the next bout of fresh hot tears away.

Using the toilet for leverage, Carrie pushed to her feet and walked to lean limply against the sink. She wet both cloths with cold water again. The one behind her neck really was helping. The urge to throw up was lessening every second.

Carrie rinsed her mouth and gently brushed her teeth, having learned that too much toothpaste only made the nausea worse. She rinsed her mouth several times until the mint flavor was gone. Then she walked carefully back to the bedroom and crawled into the bed.

When a fully dressed Michael with hair restrained behind him came back with a glass of ice water, Carrie was propped up on pillows. She sighed in relief that she wasn't going to be tortured with a nearly naked version of him again.

Day one of being alone with the man in his house was going just about as badly as she had envisioned, including having to confront the humiliation of still wanting him every bit as much as she ever had. The illusion of getting over him just kept crashing and burning every time she turned around and saw him.

"I would have helped you," Michael chastised, handing Carrie the glass of ice water and watching as she sipped it gratefully.

"And you can still," Carrie said, striving for a light tone despite how resentful she was of needing help—specifically, his help. "I left my nausea medicine in the bathroom."

Michael walked into the bathroom and returned with the pill bottle, shaking out the recommended dosage into his hand before passing it to her.

Carrie tossed the pills in her mouth and chased them quickly with the water. "Twenty minutes until I feel better," she said. "Thank you, Michael."

Michael set the bottle on the nightstand and went to the foot of her bed to sit. "Can I try some reflexology? It's supposed to help with the nausea and might make your relax."

Carrie shrugged. "Sure. Just don't jostle me too much."

Michael picked up her left foot and stroked her insole with his thumb.

"Oh God," she groaned, leaning back and closing her eyes as the tension seeped out of her body one stroke at a time. "That's amazing. Where did you learn that?"

Michael kept his head down and continued his task while trying to decide how best to answer her in the least incriminating way for him.

"I dated a massage therapist for a while," he said finally. Having never lied to her, he saw no reason to start doing so.

Carrie opened her eyes to slits and promptly closed them again.

"Sure—of course," she said flatly, letting the rest of what she was thinking remain unspoken. She'd already voiced her opinion of his dating habits. There was no reason to beat a dead horse, as her grandmother would say.

Michael sighed resolutely, the sound very audible in the quiet. He accepted that Carrie was still upset about the women he'd dated where she worked, but he didn't have to tolerate her thinking he was a totally bad guy. Because he wasn't. She had been married when he dated them, and he had barely caught her between husbands this time. Who was she to critique him?

"Maybe I should just make a list of all the women I dated where you work so we can hash it all out once and move on," he said, not able to keep the hurt out of his tone.

Michael swung both legs up into the bed and pulled Carrie's left foot snug against his crotch as he turned his attention to stroking the right one.

"You were married, and I dated," Michael said. "I couldn't chase a married woman."

"No—I will admit that you never chased me when I was married," Carrie said, not adding that the men she'd married hadn't even left an impression. "But I would never have tolerated that from you anyway."

After being used and dumped by a younger Michael in college, there hadn't been enough of her heart left for any man to break. Dating the adult version of him when their paths had crossed again had been totally out of the question and was made more unreasonable by the fact that he didn't even remember her.

Yet for as long as Carrie had known him, Michael had dated and discarded women without showing any regret. She had watched him repeat the pattern with others, just as he had with her, moving from woman to woman and bed to bed, never realizing they cried and hurt and bled over him. She hadn't let herself care about what he did enough to be offended by the pattern again until she had let herself be seduced two months ago and ended up pregnant by him.

Despite evidence to the contrary, she really wasn't by nature a masochist. It just looked that way. She'd handled the crisis in college, and she would handle this one. It wasn't like she didn't have a history of bad judgment concerning him.

"Michael, it honestly doesn't matter what you did with other women. We've already determined that it doesn't concern me long term," Carrie said sadly, not wanting to have this conversation.

"I've told you this before, but I'll say it again. You're the only woman I want. Every other woman in my life was at best practice and at worst a substitute. For the duration of our involvement, every other woman is also completely history, regardless of whether you exercise your full options with me or not. That's as clear as I can make things. I only care about you right now. You don't see me grilling you about your ex-husbands, do you?"

"Fair enough," Carrie said stiffly, not surprised that Michael had no understanding of how she felt emotionally. Why would he? He was a guy who did what he wanted, a guy like most guys she had known.

"How many men do you think I've let into my bed, Michael?" she asked.

"The men in your past don't matter anymore, but you can tell me if you want," Michael said, unable to keep the defensiveness from his voice. Hell no, he didn't want to know. He might have to go break something to work off his jealousy.

"There have only been three men, and that includes you," Carrie said, keeping her eyes closed. "I was raised to believe you married a person before you gave yourself to them physically. That was the reason I hadn't slept with Tom even though we were technically engaged. You're the only man I ever slept with that I wasn't married to."

Michael said nothing more about the third man that she had

intended to marry. That one hurt most because he hadn't even known about him the night he'd spent with her. He kept his attention on his task of rubbing her feet so he wouldn't have to glare at her over Tom.

Plus, he was a little ashamed of himself.

As sexist as it was, Carrie's lack of partners only made her more appealing to him. Knowing that she took sex so seriously told Michael that the connection between them was so strong that she had to be with him. He liked knowing he had at least that much power over her despite her ongoing refusal to date him over the years.

Michael believed Carrie's story completely when she had insisted that he had been her first, even if he didn't remember it. But he was definitely aware of how he felt about her now, he wanted to be Carrie's only sexual partner for the rest of her life. He might not understand exactly why he felt that way or why it was her, but every time he looked at Carrie Addison he wanted her.

"Your discrimination only makes me admire you more," Michael said, raising his head to meet her gaze, only to find Carrie had closed her eyes to shut him out.

"I accept that it's not your fault I violated my family's sexual programming to be with you in college or that I still feel guilty about it," she said quietly, finally opening her eyes and meeting his gaze directly again. "But I can't react with a shoulder shrug to your lack of discrimination when I got to watch most of your cast-offs crying their eyes out over you. However, I will make an effort to refrain from sarcasm about it in the future. I'll try to keep my focus just on our present situation."

While the thought of not hashing out his past dating exploits appealed to him, the thought of Carrie keeping her true feelings inside and continuing to resent him held no appeal at all. Michael had never been afraid of fighting, nor of his emotions. He for damn sure wasn't going to be afraid of the anger of the woman he intended to make his wife.

He also doubted any woman had cried more than two minutes over him. With most women, Michael had been as casual about sex as Carrie accused him of being, but he had never pretended otherwise. There was nothing wrong with consenting relationships among adults. He did not feel ashamed.

"You can ask me anything you want. I'll answer you honestly," Michael told her. "Carrie, I want our pasts resolved and put behind us, whatever it takes. I want you to believe me when I say you're the one I was looking for and waiting to be with all this time. I wasn't maliciously using those women. Hell, I was just dating. I refuse to let you think I'm the worst man that ever walked."

"I never said you were the worst man that ever walked. You're just —you're just not the kind of man I want to settle down with for the rest of my life," Carrie said firmly, laughing harshly, closing her eyes again. "Give me a break, Michael. You know I can't turn around at work without running into a woman you've slept with. Hell, Belinda is the only exception so far, and she's interested in you. She asked me if I was dating you the day you brought me the engagement ring."

Michael lifted both her feet, held them tightly against his body, and tried to show he loved her with every affectionate stroke of his hands. Carrie wouldn't look directly at him or meet his gaze, and that hurt. Her fisted hands in the bed covers were another sure sign of her ongoing distress with the subject matter.

Yet as bad as the situation was, he still refused to think of it as being irrevocable or entirely his fault. Carrie had married two other men, committed herself willingly to them. As far as he had known, she hadn't even considered giving him a chance before two months ago.

And damn her, he'd for sure had no damn desire for any woman since. Why couldn't she try to accept that? Michael tightened his jaw but swallowed the urge to fight with her more.

"I have no intention of dating Belinda. I'm sorry about the others and that you have to deal with my ex-girlfriends where you work. Truthfully, I never thought about it being an issue," he said tightly. "That's not an apology—just an explanation. You were married when I was serial dating in your company. I never cared how any of the women I dated felt about each other, but I'm starting to see how it could be embarrassing to you in our current circumstances. If I had known our situation was going to ever be possible, I might have been more discriminating."

Carrie opened her eyes and sighed. She could hear in his voice how mad Michael was becoming. Fighting was certainly not going to help them get along. The fighting only made her heart ache and her body crave peace with him.

God, what had she been thinking when she said yes to living with him? Agreeing to stay with Michael for the duration of the pregnancy was the dumbest thing she had ever done in her life outside of getting pregnant in the first place. Still, she had contractually agreed to create the illusion of a legal relationship, and she needed the help during these first months. So she simply had to find a way to live peacefully with him.

"The sickness and the medicine muddle my thinking. As I said before, who you dated doesn't really matter, or at least it shouldn't. Forget I mentioned it. I'm sure your old girlfriends will see our marriage as me winning you, rather than it just being a consolation prize for getting pregnant. I'll survive the gossip. Maybe now they'll at least stop bragging to me about how great you were in bed."

Michael set her feet aside and stood. He couldn't listen to any more without wanting to hurt her in return. As he'd told her before, it wasn't his fault the women he had dated were indiscreet. It wasn't like he went around bragging about them. Hell—he didn't even remember them. Erin was the only one he'd even dated more than once.

But he could certainly describe in vivid detail every single thing he and Carrie had done together during the one night he'd spent with her two months ago. He'd post a damn description on her company bulletin board if he thought it would help their situation. It had always been her that he wanted. Always.

"Just so our stories match, what did you tell Belinda about us?" he asked as quietly as he could, trying not to glare at her closed eyes.

"I told Belinda that you'd asked me to marry you and that I had said yes," Carrie told him, sliding down into the bed and rolling to her side. "It's none of her business about the baby."

Michael clenched his jaw at her back turned to him, but kept his tone soft as he asked the rest of what he wanted to know. If Belinda accepted it, their engagement was going to be common knowledge at Carrie's company soon. "What did Belinda say?"

"Congratulations and that the ring was beautiful," Carrie said, her voice fading as her mind floated in the need to sleep again. "I'm sorry I'm fading. This medicine makes me so tired."

"Yes, but you'll wake up hungry in an hour. I'll make you breakfast then," Michael said softly, walking to the bed and tugging the covers up over her shoulders, anger giving way to feeling sorry for her again.

"Dad may be coming by to pick up some things to take to Jessica's. He says he's moving in with her. We'll try not to wake you," he whispered, smoothing the covers down her arm.

"Thank you, Michael. The foot rub really helped me. Even the muscles in my stomach have relaxed," she said softly. "I didn't mean to snipe at you when you were being nothing but kind. I'm sorry."

Maybe she was, Michael thought, but it seemed like hell would still probably freeze over before Carrie would change her opinion of him. His frown deepened as her breathing settled.

"I'm glad it helped. Rest now. I'll see you when you wake up," he said firmly.

Michael pulled the wet cloths from her as she slipped into sleep.

CHAPTER 2

Michael was sitting at his kitchen table sipping his third cup of coffee and feeling resentful of Carrie's bad opinion of him when he heard his father coming through the front door. He got up and went to the kitchen doorway.

"Coffee?" he asked, grinning at the happiness on his father's face.

"Yes. I'd kill for some coffee. Jessica drinks tea most mornings. I tried to drink that instant stuff she bought for me, but it's just not the same," Will said. He took the fragrant cup from Michael's hand. "Thank you, son. You're my hero."

Michael frowned at that and sighed as he tromped back to his seat at the table. "Glad I can be someone's hero."

"I thought you did pretty good last night too," Will said, coming to sit at the chair across from him. "You waded into a couple of screaming, fighting women to save the mother of your child. Then you carried her inside and fed her. Jessica talked about you two for hours after we got home. It took quite a lot to get her attention focused back on us—I mean me."

Michael laughed, but there wasn't much humor in it. "Please tell me you're going to marry that woman. I need some good news today."

"As soon as Jessica agrees to a date, we'll get married," Will said smiling, studying the distress on his son's face. "Why? You thinking we could make it a double wedding?"

Michael shook his head. "No. Sorry. I can't share the limelight with you and Jessica. Carrie told me she had quickie civil ceremonies the other two times because her family was not supportive of either relationship. Winning over her family is my next hurdle. I'm planning to tackle that tomorrow. My plan is for her father to walk her down a church aisle to me this time. We're going to have the kind of wedding that sticks."

"Just because you had Celtic ancestors doesn't mean you have to treat this marriage of yours like a strategic campaign of some sort. You're not marrying the woman to acquire her money or land." Will smiled at the grin Michael gave him.

"Dad, that woman is my land. In her own words, she said she was a field I plowed. I'm just going along with her metaphor. Don't get me started on how I feel about the baby," he said, sighing at his own determination to create the kind of relationship he wanted, even though Carrie obviously didn't feel the same. "My bride might not be completely willing, but I still want our marriage to be so legal and sanctified that nothing and no one can say it's not."

Michael took a long drink and stared across the kitchen.

"One minute I'm mad as hell at Carrie for putting our pasts between us, and the next I'm compelled to take care of her because it's my fault she's so sick. I've never been so conflicted before," he complained, "and all of that just makes me more determined to marry her. It's crazy."

Will laughed. "Yeah. That sounds like real love."

"Well, real love sucks then," Michael said firmly, laughing as his father almost choked on his coffee laughing at him.

"There are some upsides," Will said, taking a more cautious sip. "My money is on you finding a way to make your situation work. After all, your future bride is actually sleeping in your bed in your house at this very moment. That's way more than your mother, Shane, or I thought you'd manage."

"Gee thanks," Michael said sarcastically, "glad to know my family has so much faith in me. Who are you to talk? What did you do this morning? Just leave your future bride home sleeping alone in her own bed?"

Will snickered, thinking how much more he enjoyed Michael's company when he wasn't constantly around him. He loved his sons, but fervently hoped he never had to live with them again.

"No. Jessica is meeting her friends Susan and Steve to mend some friendship fences this morning over breakfast. She thinks Susan might be upset at her still. If it goes well, she'll have the four of us eating dinner together soon. Frankly, I'm looking forward to smiling at Steve Lipton the whole evening," Will said, not minding that it was bragging. He felt like bragging about Jessica. "I know he didn't think my chances with Jessica were good."

"Your chances were always good with Jessica," Michael said irritably, frowning into his coffee cup.

"Oh, yeah. Sure they were," Will agreed, "that's why I had to beg her not to date and sleep with other men. If I hadn't gone to Cincinnati and seduced her that night, she'd have bedded the math teacher trying to forget me. I still owe you and Shane for that one."

"Great. Tell me how to make Carrie forget about the other women I dated," Michael said.

Will sighed. "I wish I could, but I can't."

"Thanks for nothing," Michael said, only half teasing. "No more coffee for you."

"Michael—your situation is too complicated for an easy answer. I do think you're doing well. She's here and letting you help her. That says Carrie trusts you on some level whether she is willing to admit it or not. Fixing emotional things takes time," Will told him, smiling. "Jessica asked me to marry her last night."

"When last night?" Michael said, surprised.

"Last night on the patio. Just before the lift and spin you guys were all clapping about," Will said, bragging. "I said yes of course."

Michael laughed. "I bet it was the bust that convinced her. That statue of her shows exactly how you feel about the woman. It's some of your best work, Dad."

Will nodded. "Yes. That's what your fiancée thinks as well. Carrie says I should do a show of some smaller pieces. I don't have many."

"I think that's a great idea," Michael agreed. "Make some more."

"I'm thinking about it," Will said. "I sure liked getting done with a piece in just a few weeks. I might do some torsos. Maybe some arms lifting from stone."

Will drifted off in creative thought, already imagining the work coming to life.

Michael smiled and studied the satisfied expression on his father's face. "I hope you get to look like that for the rest of your life."

"Look like what?" Will asked. "What do you mean?"

"Contented," Michael told him. "It's an emotion I long for but have never felt—well except once, but it didn't last long. If Carrie would just believe I love her, I think I could find it again."

"Contentment is one of the harder emotions to hang onto," Will said, rising to refill his mug. "It helps if you're the type of person who regularly counts blessings. Sometimes it's hard for me, but I keep working at it."

"Like being grateful Carrie is here for me to help, instead of her living alone and dealing with being sick by herself?" Michael asked.

Will nodded. "Yes. That's a good start."

"How long until I get to the contented part?" Michael asked, raising an eyebrow.

Will shrugged and laughed.

"Shane was right. You and Mom are not getting any wiser as you age," Michael said bitterly.

"You learn wisdom by surviving trials, but it looks like you'll be developing your own soon with all the challenges you've attracted to yourself," Will said, choosing not to be offended by the opinions of the two smartass males he raised. "Michael, you're thirty-four. It's time to stop being mad that your mother and I don't have solutions for you anymore."

Michael thought about his father's statement, ignoring him as he sipped his coffee. "Well, growing up sucks too then," he said, laughing despite the ache in his chest.

"I'm sorry you're having a tough morning, son," Will offered, fighting the grin that kept twitching the corners of his mouth. He shouldn't laugh, but it was hard not to. He knew his stubborn eldest was going to push, shove, and do God only knew what else to the woman sleeping down the hall. Michael honestly thought he would win the stubborn contest between Carrie and him.

Will figured it was extremely wise of him not to point out the futility of that to an already frustrated Michael. He was just glad Jessica was letting him live with her until they found a house to buy.

~

"MORE SCRAMBLED EGGS?" MICHAEL ASKED, SPOONING THEM ONTO

Carrie's plate when she nodded. "There's another piece of whole wheat toast too."

Carrie sighed. "I've had three pieces already. And I don't want to know how many eggs I've eaten," she told him. "They were really good. I feel almost normal for once."

"It wasn't as many as you think. I'm just glad you can eat. Your color is better as well," Michael told her, bringing his coffee mug back to the table.

"Did I hear your father here earlier?" she asked.

Michael nodded. "Yes. He collected most of his clothes and toiletries. I may move into his bedroom this week. It's larger than the one I'm currently sleeping in, plus I'm thinking about turning the smallest bedroom into a nursery."

"Oh," Carrie said, chasing the bite of toast she was chewing with ice water. "I guess that will need to be done. Are you going to want me to help?"

"You can if you want," he said, watching for signs of desire, but seeing none.

"I'd rather not. I think you should be the one making those decisions. I will gladly share the costs with you. I know baby gear can be expensive. My brother and sister-in-law just had a baby last year," she told him.

Michael set aside her disinterest in decorating the nursery as a debate for another time. "Tell me about your family. What should I expect tomorrow?"

Carrie set down her toast and pushed her plate away. Thinking of taking Michael to meet her family robbed her of the rest of her appetite.

"My father is a paid caretaker of the church he and Mom attend. That's his full-time job and he takes it seriously. He has some strict ideas about how a person should live, and I'm pretty much the only child of his who's not towed the family line. He's not exactly a warm and fuzzy guy where I'm concerned."

Michael shook his head. "So no swearing or dirty jokes during lunch—got it."

"My brother is pretty awful also, but I don't care what he thinks. Don't bother being nice to him. It's a waste of breath," she said.

Michael grinned when she sounded more like the woman he knew. "What else should I know?"

Carrie looked at Michael and thought that pretty much everything she liked about him was something her family was going to hate. "The list is too long. Plus it doesn't matter if they like you or not. Their opinions are not going to affect my decision to marry you. They didn't approve of the other men in my life either, and they were both fairly conservative. I certainly don't expect them to approve of you."

"Maybe I should cut my hair," Michael said, pulling his hair out of his ponytail and running his hands through it. "I know I look less respectable with hair this long. It wouldn't kill me to cut it shorter for a while."

"That's silly. You're not cutting your hair," Carrie said tightly without stopping to filter her disgust over the idea. She looked at Michael, saw a question in his gaze, but looked away without answering it.

"Why shouldn't I?" Michael asked, wondering if she was thinking about the same reason he was. "It's just hair. It will grow back eventually."

Carrie flushed as she thought about the only real argument she had. Since her preference was a result of their recent night of madness, she couldn't share that with the source. But even setting that aside, it still wasn't right for Michael to cut his hair just to please her family.

For one, nothing he did would please them anyway because they were impossible to please. She had been failing to do so for years. For another, Michael's hair was innately a part of him. It suited his nature. It suited his art. It suited him, period.

So no, Carrie wasn't going to let him cut his hair off.

"Just don't do it, okay? Don't change anything about how you look. It's a waste of energy to try and please my parents," she said flatly.

"Cutting my hair is a small concession if it makes it easier for you to sell me to them as a potential husband," Michael said carefully.

"You are not cutting your hair, Michael. End of discussion," Carrie said, standing and stalking to the sink with her dishes. "I think while I'm feeling better, I'd like to run to my apartment and pick up some things."

"Great. I'll drive and you can keep briefing me on your family. I want to know about all of them," Michael said, standing and taking his own dishes to the sink.

If Carrie turned to face him, he would barely have to bend his head to kiss her. He had all but forgotten there was only few inches difference in their heights. It gave him so many ideas that he couldn't push them away, especially the ones about repeating their night together.

"I won't cut my hair since I know you like it long," he said softly, almost whispering it in her ear.

Carrie's gaze swung to Michael's, her irritation at his statement obvious to both of them.

"I didn't say I liked your hair. I just said there's no need to cut it," Carrie said, defending her words.

"Oh, well if you don't like my hair, then there's no reason not to cut it," Michael countered. "I'll call Shane to come over and take off a few inches. He's cut it for me before."

"Michael, you are *not* cutting your hair, so stop talking about it," Carrie ordered.

"Oh. There you are," Michael said, grinning at her tone and the hands on her hips. "I've really missed you, General Addison. Glad to see you're feeling better."

"Up yours," Carrie said smartly, to his resounding laugh.

But when she turned to walk away, the room spun. She reached out but there was nothing to grab but air.

Then suddenly, there was Michael wrapped around her and holding her up.

"Whoa," he said, alarmed. "That was almost fainting. I'm sorry if I stressed you with my teasing. I'm not cutting my hair, honey. How could I cut it? I still remember your hands in it when you held me still and kissed me so fiercely. I thought I would die from the pleasure of feeling like I belonged to you."

"Michael, please stop torturing me with memories," Carrie begged, leaning weakly against him because she had no choice. And all the while her mind reeled and reeled from knowing Michael remembered the same things she did about their night together.

"Can't you even admit that's why you don't want me to cut my hair?" Michael asked fiercely, his voice a tense whisper. "I haven't even had a stray thought about anyone but you since that night. Give me a little hope here."

When Carrie's mind cleared of the blackness threatening to take her under, she was still leaning against Michael, still in his arms. And it made her mad as hell that Michael was asking for something more from her—as if the man hadn't already taken away everything—including her self-control. Full out angry now, Carrie reached behind Michael and wrapped a hand in his long, loose hair, using it to pull his head back while she stared fiercely into his face.

"You've had all of me you will ever have, Michael Larson," she vowed, eyes flashing as she yanked down hard to emphasize her point.

Michael felt desire heating his blood as he resisted Carrie's tugging, and he welcomed the fire it was building. This woman called up emotions in him that no one else ever had. Not all of them were reasonable, but it was impossible to be calm as he looked into her furious face. She was just damn lucky he had a leash on himself this morning.

"Yes, I *have* had all of you, Carrie Addison. And I intend to have all of you again," Michael told her, his gaze as fierce as hers.

Then he bowed his head to Carrie's mouth despite the strength of her tugging behind him. He chased the fire burning between them across her lips with his, the passion of their kiss shocking with the raw need it revealed. Two months ago was nothing. That was yesterday. His need for her was now.

When she pulled away, Michael said her name, half question and half demand. How could she keep pulling away from him—from *this*?

When Carrie felt her mouth wanting to open under Michael's, she yanked her lips from his in panic. She released his hair immediately, but had to untangle her fingers as she tried to back away. His body was hot and hard against hers. And he was strong, very strong. Carrie knew if Michael didn't let go willingly, there wasn't much she could do about it.

When she felt Michael easing his grip, she tentatively stepped back. Humbled when she almost fell again, Carrie was mortified when Michael had to catch her a second time.

Then she was only angry that she had ended up back where she started in his arms, pressed against him as proof of his desire pressed insistently against her.

"Obviously, I'm in no position to stop you from taking advantage of this situation, but I can promise you our sleeping together again won't matter in the long run. I will still walk away from this craziness I feel for you just as fast, no matter how many times I have to climb out of your bed," Carrie warned, her body shaking with fury, hurt, and shame because Michael could seduce her so easily.

Michael straightened and held Carrie away, but he couldn't make himself let go. Even with Carrie's rejection stinging his ears, he needed to be sure she wasn't going to fall. So he couldn't let Carrie go completely, even when part of him wanted nothing more than to push her away from his body to ease his own pain.

"When you're strong enough to stand alone and we're sure you're not going to faint again, I'll let go," Michael said, the words torn from him. "Take your time. I'm—I won't touch you again. It just happened. You started it when you grabbed my hair."

Carrie slid her hands down his arms to Michael's hands and grabbed them to steady herself as she finally moved away.

"I knew staying here was a bad idea. Now I know how bad, but I still have no choice. I can't ask either of my sisters to drop out of school and move back here to help me. Plus there's the whole marriage thing. I'm not a fool. I know I won't be able to stay away from you forever if we're in the same house, but don't weave any fantasies, Michael. Wanting you does not mean you get to make me miserable for the rest of my life," Carrie told him, easing away further, grateful when the dizziness didn't return. "I'm going to go lie down again. Don't follow me."

Michael stood where she left him, afraid to move, afraid of what he might do if he did. He was wound up enough to prove to them both just how it was between them.

He listened to Carrie sliding her hand down the hallway wall to brace herself as she headed to the bedroom, chastising himself for having vicious thoughts about a woman in her condition. When he heard the door click shut behind her, Michael closed his eyes and swore until the kitchen air was full of his whispered oaths.

He couldn't work out his frustration on his art because the banging would wake her, and Carrie needed to rest. He couldn't leave the house for fear she'd fall without him there to help. He had never felt so out of control in his entire life, and he hated the feeling.

And still all he wanted was to walk down the hallway and crawl into bed with Carrie to hold her while she slept.

Part of him even felt he needed to apologize again, but hell—he still didn't know what for. She was upset about the baby and being there, but he was still happy to have her there for any reason.

What the hell was the matter with him?

He was sick, had to be sick to want to tie himself to a woman so unforgiving and so unwilling to see what could be. She knew how it was, how strong it was. Hell, she had married other men to avoid what was between them. He knew that was the reason. Didn't she understand that their desire for each other was what people looked for all their lives, longed for with every breath?

She carried his child. They were his—both his—the woman and the child. All he wanted was the chance to love them. Why couldn't she accept that?

And how was her family ever going to if she didn't?

Well, he wasn't going to let Carrie just toss what they had aside, Michael decided. Somehow—some way—he *was* going to get through to her.

In the meantime, he was just going to take a cold shower to soothe his temper and maybe a grab a nap himself. He certainly hadn't slept much last night knowing Carrie was such a short walk away from him.

When they both were calmer later, he would take Carrie to get her things and then bring her the hell back here where she belonged —with him.

Tomorrow—Michael promised himself—tomorrow he was going to win the approval of her family. He knew her father had not approved of the first two husbands. But the man would accept him. He would have to when he saw that Michael was the right man for his daughter.

Not that it would change his mind if Carrie's father refused to give his blessing, Michael decided, but winning her family might be the key to the lock on Carrie's heart.

And for a chance at that, he would try anything.

CHAPTER 3

"So your father is very strict, and your brother is mean," Michael restated, noticing Carrie was keeping her face turned to look out the car window and not looking at him. "What's your mother like?"

"She supports my father in everything regardless of circumstances," Carrie said flatly, keeping her gaze on the beautiful horse farms they were passing on the way to Sunday lunch with her family. "That's really all there is to Margaret Addison."

"Are you not close to your mother?" Michael asked.

"When I lived at home, my father made decisions for all of us, usually without asking what we thought or felt about the situation. Even when I knew my mother disagreed, I only saw her stand up to him once or twice," Carrie said sadly. "I love her, but I don't really like or respect her the way you do your mother. I think I've put a lot of energy into making sure I didn't turn out to be that kind of woman."

Michael fought the urge to sigh. He hadn't even met Carrie's family, but already he didn't like them. From the way Carrie talked about them, he didn't think she liked them much either.

"What about your sisters?" he asked.

"They're great and happy to be in college," Carrie said, turning her head back to look at Michael's profile as he drove. "There's seven years difference between Darla and me. Alison is not quite eighteen months younger than her. Kevin is two years older than me. It's like my parents had two completely different sets of children. My brother is a pain, but I actually like my younger sisters. I was the one who talked them into moving to Bowling Green and away from home."

"You were trying to help them have a better life?" he asked.

"I was hoping they would meet enough people to learn that not all families are as judgmental as ours," Carrie corrected. "Darla is completing her master's degree in education. Alison is just beginning hers. They're both planning to be teachers."

"You sound very proud of them," Michael commented, not missing her quick satisfied smile as she nodded.

"Yes, I am," she confirmed.

"So what's the deal with your brother? You don't have to tell me if you don't want," Michael said, thinking if she didn't, he'd just make his own decision when he met the man.

"Kevin always tried to be Dad. Every time I went on a date, Dad would first lecture the boy I went out with on good behavior. That was bad enough. Then Kevin would beat up the guy the next day at school if he even suspected we'd been making out. I couldn't get a date most of my sophomore year in high school because of my brother."

Carrie turned to stare out the window again.

"It was poetic justice when Kevin got a girl pregnant his senior year. That put a stop to his controlling behavior where I was concerned. They were planning to get married, but the girl lost the baby. It was a relief to me when Kevin graduated. From my junior year in high school on, I pretty much avoided Kevin until he met and married Crystal three years ago. She's made him almost tolerable," Carrie said wryly.

"Your brother sounds like a normal screwed-up guy to me," Michael said. "Don't you feel sorry for him even a little bit?"

"Not usually, but Kevin did pay dearly for his mistake in high school," Carrie said, continuing her story when she realized Michael was still following along intently. "Dad and Mom made his life hell the whole time he was in college. He got lectures about his sex life every time he came home. Darla and Alison used to call me to tell me. They were in middle school and always banished from the room, but they loved to eavesdrop. I decided not saying anything was the way to go. So I lied to my parents in college and said I was too busy to date."

Michael suddenly had a very clear understanding of why Carrie had chosen to handle her unplanned pregnancy alone.

"Based on what you've said, I don't blame you for keeping things from your parents. I did too, but it was really hard with them both being teachers. Still, they weren't too bad. My parents would pronounce their disappointment, tell me I had to fix things, and then hug me as they pushed me out the door to do it. Even now, if I don't fix things to their standards, I hear about it. Since I hate to disappoint them, I try never to screw up," he told her on a laugh.

"I can't even imagine my parents fussing and hugging the way yours do. Not that I don't think your family is just as crazy as mine, especially your mother and future stepmother," Carrie said, smiling a little at the memories of the women calling each other names. Then later they had stood at the sink doing dishes together as if they'd been friends forever. "But I guess I admire the way they rise above their problems with each other for the greater good of the family unit."

"My father always says that most people are basically good despite their flaws," Michael said. "My stepmother is a great person. My mother is a good person too. She tends to be judgmental—wait, that's not fair. She's not so much judgmental as just anti-sentimental about what she doesn't understand. I'm learning that about her. Take my art for example. My mother thinks it's a crazy thing that people would pay me for my art."

Carrie whipped her startled gaze to Michael's profile. *"You're kidding me. Your mother doesn't like your art?"*

Michael winced and shook his head. "No. When we were kids, she used our art projects as doorstops. Dad still gets mad when it comes up in conversation. He has always supported our art. My stepmother gets it too. Dad picked a winner in her."

"How do you still manage to like your mother?" Carrie asked, truly perplexed.

Michael shrugged. "In every other way, Mom is a great mother. She used to sing us to sleep and was very kind when we were sick. She and Dad used to take us on trips and we'd have great adventures. She just doesn't get art. Not mine, not Dad's—which sucks, but it's not a fatal flaw."

"But, Michael, *art is your life,*" Carrie said emphatically. "And your art is—your art reflects you. There is a true power in your pieces. I've always felt—"

Carrie broke off what she was saying, a bit embarrassed when she noticed Michael staring at her more than the road.

"Felt what?" he asked. "Tell me. Please. I'd like to hear what you think."

Carrie swallowed. "Because of my success in promoting your work, in the last three years I've also worked with several other artists. Lots of artists have talent, but not all art has—well, *real* passion or life visible in it. Your work contains energy. Your father's does as well. That makes your kind of art the best kind. That's why people want it."

"Thank you for sharing that. Your opinion about my art means a lot to me," Michael said softly, nodding because his throat was tight.

If they had been home, he would have had to walk away to cry. It was extremely validating to know that the woman he loved sincerely liked his art. Maybe he'd always seen that. Maybe that's why he loved her. It was hard to know which came first.

Trapped in the car with her, all Michael could do was turn his full attention back to the road and add her liking his art to the list of things to discuss when they were getting along better.

Carrie bit her lip. "I've never not been a fan of your art. I—," she paused, knowing to say what she wanted to say would only nail the coffin she was in with Michael tighter around her, but the man had the right to know his art was more than merely good.

"Michael—it was always very easy for me to promote your work because I understand it. I don't even have to sell it. I just have to find the right people who want it. I met with the city board in Cincinnati, intending only to offer them the other piece you did similar to the one at the Louisville fairgrounds. There was a woman on the board who asked me what I saw in your art. I told her I saw raw power and the ability to communicate great passion. Two weeks later, I heard they commissioned the custom piece for the park."

"No one said that commission was because of you. I made twenty thousand on that piece. You didn't even take a cut," Michael told her. "Why didn't you tell me? Why didn't you tell your boss? All you said was they didn't want the piece that was done."

Carrie shrugged and laughed. "Because they didn't want the piece that I was selling, and it wasn't me that sold the commissioned work. Your art is the draw. All I did was share my honest opinion. The rest was between you and the city of Cincinnati."

"Carrie . . . ," Michael said, his voice rough with emotion. She supported his art because she believed in it, even when she was married to other men, even when she allegedly hated him. What was he supposed to do with that information?

"Turn by the chapel ahead," Carrie told him, her attention drawn out the window. "The house is a mile up the lane beside it."

Michael made the turn, swallowing the urge to demand more of an explanation. He could see Carrie was visibly drawing her personality inside herself. Normally she charged into confrontations, but at the moment her eyes were going flat with dread. What could her family possibly do that was so awful?

She looked—well, she looked like she had the day she'd shown up to tell him about the baby, which was even worse because Michael hadn't seen her look much like her real self since.

"Carrie—I'm not here for your parents' sake. I'm here for you. I won't let them use me to hurt you," Michael told her, hoping he could pull it off.

He would fight his impatience and dig for the tolerance it would take. He'd channel his father, the calmest man he'd ever met in his life. He would be calm and polite.

"I appreciate your noble thoughts about being on your best behavior for my sake," Carrie said sarcastically, as they pulled into her parents' extended graveled driveway. "It will just be wasted on this group. Don't worry. I know how to handle them. We won't stay long, and they won't expect me to. After bringing home a few dates, I stopped bringing men here. It wasn't worth what my family put them through."

When she climbed from the car, Michael frowned at the resigned look in her eyes. Her shoulders were drooping so much, she was practically bent forward. She kept her eyes on the ground as she walked, never lifting them to the early September sunshine or the wind blowing in the trees. Michael thought Carrie didn't even look like herself.

He was already mad at her family before he even crossed their threshold.

~

CARRIE TAPPED ON THE FRONT DOOR OF THE LONG BRICK RANCH HOUSE she'd grown up in, and opened it quietly.

"Hello," she called, stepping inside with Michael close on her heels.

Her mother dashed out of the kitchen to the hallway, arms open as she came to them.

"Carlene, why have you stayed away so long? Have you lost weight? You seem thinner," Maggie Addison said, wrapping her arms tightly around her oldest daughter, fighting not to be hurt when there was no answering hug.

"Mom, this is Michael Larson. Michael—this is my mother, Margaret Addison," Carrie said, stepping aside to let Michael shake her mother's hand.

"Pleasure to meet you, Mrs. Addison," Michael said politely, taking the woman's hand in his.

He was surprised to find her grip a lot firmer than he would have imagined judging from the fact her gaze wouldn't even hold his for more than two seconds. She was about Carrie's height and looked very much like an older version of her daughter, except for her very blonde hair laced with even brighter silver strands.

Michael Larson wasn't very tall, Maggie thought, but he was very broad shouldered and had a grip of iron. Her husband Ethan wasn't going to intimidate this one so easily, she thought, ultimately deciding that was a bonus for Carlene. She searched Michael Larson's face, seeing dark determined eyes assessing her back. It made her a little nervous the way he kept his gaze locked on hers, never looking away.

"Everyone's in the back yard. I was just finishing up lunch," Maggie said, shaking off her nerves. "Take Michael out and introduce him to everyone, Carlene. I'll be out in a moment with some tea."

Carrie reached down and picked up Michael's hand with her cold one. He looked at her but said nothing as his warm fingers closed around hers.

Darla and Alison were on the patio when Carrie slid the door open. They fairly jumped into her arms to hug her.

Here was warmth and love, Michael thought, smiling as the younger girls hugged Carrie and patted her face. They chattered on about school and things while he took in their similarities to their sister. They would have looked like a set of triplets except for Carrie's brunette locks. Obviously, her sisters had taken after their mother in appearance.

Carrie turned to Michael and made introductions, not surprised to see both her sisters perking up considerably as they took in Michael's appearance. His masculine looks were rustic and earthy. He looked exceptional today in new jeans and a crisp striped shirt that highlighted his shoulders. Carrie wanted to laugh watching Darla and Alison try to rein in their interest, but had to put a hand to her stomach as a nausea wave rolled over her.

Michael instantly stepped into her, putting an arm around her and a hand over hers on her stomach. "When was the last time you took your medicine?"

"It's probably just the stress. I'm still on schedule," she said, trying to dislodge his hand from her stomach as her both her sisters stood open-mouthed staring at them.

Her family wasn't big on public displays of affection and Carrie shook her head at the questions in her sister's eyes. "I've had some stomach problems lately. No need to worry. I'm fine. Michael is just nervous. I've gotten sick on him a couple of times."

"I'm not the only one nervous. You're practically shaking," he whispered, looking over her shoulder at two men glaring at him. "So tell me, is that your brother and father glaring at us?"

Carrie turned slowly and looked out in the yard. Her sister-in-law, Crystal, was off playing with her one-year-old nephew, Jason. Her father and brother stood with arms crossed, staring at the group on the patio.

Carrie rolled her eyes and sighed, recognizing their body language and what it meant. They were already upset, and all Michael had done so far was touch her out of concern for her health. They had probably seen his long ponytail and concluded he was a heathen. The rest of their judging would have followed from that.

"Yes," she answered, her tone as hard and unfriendly as their glares. "Those two are unfortunately the men in my family."

"Interesting. They're both blond. Are you the only brunette?" Michael asked, hoping to distract Carrie from her nervousness with inane questions about details. Plus he was kind of curious how a family of total blonds produced a chocolate brunette with red highlights.

"Yes," she answered flatly. "I'm the only brunette. Look, don't be surprised at anything the men in my family say to me about my appearance or us. They think they have the right to control everything and everyone that goes by the name Addison."

"Are you afraid of them?" Michael asked softly, his tone taunting on purpose. He grinned when Carrie glared at him.

"No. I'm not afraid of them. I just dread the inevitable confrontation over you. I hate confrontation," she said, crossing her arms and glaring at Michael herself.

"No you don't. You wade into confrontation," Michael corrected. "You stopped my mother and future stepmother from killing each other Friday night without even thinking that you might have gotten physically injured."

"I stopped them *because* I hate confrontation," Carrie insisted.

Michael laughed. The woman had held him captive by his hair just yesterday, and his scalp was still feeling the after effects today. "Boy are you in denial. You need to talk to my brother, Shane, though you might want to wait until December when his doctorate is official."

"Fine. Be a comedian, but this is not funny. You want to know what I'm avoiding? Come along then. Let's introduce you to the men in my family and you can form your own opinion," Carrie declared, picking up his hand to drag him out into the yard with her.

"Nice to meet you," Michael said to her sisters, who smiled and waved as he let himself be dragged away.

He didn't miss the sympathy in their gazes and wondered if his mouth had gotten him into trouble again.

OTHER BOOKS BY THIS AUTHOR

The Perfect Date Series

Never Is A Very Long Time

Never Say Never

Never A Dull Moment

Never Ever Satisfied

Never Too Late Series

Dating A Cougar

Dating Dr. Notorious

Dating A Saint

Dating A Metro Man

Dating A Silver Fox

Dating A Cougar II

Dating A Pro

Art Of Love Series

Carved In Stone

Created In Fire

Captured In Ink

Commissioned In White

Covered In Paint

Visit Donna's website to see more books.

ABOUT THE AUTHOR

DONNA MCDONALD

After 35 years of doing everything for a living except writing books, Donna McDonald published her first romance novel in March of 2011. Fifty plus novels later, she admits to living her own happily ever after as a full time author.

Her work spans several genres, such as contemporary romance, paranormal, and science fiction. Humor is the most common element across all her writing. Addicted to making readers laugh, she includes a good dose of romantic comedy in every book.

How To Connect With Donna...

www.donnamcdonaldauthor.com
email@donnamcdonaldauthor.com

Printed in Great Britain
by Amazon

19786487R00155